W9-AZA-275

A GLOVE SHOP IN VIENNA
And Other Stories

By the same author

A Countess Below Stairs
Magic Flutes
A Company of Swans
Madensky Square

A GLOVE SHOP
IN VIENNA

And Other Stories

Eva Ibbotson

St. Martin's Press
New York

Library of Congress Cataloging-in-Publication Data

Ibbotson, Eva.
    A glove shop in Vienna / Eva Ibbotson.
        p.   cm.
    ISBN 0-312-06983-9
    1. Love stories, English.   I. Title.
    PR6059.B3G57   1992
    823′.914—dc20   91-33836
                                                          CIP

First published in Great Britain by Century Publishing Company
Limited.

First U.S. Edition: February 1992
10 9 8 7 6 5 4 3 2 1

Contents

A GLOVE SHOP IN VIENNA
And Other Stories

VICKY AND
THE CHRISTMAS ANGEL

IT WAS mid-December and a night of snow. All day the thick, soft flakes had fallen quietly, covering the blank-faced nymphs and satyrs on Vienna's innumerable fountains; blanketing the bronze rumps of the rearing horses on which dead warriors of the Habsburg Empire rode forever; giving the trees along the Ringstrasse a spare, Siberian splendour.

Sounds in the snow were muffled. The sound of carriage wheels on the cobbles, the sound of street sellers crying their wares – even the sound of church bells, so much a part of Vienna in those days before the First World War – came far more gently in the snow.

The gas-lamps threw rings of brightness into the squares, the smart shops along the Kärtner Strasse looked like stage sets. In the big apartment houses, those grand, slightly crumbling Viennese houses which look like Renaissance palaces but house simply doctors and lawyers and other self-respecting members of the bourgeoisie, the closed shutters were pierced by rays which the snow threw back in unaccustomed brightness.

One window, however, in one such apartment house, remained unshuttered so that its square of golden light went untrammelled into the dusk. It was a bathroom window and, surprisingly for a bathroom, it was occupied not by one person but by three.

The eldest of these was a girl of about eight. She sat enthroned – and literally so, for there was no doubt about her kingship – on a linen basket from which her legs, in white ribbed stockings and kid boots, stuck out at an angle, for they were a good six inches off the floor.

Her subjects, twins about three years old, were arranged on either side of her on gigantic, upturned chamber-pots. Epically fat, seraphically golden-haired, they sat gazing upwards at their sister. Only Tilda's half-swallowed thumb, Rudi's strangulated ear as he twisted a silken curl tighter and tighter round the lobe, revealed the strain they were undergoing: the strain – at that age – of totally *listening*.

Earlier in the year, listening had not been such anguish. 'Snow White,' 'Hansel and Gretel' or Vicky's own creation – the mighty but gentle giant, 'Thunder Blunder,' whose ill-mannered stomach rumbles caused the thunder which, before they knew this, had so much frightened them . . . all these were so familiar they could be understood without this terrible concentration, this agonising immobility.

But what Vicky was telling them now was different. Somehow more important; more . . . true. It was about Christmas, which was coming ('Soon, now,' said Vicky, *'properly* soon'.) Christmas, a concept so staggering that the twins could hardly grasp it, involving as it did everything they had ever warmed to: food and smiling people and presents – and, most mysterious of all, the *tree*.

'A *great* tree,' said Vicky. 'Mama will buy it at the Christmas Market. But it will be nothing. Just a fir tree. And then. . .'

And then . . . The twins sighed and swayed a little on their seats as Vicky told them the story that every child in Vienna knows: the story of the Christ Child who comes on Christmas Night when the children sleep, to bring the presents and decorate the tree.

But because it was Vicky, in whom the flame of imagination burnt with an almost dangerous brightness, the fat and placid twins saw more than that. They saw the gentle, tiny babe in the manger turn, on Christmas Eve, into a great golden-winged angel who flew through the starry night bearing the glittering array of baubles for the tree; heard the beating of his wings as he steadied himself; felt the curtains stir as he flew in from the mighty heavens to make *their* tree wonderful, leave *their* presents in lovingly labelled heaps beneath its beauty.

'It's the *angel* does all that?' said Tilda, removing her thumb.

'Of course. The Christmas Angel.'

'Can he carry all the presents?' demanded Rudi. 'If I get a big engine can he carry that?'

'He can do everything,' said Vicky. *'Everything.'*

But the angel in the household of Herr Doktor and Frau Fischer had help. In the kitchen Katrina, fat and warm and Czech like all the best cooks in Vienna, produced an ever-growing pile of gingerbread hearts and vanilla crescents; of almond rings and chocolate *guglhupf*. Vicky's mother, pretty and frivolous and very loving, helped too, whispering and rustling behind mysteriously closed doors. As for Vicky's father, erupting irately from the green baize door of his study shouting, 'Bills! Bills! Nothing but bills!', he possibly helped most of all.

A week before Christmas the Christmas visitors began to arrive. First came Vicky's cousin, Fritzl, just a year older than she was, with his mother Frau Zimmermann.

Frau Zimmermann, her father's sister, was something Vicky did not understand; something called a 'Free Thinker'. It meant having to go and speak to the servants when other people were saying their prayers, and taking Fritzl to see the skeletons in the Natural History Museum when everyone else was going to hear the Vienna choirboys. Since Vicky loved both the skeletons and the choirboys, she could never decide whether Free Thinking was a good thing or not.

It was the same with Fritzl. Mostly Fritzl was her friend – inventive and talented. After all, it was Fritzl who had lowered a stuffed eel down the ventilation shaft into Frau Pollack's flat below. But at other times . . .

This time, particularly, the odd, restless and obscurely frightening side of Fritzl seemed to have got worse. He had hardly unpacked before he made her come into the linen cupboard and told her all sorts of things – things which weren't actually very interesting because Kati, the washerwoman, who was her friend, had explained them to her already and anyway they were obvious enough to anyone who used their eyes. But Fritzl added other things which were to say the least of it unlikely because the Kaiser simply wouldn't have done them – and anyway, she didn't like Fritzl's hot and hurried voice or the way he stammered over the words.

But it was in the bathroom at story time that he worried her most. During 'Snow White', or 'Daniel in the Lion's Den,' or 'Thunder Blunder', Fritzl listened well enough, sitting between Tilda and Rudi with his back against the bath. But when it came to the story which mattered more than any other because literal and actual and *true* – then Fritzl made her nervous, fiddling with the loofah, tapping his feet on the tiled floor until Tilda, through her sucked thumb, said moistly and reproachfully, 'Shh, Fithl; she'th telling about the *angel*!' And even then he would sit with his dark, too-bright eyes boring into Vicky and make her go on too quickly, as though only by reaching the end of the story could she find safety. But safety from what?

The last of the Christmas visitors was Cousin Poldi.

Cousin Poldi arrived, as inevitable as the sunset, on the Friday before Christmas Eve, having travelled from Linz where she lived alone above the milliner's shop in which she worked.

Nothing, by then, could put a blight on the Christmas spirit, but Cousin Poldi usually achieved a kind of halt in the general ecstasy, making it necessary for Vicky and the twins, and even her parents, to recharge themselves so to speak after the impact of her arrival.

For Cousin Poldi was, in every way, most decidedly a 'Poor Relation'. Dressed in fusty, dusty black with button boots which looked as though the cat had spent the night on them, she wore a bracelet consisting of a sparse plait of grey hair which had been cut from the head of her mother after death. While there was nothing particularly tragic about the death of Cousin Poldi's mother, who had passed away peacefully in her bed aged eighty-six, the circumstances and the strange smell of preservative which clung to the bracelet made it an object of terror to Vicky, for whom kissing Cousin Poldi when she arrived was a minor kind of martyrdom.

And now, with everyone safely in position, the household of Herr Doktor Fischer could march forward to the great climax of Christmas Eve. A frenzied last-minute clean-up began, the maids gliding silently up and down the already gleaming parquet with huge brushes strapped to their feet. Carpets were thumped, feather-beds beaten, and in the kitchen . . . But there are no words to describe what went on in a good Viennese kitchen just before Christmas in those far-off days before the First World War.

Bed-time prayers, for the children, became a laborious and time-consuming business. Vicky, obsessed by her angel, devised long entreaties for his safe conduct through the skies. The twins, on the other hand, produced an inventory which would not have disgraced the mail order catalogue of a good department store. And each and every night their mother got them out of bed again, all three, because they had forgotten to say: 'And God bless Cousin Poldi.'

Five days before Christmas, the thing happened which meant most of all to Vicky. The tree arrived. A huge tree, all but touching the ceiling of the enormous drawing room, and: 'It's the best tree we've ever had, the most beautiful,' said Vicky, as she had said last year and the year before and was to go on saying all her life.

She wanted presents, she wanted presents very *much*, but this transformation of the still, dark tree – beautiful, but just any tree – into the glittering, beckoning candle-lit vision that they saw when one by one (but always children first) they filed into the room on Christmas Eve . . . That to her, was the wonder of wonders, the magic that Christmas was all about.

And though no one could accuse the Christ Child of having favourites or anything like that, it did seem to Vicky that when He came down to earth He did the Fischers especially proud. There never did seem to be a tree as wonderful as theirs. The things that were on it, such unbelievably delicate things, could only have been made in Heaven: tiny shimmering angels, dolls as big as a thumb, golden-petalled flowers, sweets of course – oh, every kind of sweet. And candles – perhaps a thousand candles, thought Vicky. Candles which caused her father every year to say, 'You'll see if the house doesn't catch fire, you'll see!', and which produced also a light whose softness and radiance had no equal in the world.

The twins grew less seraphic, less placid as the tension grew. 'Will the angel come tonight?' demanded Tilda at her prayers.

'No,' said Vicky. 'You've got to go to sleep for two more nights.'

'I want him to come *now*' said Rudi, '*Now*. . .'

For the last two days, the time for the young ones passed with unbearable slowness. Even Vicky, clothed in her own mantle of imaginings, grew restless. Only Fritzl, who did not have to bless Cousin Poldi because he was not allowed to say his prayers, retained his cheerfulness, looking at Vicky often with that strange and glinting brightness which she could not understand.

But at last it was the twenty-third and on that night her mother turned the key in the huge double doors which led to the drawing room. And at this sound the chrysalis which had been growing inside Vicky all these days broke open and Christmas, in all its boundless and uncontrollable joy, broke out.

She had not expected to sleep but she must nevertheless have slept, because she didn't hear Fritzl come in and yet suddenly he was there bending over her in his nightshirt, shaking her.

'He's there!' said Fritzl, his voice hot and eager as it had been in the linen cupboard. 'Come on, get up. I'll show him to you.'

'Who?' she asked, still stupid from sleep.

'Who do you think? The Christmas Angel. The Christ Child. The one you're always going on about. He's in there, decorating the tree.'

Vicky sat up. Even by the subdued glow of the night-light, Fritzl could see her turn pale. 'But then . . . we shouldn't.'

'Oh, don't be so soft. We wouldn't go in. You can see quite well through the keyhole.'

So Vicky got up and felt for her slippers and crept after Fritzl down the long parquet corridor, careful to make no sound. Her heart was pounding and she felt sick, and this was all because soon now she would see a sight so blinding, so beautiful . . .

That was why she was afraid. That was the reason. Not that odd glitter in Fritzl's eyes, not that shrill edge to his voice. Not anything else.

They were up to the door now. Fritzl was right, the key had been taken out, the hole that was left was big enough . . .

'Go on, have a look,' said Fritzl, giving her a push.

Vicky stepped forward.

'Fritzl! Vicky! How *dare* you!'

Her mother's furious voice sounded from behind them; her arm came out and wrenched Vicky away from the door.

But Vicky had already seen.

Seen the step-ladder, the bunched skirt pulled up to reveal, above the dusty button boots, a desperately unfragrant length of stocking. Seen Cousin Poldi, her mouth full of pins, reach up to hang the star on to the tree.

There was little anyone could do. Her father, frightened by her pallor, her stony silence, gave her a white powder; her mother sat by her bed chafing her hands and wishing as she had not wished anything for years, that Vicky would cry, wail, reproach them for lying – anything to show that she was still a child. But Vicky said nothing. Nothing to Fritzl slinking off to his room, nothing to her parents. Nothing to anyone, because there was nothing at all to say.

Even so, she must have slept once more because she was woken by the sound of sobbing. Not the twins' sobbing, not a child's sobbing at all, but an ugly tearing sound. A sound which frightened her.

She got up and went on to the landing. Though she'd known really what it was, she stood for a while outside Cousin Poldi's door as though hoping for a reprieve.

Then she turned the handle and went in.

Cousin Poldi was sitting upright in a chair. Her starved looking plaits hung down on either side of her blotchy face and there was something dreadfully wrong with her mouth. On the table between the glowing, shining things: snippets of silver ribbon, wisps of gossamer lace, lay the hair bracelet, curled like the tail of some old, sick animal.

Vicky took two steps forward and stood still.

'Your mother is right,' mumbled Cousin Poldi, her hand over her mouth. 'I'm an old idiot, fit for nothing. Every year she reminds me to block up the keyhole – and then I forget.'

Vicky said nothing.

'I get excited, you see . . . All year I prepare . . . So many things are wasted in a milliner's shop, you wouldn't believe; pieces of stuff, bits of ribbon. I keep them all and then in the evenings I make things for the tree. It's a bit lonely in Linz, you see . . . It keeps one busy.'

Vicky took a sudden step back. She had seen the teeth in the glass beside the bed and understood now what was wrong with Cousin Poldi's mouth.

'Every year I've done the tree for your mother. It was so nice being able to help . . . she's so good to me, so beautiful. If it had been her you'd seen. . .' She broke off. Then forgetting her naked gums she dropped her hand and looked at Vicky with a last entreaty in her rheumy eyes.

'I've spoilt it for you for ever, haven't I?' said Cousin Poldi.

And Vicky, implacable in her wretchedness, said, 'Yes.'

In every family there is apt to be a child around whom, in a given year, Christmas centres – not, of course, because that child is more greatly loved than the others, but because of something – a readiness, a special capacity for wonder, perhaps just a particular age – which gives that child the power of absolute response.

In the Fischer household that child had been Vicky. Now, with the centre dropped out of their Christmas world, Herr Doctor and Frau Fischer nevertheless had to push the day relentlessly along its course.

Fritzl, moody and ill-looking, was no help. It was the twins with their sublime unconcern, their uncomplicated greed, who made it possible to carry on; Rudi wriggling through morning mass in St Stephen's cathedral, Tilda screeching up and down the corridors waiting for dusk.

And then at last it was over, the agonising waiting, and the moment had come. The moment when they all assembled in the dining room and listened to the sweet soft tones of the old cow-bell with which their mother summoned them. The moment when the door was thrown open and, the children first, the adults afterwards walked in, dazzled, towards the presents and the tree.

With a last despairing glance at Vicky's face, Frau Fischer reached for her bell. And then: 'Stop!' said Vicky. 'We're not all here.'

Everyone looked at everyone else. 'I'm here,' said Rudi, reasonably, sticking to essentials. So were Tilda and Fritzl; so was Fritzl's mother. Herr Doktor Fischer with his home-made fire extinguisher was there; so was the cook, so were the maids.

'Cousin Poldi isn't here,' said Vicky.

Herr Doktor Fischer and his wife exchanged glances.

'She's gone, Vicky; she's going back to Linz. She thought it would be better.'

'Then she must be fetched,' said Vicky.

'But, Vicky. . .'

'We can't go in till we are all together,' said Vicky, still in that same inflexible, unchildlike voice. 'She'll have to be fetched.'

Herr Doktor Fischer took out his watch. 'The train doesn't go until four,' he said to his wife. 'I could probably get her still. But it would take some time.'

Vicky said nothing. She just stood and waited and for the first time since Fritzl had stolen to her in the night, there was a glimmer of tears in her eyes.

'You had better go,' said Vicky's mother quickly. 'We can wait.'

The word *wait* fell on the twins' heads like a cartload of boulders.

'No,' wailed Rudi, 'Rudi *can't* wait!'

'Nor can't Tilda wait neither. Tilda wants her presents now!'

'Hush,' said Vicky sternly. 'How *dare* you act like that on Christmas Eve? And anyway, I'm going to tell you a story.'

Still sniffing, doubtful, they came closer. 'In the bathroom?'

'No. Here.'

Vicky looked over at Fritzl, ready to measure herself against him, and then looked away again because somehow there was no longer any threat.

'What story do you think?' she said to the twins. 'On a day like this? The story of the Christmas Angel, of course. The one who came last night, to bring the presents and decorate the tree.'

And she told the story. Told it so that Frau Fischer had to move over to the velvet window curtain and hide her face. Told it so that the sound of Herr Doktor Fischer's footsteps, the squeak of Cousin Poldi's returning button boots, were almost an intrusion.

No one said anything. Only when at last the great doors did open and Vicky moved forward to follow Fritzl and the ecstatically tottering twins into the room, her mother held her back.

'No, Vicky,' she said softly, 'let the children go in first. We adults . . . we *adults* will come on afterwards.'

And then very slowly, she led her daughter forward towards the shining glory of the tree.

DOUSHENKA

THERE WAS nothing odd about finding a photograph of Great-uncle Edwin wedged at the back of a bureau drawer. It was a day for finding wedged great-uncles, crumpled brides cut from local newspapers, albums of yellowing babies . . . I was in my last year at Oxford and had come up to London to help my parents move house.

But Great-uncle Edwin . . . ? He had been a grocer, I thought, in a South London suburb. Wimbledon? Teddington? So why this photograph in which he wore a high-necked *boyar* blouse, felt boots and a round fur hat? Beside the mild, slightly surprised figure in its Russian clothes was the usual draped table on which he rested a light hand. But where was the aspidistra? Where the picture of the Queen? That wasn't . . . but of course it was. A samovar!

I put the picture in my pocket, but I had to wait until the following Christmas for the visit of my mother's eccentric older sister, my Aunt Geraldine, to get the story.

'Edwin?' she said. 'Ah, yes, poor Edwin! Dear God, what a romantic that man was! And then to marry Edith . . . And yet. . .'

'Would you tell me?' I said. We were walking along the Embankment towards Chelsea Bridge. Beside us, the Thames snuffled gently against its walls, a slow barge went down towards Greenwich. It was all very English, very peaceful, very grey.

She looked at me, surprised, pleased perhaps that I – uncouth and masculine and young – should seem to care about the past.

'He was obsessed,' she said. 'I don't know how it happened. Perhaps a label on a crate of smoked sturgeon from the Volga, a delivery note for Ternov ham . . . He kept a grocer's shop in Putney.'

'Russia?' I said and shivered as she nodded, because it is a devastating experience, finding a fellow-sufferer from the same disease.

'If he was walking along here with you,' said my Aunt Geraldine, 'he wouldn't see this river.'

'I know,' I said. 'He'd see the blue ice beginning to break on the Neva, the pale façade of the Winter Palace, Rasputin's unspeakable head bobbing on the water. . .'

My aunt looked at me. A long look. 'I see,' she said. 'Though of course in those days Rasputin was still alive.'

'One can't choose one's obsessions,' she went on, and I think she meant to comfort me. 'I myself spent the first three years of my adolescence as Third Daughter in the House of the Four Winds in the province of Soo Chow. Outwardly, of course, I was Geraldine Ferguson, the only girl in the Upper Fourth with acne *and* bunions. But inwardly I was Golden Bells whose verses did not displease the Emperor.' She stopped for a moment and we leant over the Embankment Wall. 'Something to do with reincarnation, perhaps,' she said.

'And Uncle Edwin?' I prompted.

'Ah yes. Well, he had it very badly. Words like "*droshki*" or "*troika*" would send him into a sort of trance. I imagine he must have been the only grocer in London who climbed to his haricot bean jar on three volumes of Lermontov. But of course he never had a hope of going and he found the language almost impossible to learn.'

'And then he married Edith?'

My aunt nodded, staring at the gentle, unfrozen, incurably un-Russian Thames.

'I shall never know what made him do it,' she said.

'What was she like?'

'If I know what she was like, it is because I was with Edwin when he died. It was only in the last days of his life that he spoke freely. Before that he never complained.'

I waited.

'She was a "not tonight, dear" woman,' said my aunt. 'They're extinct now, I gather, and thank God for it because they're killers. Slow killers. Poisoners. Edith didn't just have nights when it was too hot and nights when it was too cold and nights when she had cream on her face. She had nights when her stays had left her tender and nights when the neighbour's mother-in-law was asleep the other side of the wall. . .'

'Poor Edwin.'

'Poor Edwin indeed. Of course it just made him worse. He'd read Pushkin: "soul of my soul, light of my heart", sitting there on a barrel of pickled cucumbers, and then go upstairs and find Edith with her mouth shut like a trap because it was the anniversary of the Prince Consort's funeral.'

'So what happened then?'

'What happened then,' said my Aunt Geraldine, 'was that a man called Mr Frobisher shot himself.'

'He hadn't,' she went on, '*meant* to shoot himself. He'd been after pheasants on his home moor when he tripped and fell and the gun went off. Mr Frobisher was a retired haberdasher who'd done extremely well out of a patent spring-clip for bow ties. He was also Edwin's godfather and when the will was read, it turned out that he'd left Edwin a thousand pounds.'

I stopped dead, a few yards from the Albert Bridge.

'No,' I said. 'He didn't?'

My aunt nodded. 'Yes,' she said. 'He was a brave man. He went to Russia.'

'Brave?' I said. 'Idiotic! Insane!' To put all those dreams to the test . . . to travel on trains to whose wheels still clung ghost shreds of Anna Karenina's muff. . . to let the sapphire curtains of the Maryinsky part on the fabulous Kschessinskaya, mistress of the Czar . . .

'He left his assistant to look after the shop,' said my aunt, 'sent Edith back to Mummy in Clapham (and weren't they both pleased!) and arrived, at the end of April, at the Finland Station in St Petersburg.'

Like everyone who dreams of Russia, he had seen it always under snow. But now it was spring. In the Alexander Gardens, where the English governesses sat watching diminutive princesses roll their hoops, the lime trees were green and gold. The Neva sparkled and danced between its granite banks, the air blew softly from the Gulf of Finland. From his hotel he could see Peter the Great, bronze and invincible, astride his rearing horse; in the drawer of his writing desk, impressing him vastly, he found the visiting card of the room's former occupant: Lord Broomhaven of Craghill Castle, Yorks.

Edwin had no plan for his days. He just walked and walked, as pleased with the marble and jasper sarcophagi of the dead Romanovs as with a stall selling gingerbread from Tver.

And then one evening he was walking down Theatre Street . . .

My aunt paused. 'You've heard of it?'

'Oh, yes.' I'd heard of it all right. A wide and elegant street running between the Alexandrinsky Theatre and the Fontanka river. A street peopled with limbo's most graceful ghosts: the young Pavlova running to the Summer Gardens to feed her swans; Karsavina, after her début, ecstatic at Petipa's praise; sledgeloads of nascent cygnets or Sugar-plum fairies driving to rehearsal at the Maryinsky . . . For on one side of Theatre Street, half huge and splendid palace, half nunnery, is the place where it all began: the Imperial Ballet School.

Edwin was no balletomane. It was the hour of the evening meal, the street was empty and he was on the way back to his hotel. What stopped him was a sound: perhaps the most forlorn sound in the whole world. The sound of someone *not* crying.

He turned. Leaning against a closed doorway in the side of the huge building was a young girl. She wore an old-fashioned brown cloak a little small for her; an ancient carpet-bag lay like an unwanted animal across her feet, and on her long, dark lashes he could see the tears held steady by her bursting will.

'Are you locked out?' Edwin managed in his clumsy Russian.

She lifted her face to his. 'Yes,' she said. 'But for ever. I have been expelled for ever from the Imperial Ballet school.'

Her name was Kira. Edwin took her back to the hotel. And began, he said, his life.

'If you consider,' said my aunt, 'you'll realise that always, in every age, there's been a romantic ideal: a kind of girl whose looks, whose whole way of life, appeases that yearning for chivalry and tenderness that even the most sophisticated men don't seem able to stamp out of themselves. All those Paris *midinettes* with their poverty and hearts of gold; those demure oppressed Victorian governesses . . . And of course, then as now, the girls of the ballet.'

Kira was barely seventeen, small-boned and supple as a willow. Not at all beautiful, Edwin told my aunt, desperately proud of this piece of detachment. Not beautiful, then: a narrow face with immense Byzantine eyes, smooth hair pulled up behind faun's ears. 'And when she sat down to listen to you,' Edwin said, 'it was her *feet* she folded.'

As soon as he took charge of Kira, Edwin changed. He might really have been the Lord Broomhaven of Craghill whose visiting card he had taken to carrying in his pocket. He ordered a room for her in the hotel, was told there was no room, insisted – and got one. He asked for a meal to be served to them upstairs, was told it was too late, and presently sat with her by his window over grilled sturgeon and sparkling Crimean wine.

And afterwards, lying on his bearskin rug, shredding its loose fur into petals with her narrow, nervous hands, Kira told him her story.

'How did he understand her?' I asked, 'if his Russian was so bad?'

My aunt shrugged. 'He understood her because he *had* to understand her,' she said.

Kira was in her last year at the Ballet School, due to leave soon and join the *corps de ballet* at the Maryinsky. She made him see her life there very clearly: the huge, empty rooms where they practised, the vast dormitories each with its own governess in her curtained bed; the windows to the street made of frosted glass because once a pupil had eloped with a young hussar. The discipline, the austerity was what came over most. But she was happy.

And then her father, an idealistic country schoolmaster, wrote a book which was regarded as seditious and was sent to Siberia. A few months later her brother, a student at the Conservatoire, got himself mixed up with a group of revolutionaries and was imprisoned in the dreaded fortress of St Peter and St Paul.

Even then, she said, they wouldn't have done anything to her. The ballet was outside politics in Russia, it was their pride to have it so. But she had lost her head.

'It was knowing he was so near,' she said, lifting her head to the window where the thin gold spire of the fortress cathedral still pierced the pale light of a northern evening. 'Just across the river.'

She started creeping out at night to meet his friends, a group of hot-heads who were making plans to free him. Inevitably she was discovered. And dismissed . . .

'But where will you go?' asked Edwin. 'Is your mother still

alive?'

Kira shook her head. There was only her Aunt Lydia, who lived in a small town near Kazan. A dreadful town, Kira said: two dusty streets, endless fields of sugar-beet. 'And chickens. You've never seen so many chickens.'

It was this aunt she had been vainly awaiting when Edwin came.

'I need hardly tell you,' said my Aunt Geraldine, as we made our way back along the river, 'that Edwin behaved with perfect propriety. . .'

He sent another telegram to Kira's Aunt Lydia, installed Kira in his own room while he moved to a smaller one overlooking a courtyard, and prepared to make tolerable for the shocked and lonely girl the time of waiting.

He began formally enough with drives to the Islands, visits to museums. But soon he found that she liked, as he did, just to walk the streets, just to look and listen, and explore . . .

So they fed the pigeons in the Summer Gardens, bought hot *piroshki* and ate them leaning against the bronze horses of the Anichkov Bridge . . . In the evenings they strolled along the embankment and listened to the students playing their mandolins, or drank lemonade on one of the barge cafés moored along the Quays. And always, without seeming to do so Edwin managed, in this city which was wholly strange to him, to avoid any place which might give her pain. Not just the Maryinsky Theatre, but all the theatres in this pleasure-loving town. Not just a poster announcing a ballet programme – even the portrait of a dancer in an art shop he could somehow smell out and keep from her.

Gradually her natural gaiety came to the surface, her eyes lost their shipwrecked look. On the day she laughed out loud at a tiny Maltese terrier, like a white wig on casters, which was chasing a huge Borzoi across Mars Meadow, he felt as though he had been given a million pounds. And already, knowing what the future would bring, he began to hoard those small, unimportant details which memory uses to unlock the doors of love. The way she cupped her bowl of coffee, holding its warmth against her chest; the despairing shake of her head when he mispronounced, yet again, a poem she was teaching him about a crocodile walking down the Nevsky Prospect . . .

She was a thief, too, unashamedly stealing sugar from the café tables to feed to the tired old *droshky* nags.

And every day as they returned to the hotel Edwin would hold his breath, expecting to see the waiting figure of Aunt Lydia, whom he imagined always as a vast peasant woman in felt boots and sacking, with a basket of chickens in her lap. And when she wasn't sitting there, he felt weak with relief. Another day's reprieve. Another day of idyll.

For what happened next, Edwin always blamed himself. He should have taken more care, supervised what she drank . . .

'One morning,' said my aunt, 'Kira woke flushed and feverish. She couldn't eat. By the evening she was very ill.'

It was typhoid fever. The hotel insisted she be moved to hospital. Edwin bribed and cajoled and blustered and they put up blankets dipped in disinfectant and let her stay. Edwin nursed her and let no one near. Two days earlier he had been shy of touching her elbow to guide her across the road. Now he washed her, changed her nightclothes, held her head when she vomited. When the old-fashioned English doctor wanted her hair cut, Edwin himself cut the long black tresses, strand by strand, while she slept.

In her delirium, Kira went back into early childhood. She wept as the chickens of Kazan pecked her small fingers, ran after her brother begging him to wait, oh, *please* to wait for her, screamed as her mother's grave was filled again with earth. And always, like a brook running through the centre of her experience, was this *leit-motif*, the work of the ballet, as she murmured: '*Plié* . . . *battement tendu* . . . *soutenu*. . .', counted her beat and in her cracked and fever-ridden voice hummed snatches of music.

Edwin never left her, day or night. Before, he had had the luxury of a romantic and tender emotion; he had been 'in love'. Now he cut right through that. Kira became his unborn child, the wife he had never had, the woman she would be when she was old. When it was over, he said, he *knew* her.

At the peak of Kira's illness, Aunt Lydia arrived at the hotel. He had imagined her quite wrongly. She was a thin, anxious woman in an exhumed-looking black coat – the village schoolmistress. All the time he spoke to her she kept a handkerchief soaked in carbolic across her mouth. Illness terrified her; she dreaded being asked to stay and nurse her niece.

Edwin reassured her, gave her money for the journey back, told her he would bring Kira himself when she was well. And forgot her.

It is a slow illness, typhoid fever, and nearly a month passed before Kira was out of danger. Then suddenly she was sitting up in bed, convalescent. She had a passion for jigsaw puzzles. There was one in particular, of the Czarina and the four little Grand Duchesses . . . 'A real stinger, that was,' Edwin told my aunt. 'We must have spent hours looking for Anastasia's hair-ribbon.'

Her illness seemed to have washed Kira free of her distress about the Ballet School. She asked no questions about the future, obeyed Edwin like a trusting child, seemed content to drift.

One beautiful day towards the end of May, with the sunlight streaming into the room, he picked her up and carried her from her bed to the open window.

'*Oh!*' she said. 'Oh, Edwin, look! The river! The sky! Oh, isn't it *marvellous* that I'm not dead!'

And she turned in his arms and kissed him.

'Edwin was no fool,' said my aunt. 'He knew exactly what that kiss was about. Gratitude for a return to health, artless affection, nothing more. All the same, as a result of it, he decided to change his life.'

Two days later he left Kira with some magazines, went along to the English grocer in Gogol Street and asked for a job. They needed English-speaking staff, were impressed by his knowledge of the trade and told him he could start the following month.

Edwin didn't go back to Kira straight away. He walked back across Palace Square and sat down on one of the benches in the Alexander Gardens.

It was a beautiful day. Babies in perambulators passed him, pushed by nurses with streamers in their caps; beside him on the grass a small girl in a white dress built a stick-house for a captured beetle. And Edwin closed his eyes and looked into the future.

He was a modest man, but he knew that he was better than

Aunt Lydia and the chickens of Kazan. And sitting there, the sun on his face, Edwin lived through the life he would have with Kira.

He saw their little flat on the other bank of the Neva where everything was cheaper; two rooms, a window box, a canary to sing for Kira when he was out at work. He saw her sitting opposite him in the morning, cupping her bowl of coffee, while he told her how much, how very much it had grown in the night – her poor, shorn, duckling-feather hair; saw her running towards him in the evening in an apron too big for her. He felt her hand creep from her muff into his pocket as they walked the snowy streets to buy their Christmas tree; dusted the pollen off her nose after he had brought her the first king-cups. By the gay and gilded fountains of Peterhof they bandied preposterous names for their unborn child. At night, in their big wooden bed, he watched her spoon cherry jam into her tea and told her that her habits were disgusting, that he loved her more than life itself.

'When he was dying,' said my Aunt Geraldine, jabbing the tip of her umbrella into a cracked paving-stone, 'he told me that of all the hours of his life, that hour in the Alexander Gardens was the one he would most like to have again.'

It was noon when he returned to the hotel. He was a quiet man, always, and now, opening the door of his room, he made no sound. Kira's back was to him. She was standing by the open window through which there flowed, badly played, relentlessly rhythmic, the sound of someone practising a Schubert waltz. Kira's feet were folded in the fifth position; her arms were curved in to her side. And then as he watched, slowly, so shakily, with the ghost of her former strength, she began to go through one of her old routines: *glissade . . . jeté . . . attitude en avant . . .*

Edwin stood very still, holding on to the knob of the door. He could see only her back and the nape of her neck with its heartbreaking, sawn-off hair, but he knew . . .

'You're crying,' he said.

Her arms dropped. Her foot glided to rest like an autumn leaf.

'From the back of my neck you can tell I'm crying?' she said wonderingly.

Probably she grew up at that moment. At any rate she turned and came towards him and lifted her face to his, and he kissed her wet eyelids, her mouth, while everything inside him crumbled slowly into dust.

The next day he went to Druce's in the Nevsky Prospect and bought a pair of incredibly expensive English gloves. He said he didn't think he could have done it without those gloves. Then he took out Lord Broomhaven's visiting card and drove to Theatre Street.

'I'll never know how he managed it,' said my aunt. 'You'll notice I've used the same words about him again and again: "meek", "quiet", "gentle". All the same, he confronted the Principal and persuaded her that he really was an English aristocrat whose *entourage* had been horrified to find a member of the Czar's famous Ballet School abandoned and at death's door. He hinted at a scandal in the English press, implied a special interest in Kira on the part of a high-ranking diplomat —and just at the right moment became a supplicant, stressing Kira's remorse and change of heart.'

The decision to expel her had not been unanimous. Now it was reversed.

And so, on a still grey morning, he drove Kira back to Theatre Street. At the last minute she was afraid and by the same door at which he had found her she clung to him and said, 'No! No! I want to stay with you!'

But he was beyond everything by now and gently he loosened her arms and picked up the great brass knocker shaped like the Imperial Eagle of the Czar, and then he just stood there very quietly and watched her go.

My aunt stopped talking. She had finished her umbrella-jabbing and we stood side by side, our elbows on the parapet, looking at, and not seeing, the river Thames.

'That's all?' I said at last.

She shrugged. 'He'd meant to go on, to see Moscow, Kiev, the Crimea. But his money had run out, of course, and anyway. . .'

'So he went back to Edith?'

My aunt nodded. 'Edith,' she said, 'was tired after the

journey from Clapham. She was sitting up in bed with cream on her face and —'

'No! She didn't! She didn't say it to him. Not that first night!'

'She said it! And Edwin went up to her and said: "Yes. Tonight. And any other night I choose." And went on living with her for thirty years.'

'Oh, *hell!*' I said. 'He had so little. For so short a time.'

'No,' said my aunt. 'You're wrong. Edwin was all right.'

I waited.

'I was with him at the end, as I told you. And just before he died, suddenly . . . he lifted up his head. . .' She broke off. 'I have never,' she went on, 'seen such a look of happiness on any human face. And then he said this one word. I didn't know what it was; I had to look it up.'

'*Dousha*,' I said. 'Was it that? *Doushenka?*' And suddenly it seemed desperately, frantically important that I had guessed right.

My aunt looked up, started. 'That was it. It's an endearment, of course.'

'Yes.' It's an endearment, all right, and for my money the best ever, the ultimate. 'My soul', 'My little soul' . . .

'So you see,' said my aunt, unfurling her umbrella, 'that he really was *all right.*'

And we turned and left the quiet, grey, incurably English river and went home to tea.

A GLOVE SHOP IN VIENNA

I MUST have flown over Vienna a dozen times and scarcely stirred in my seat. So why, this time, did I peer forward so eagerly into the darkness, searching the haphazard sprinkling of lights below me for . . . what? The city of my boyhood? My youth?

No, it wasn't the Vienna of the chestnut trees, Strauss in the Stadtpark, *guglhupf* at Sacher's that I groped for, devastated by the sudden, embarrassing nostalgia of middle age. It was something more specific; a particular collection of . . . ghosts, I suppose. The ghosts of my ancestors.

Only of course they weren't ancestors then. Just my relations. And could anyone have made ghosts of them though they were long, long dead?

My Tante Wilhelmina, who threw me bodily over a laurel hedge in the *Tiergarten* to shield me from the sight of two ancient llamas making sudden love? Or Gross Tante Gretl, overcome by Goethe, walking skirtless in the Brahms Platz, the *Nature Lyrics* open in her hand?

No, they would have made lousy ghosts, those gloriously batty aunts of Old Vienna. I can see them now, each embalmed, timeless in their own moment of legend: Great-aunt Netta, overcome by grief on the day that Crown Prince Rudolf shot himself, rolling her false grey plait into the *Apfelstrudel*. Great-aunt Trudi carrying the waistcoat button which had belonged to Beethoven to concerts in the Bosendorfer Saal.

There wasn't much wrong with my uncles either. Uncle Ernst, who ate eighteen *Zwetschkenknödel* on the day he died. Great-uncle Gotlieb, agonisingly shy, who spent his wedding night sitting alone beneath the equestrian statue of the Archduke Charles. Great-uncle Frederick, hurling – on the barricades in '48 – a barrel of salted gherkins at the Imperial Guard.

But mostly, as the plane flew quietly through the night, I found myself thinking of one man in my past – my very distant past – Great-uncle Max.

Great-uncle Max was a very old man indeed when I was a boy and he was famous by that time not for any particular eccentricity or time-defying *bon môt*, but for something both less spectacular and more remarkable: a Great Love.

Needless to say, in the matter of a Great Love there are bound to be elements of secrecy, of mystery . . . As a boy, overhearing the women gossip in my mother's drawing room, the story bored me. A Great Love seemed to me in every way less interesting than the ability to swallow eighteen *Zwetschkenknödel* or throw pickled gherkins at the Imperial Guard.

Now, close on half a century later, I was no longer quite so sure.

The story of my Great-uncle Max's Great Love is unusual in that it has not only a happy ending but a happy middle. The beginning, however, was sad.

Max Bergmann was thirty-nine, unmarried, a successful solicitor, small, blue-eyed and just a little bald when he attended, on a historic night in May, a performance of *Rheingold* at the Opera House.

Rheingold, if you remember, is the first work in Wagner's great operatic cycle, *The Ring*. Uncle Max, slipping into his box and bracing himself a little (for Wagner made him nervous) thus saw the curtain go up on what the programme referred to as 'the underwater bottom of the Rhine'.

The Vienna Opera at the time prided itself on the realism of its stage effects. Cardboard waves undulated laboriously from left to right and back again: jagged rocks pierced the watery gloom; undefined but undoubtedly sub-aquatic plants wreathed upwards towards the proscenium arch.

And dead centre, triumphant, the *pièce de resistance*: the three Rhinemaidens, lowered from steel cables to hang suspended some twenty feet above the stage.

Mermaid-tailed, scale-covered, golden-haired – the size of

half-grown hippopotami – they swayed and sang, immortal sirens of the deep, beckoning men to their doom.

'*Weia Waga, Woge du Welle*,' sang the centre maiden, a lady named Helene Goertel-Eisen, not because she was off her head but because that was what Wagner, in his wisdom, had given her to sing.

The rest is operatic history. The ghastly twang of snapping steel; the orchestra, at first unheeding, pursuing its relentless Wagnerian *leitmotif*; then breaking into splintered sound, silence . . .

While Helene Goertel-Eisen, pushing forty, topping the scales at one hundred and twenty kilos, came crashing to the ground.

She was not, in fact, greatly hurt. Shaken, of course. Bruised. Angry; very. And the lawyer she called in to help her sue the Opera Company was Uncle Max.

Max had been deeply upset by the incident. The vast, invincible figure hanging aloft in shimmering silver, and then the flailing limbs, the crumpled body, the broken mermaid's tail rolling into the footlights . . .

He never attended a performance of *Rheingold* again. And six months after the accident, he married Helene Goertel-Eisen.

Whether my Great-uncle Max and my Great-aunt Helene were happily married I cannot say, for it was a question which, in the Vienna of my childhood, no one asked, let alone answered. In those days (when the infant Freud, I daresay, was still bowling his hoop along the Pfeffer Gasse) one wasn't happily married. One wasn't unhappily married either. One was married.

Certainly my Uncle Max was very good to her. To the end, he called her his 'Rheinmäderl' and denied her nothing. As for my Aunt Helene, she gave up her career and settled down contentedly in the big yellow villa in the suburb of Hitzing which Max bought for her, furnishing it in the Makart style which was just sweeping Vienna: peacock feathers, shell ornaments and large numbers of small stuffed animals under glass. Freed from even the minimal restraints of her career, she was able to indulge her passion for Karlsbad plums and *Linzer Torte* and became, even by current standards, not just very, but extraordinarily fat.

After a year or two, being of a rather indolent nature, she

brought her Cousin Lily to live in Hitzing, to take over the housekeeping.

Cousin Lily belonged to that now extinct band of faintly-etched and unassuming spinsters whose own lives never quite break into flame and who live at the periphery of others – often indispensable, as often ignored. She was pale, long-nosed and ageless and wore round her neck a necklace of the milk teeth of all the children in the family. It was a disquieting necklace: brownly mottled in places, never quite free of the suggestion of dental caries and tiny flecks of dried blood.

Milk teeth or no, Cousin Lily was an excellent and un-obtrusive housekeeper, keeping Uncle Max's clothes in order, supervising the maids. And my Uncle Max, now a vigorous man in his early forties, thus had a beautifully run home, a prosperous business, an undemanding wife . . .

Had, in short, everything.

Well, nearly everything. For to tell the truth, Aunt Helene was a trifle *too* undemanding. Probably it was quite simply a matter of her bulk. One imagines her, in the matter of sex, prepared in every way to do her duty but feeling, perhaps, that it was all happening a long way off; possibly even to someone else.

If Freud had by now stopped bowling his hoop along the Pfeffer Gasse, he could not have got much further than examining his incipient moustache in the bedroom of his parents' house. It was therefore in the conventions of his own day that Uncle Max solved this most conventional of problems.

He took a mistress.

In the old Habsburg Empire there was a precedent for everything. From Bohemia one got the best cooks, the finest glass. From Hungary one imported horses and violin players for the Philharmonic.

But for a mistress . . . somehow, for a mistress you couldn't do better than a real, a proper '*echt*' Viennese.

My Uncle Max, searching the chorus at the Folk Opera, the little dressmakers scuttling by with cardboard boxes, found what he was looking for at last, in a glove shop in the Kärntner Strasse.

Susie Siebermann was everything a mistress should be: golden-haired, blue-eyed and not too young. Uncle Max, detecting an unexpected rip in his grey kid gloves, had been despatched by Tante Helene to replace them before an important dinner. Susie did nothing except sell him another pair, but it was enough.

He offered her a villa in the Vienna Woods, but she was modest and sensible and took instead a small apartment in the unfashionable district beside the Danube Canal. This she furnished simply, in the old Biedemeyer style, with painted furniture, white-looped curtains and geraniums in pots – for there was nothing of the courtesan in Susie, who recalled a simpler, more pastoral kind of mistress: Giselle in her forest hut waiting for Prince Albrecht: Gretchen at her spinning-wheel . . . Only one object linked Susie's love nest with the grand villa in Hitzing: a large, mildly malodorous stuffed squirrel (a present from an anonymous admirer) on which Uncle Max, when he came to visit, hung his hat.

The apartment faced inwards, towards a cobbled courtyard with an old pear tree in the centre, and when the shutters were closed (and of course they always were closed when Uncle Max was there) the call of the street sellers, the carpet-beating, the sound of tug-boats hooting up the Danube, came as the gentlest, the most undisturbing counterpoint to their secret and illicit love.

And indeed their love *was* secret. Very secret. It had to be. Let no one imagine that the Vienna of those days was a permissive '*oh-la-la*' sort of place. In the Imperial Hofburg, sixty-seven or so moribund Archduchesses tottered about on Spanish heels, sniffing out imperceptible breaches of etiquette. Vast armies of monumentally incompetent civil servants nevertheless managed to keep tabs on the bourgeoisie. No, in the Vienna of my Uncle Max's youth, a prosperous solicitor who wanted to stay that way did not exhibit his mistress in public.

And then, of course, there was Helene. Helene who, in one doom-filled moment, had been thrown so tragically from her steel cable above the underwater bottom of the Rhine and who must never, never be hurt again.

And she was not. My Uncle Max and his Susie were incredibly careful. He never took a *fiacre* to the apartment but walked, his hat over his eyes, or took a horse-bus two stops further before doubling most cunningly back. To the *concierge* he was Herr Finkelstein from Linz, and it was as Herr Finkelstein that Susie addressed him when she opened the door, even if the corridor was entirely empty. Nor did he ever, however much he might be tempted, visit Susie more than twice a week: on Tuesday evening when Helene held a card party, and on Saturday afternoon when she visited her relations.

So much is fact. What happened next – how the change in their relationship came about – no one will ever know for certain.

For my part, I think it happened very slowly. I think for days and weeks and months my Uncle Max came and hung his hat on the stuffed squirrel and sat politely, first in Susie's kitchen drinking coffee, because after all it was a business arrangement and neither of them was all that young. And then one day, perhaps, he put down his coffee cup too quickly, staining the cloth, and when Susie rose to dab at it he caught her and held her and began then and there to pull the hairpins from her piled-up golden hair. I think the day came when, returning to his office after lunch, he took a long and pointless detour past the glove shop in the Kärntner Strasse – not to see her, of course, or wave to her through the glass – just to know that she was there.

He was not a very imaginative man. Susie was even a little stupid. There cannot, on the surface, have been much spiritual content in their love. He called her his '*Putzchen*', his '*Mauslein*',: she, no doubt, giggled and squealed during moments when exaltation would have been more proper.

And yet, as he walked through the dusk towards his abode of shame and found the May-green lime trees limned in lamplight almost too beautiful to be endured, he must have begun to suspect that he was getting more than he was paying for. Until one day, lying behind closed shutters in his Susie's arms, listening to the soft cooing of the pigeons on the roof, it must have dawned on my modest, unassuming Uncle Max that he had found what half the world was looking for in vain: a Great Love.

With this realisation came sudden black despair. What was he doing to her, his Susie, his treasure? Hiding her away behind closed shutters and barred doors! What was he doing to himself? Tearing himself from her for days at a time, confining his passion to the inhuman restraints of the calendar! How bitter it all was, how cruel!

'*Ach*, Suserl,' my Uncle Max would say as the scent of lilac, piercing the shutters, drifted towards the bed on which they lay, 'how I would like to take you driving in my carriage to the Prater.'

'Just once,' Susie would confess, rubbing her cheek against his. 'Just once I would like to walk on your arm down the Ring-Strasse and nod to all my friends. I am so *proud* of you.'

But of course they knew it could never be. Sweet and precious their love might be but also, and for always, secret, unhallowed, furtive.

And this was the way things stood until the day of Tante Helene's epic picnic in the Vienna Woods.

The Vienna Woods, even as late as my own childhood, deserved every impassioned stanza from Austria's minor poets, every waltz-beat paean from the pen of every Strauss. A blue-green halo for the city, tender with beech trees, studded with flower-filled meadows, it had everything: viewpoints and castle ruins; rivulets and roe deer and, in the taverns, a wild, green wine . . .

My Tante Helene's picnics were famous. Seldom fewer than three carriages as well as unbelievable quantities of food set out from Hitzing. On this particular Sunday there was Tante Helene herself, a tenor resting from the Opera on account of nodules on his larynx, a string quartet from Buda-Pest, my Uncle Max, his articled clerk – and of course, Cousin Lily.

The party disembarked. The food baskets were carried to a forest clearing and with nature-loving cries, the party plunged joyfully into the woods. Only Cousin Lily remained, half-concealed by the lid of an enormous hamper, her button boots pointing skywards, her milk teeth necklace paled by the September sunshine as she patiently buttered rolls, sliced salami, spread *topfen* cheese upon the pumpernickl . . .

For a while, only the sound of distant bird-song threaded the air. Then, from the depths of the forest, came a loud and triumphant shriek.

'*Herrenpilze!*' screamed my Tante Helene and plunged thunderously into a thicket from which the yellow, shining caps of the edible boletus beckoned.

The tenor with nodules followed. So did the string quartet, although their shoes were thin. Uncle Max joined them.

It is difficult to convey the wild, primeval excitement which, even to this day, the sight of edible fungi arouses in the bosom of the Austrian middle class. Perhaps it is the last expression of a blood-lust which the English, possessing such things as a coastline and moors full of grouse and partridge, are able to express in other ways.

The party, at all events, went wild. They gathered *herrenpilze*, they gathered *steinpilze*. They gathered *baehrenpatzen* and *chanterelles* and all the other slimy horrors which the Viennese eat and which even now, forty years later, can bring the bile to my throat as I remember them.

Over one toadstool, however, there was argument.

'No, Helenchen, not that one!' admonished Uncle Max.

'But yes, Maxerl, don't fuss. We always ate that one as children in the Dorflital.'

'Please, Helene, don't let Bettinka put that one in the soup,' begged Cousin Lily later that evening, as they returned triumphantly to Hitzing.

But it went into the soup. The maids wouldn't eat it. Uncle Max and Cousin Lily, with unaccustomed firmness, declined it also. But Helene ate every mouthful.

Twenty-four hours later, she was dead.

Uncle Max was shattered. He suffered. He blamed himself. Long after the black horses with their fearful, nodding plumes had carried his Rhinemaiden to her last resting place, my Uncle Max crept desolately between his villa in Hitzing and his office in the Wipplinger Strasse. It was left to Cousin Lily, from whose dusty black pockets crumpled mauve handkerchiefs protruded like terrible boils, to manage the household and offer – between bouts of weeping – to return to Graz.

My Uncle Max did not visit his Susie for over a month after the funeral. When he did they made love in muted undertones, embarrassed by their unquenchable compatibility. After a few weeks, however, there occurred to Uncle Max the thought which would have occurred a great deal sooner to somebody less nice.

He was free! Free to drive his Susie in a carriage through the Prater, free of Herr Finkelstein from Linz, free to visit her whenever he wished with the shutters open to the sky!

No, idiot that he was, what was he thinking of? Free to marry her!

'Susie, *Putzchen, Liebchen!*,' my Uncle Max must have cried when next he saw her, throwing his hat joyfully on to the squirrel. 'Don't you understand, my little *schatz*? No more secrecy, no more pretending and hiding away!'

Susie, who had grasped this within three seconds of hearing of Tante Helene's death, looked shyly up at him.

'Oh, Maxi, I know. Isn't it wonderful?'

'Wonderful,' echoed Uncle Max. He began to pull the pins out of her hair, a thing which gave him the same intense, uncomplicated pleasure he had experienced when picking wild strawberries as a child.

This time however he faltered, stopped. Susie, too, drew away a little.

'It will seem so strange,' said Susie presently, 'not having to call you "Herr Finkelstein". Not ever again.'

'But nice? You'll like it?'

'Oh yes,' said Susie hastily. '*Very* nice. I shall like it very much.'

'I can hardly believe it myself,' said Uncle Max. 'Just getting into a *fiacre* and giving your address. In broad daylight!'

'You'll enjoy it, though?'

'But of course,' said Uncle Max. 'Of course I shall enjoy it. I shall enjoy it very much. It will all be so . . . simple.'

And they stood and looked at each other, subdued and a trifle silent as they contemplated the undoubted and perpetual bliss which faced them. Contemplated it so long and so solemnly that in the end Uncle Max left without taking advantage of her unpinned hair. It was the first time he had ever done so: a foretaste of their future life together: unhurried, respectable but not, of course, even *remotely* dull.

Helene had died in the autumn. Max and Susie's wedding was fixed for the following spring. A very quiet wedding, needless to say. All the same, one likes to think of Susie scuttling up and down the Kärntner Strasse buying material for the wedding dress. Not white, exactly, for she was a tactful girl, but pink, I daresay, or pale blue – and somewhere, one imagines, rosebuds.

And then, less than a month before the wedding, Tante Helene's will was read.

There had been a delay in the settling of her affairs, for etiquette forbade that she should trust her estate to her own husband, and the lawyer she had chosen had caught typhus shortly after the matter of the toadstools and was only now recovered.

The will was straightforward. She left a small legacy to her Cousin Lily. The rest of her property went unconditionally to her 'beloved Max.'

There was, however, a *letter*.

'I need not inform a colleague of your eminence,' the lawyer now said to Uncle Max, 'that this letter is in no way binding by law. Nevertheless, it was your wife's most earnest wish that you should consider the contents as . . . a kind of testament.'

And overcome by embarrassment, he fell to polishing his pince-nez. After which, in silence, he handed a large, sealed envelope to Uncle Max.

The next part hardly bears thinking of. My Uncle Max running up the stairs of the little apartment . . . Susie on the sofa, perhaps sewing a muslin flounce on to her wedding dress. And Uncle Max, ashen-faced, holding out the letter in a shaking hand.

'Oh, Maxerl! Oh, my darling, my *Liebchen*! Oh no, you can't do it! She can't ask it of you!'

Together they clung, rocking in agony, while the crumpled wedding dress fell unheeded to the floor.

'Cousin Lily!' wailed Susie. 'Oh no, no, no, no!'

'She is alone in the world, you see,' explained Uncle Max, brokenly kissing his Susie behind the ear.

'So *dreadful* for you!'

'Not dreadful, really,' said Uncle Max bravely. 'She runs the house. And she wouldn't expect . . . Only on the Kaiser's birthday, perhaps. But it's *you*, Susie, don't you see?'

'You mean we would have to be so secret again? To pretend, to hide away from the world?'

Max nodded, sorrow making him speechless. Clinging together, they faced it in all its tragedy: the brief and stolen hours, the secret bed behind closed shutters, Herr Finkelstein from Linz . . .

'Susie, this is a terrible blow. It is the most terrible blow we have ever faced together,' said my Uncle Max. 'But we *can* face it. We can conquer it!'

'Oh, yes, Maxi!' cried Susie, illumined by sacrifice. 'We *can*. Together we can conquer everything.'

And because time was short, and always would be short, because their plight was really very desperate, it was Susie herself who pulled the hairpins from her long and golden hair.

And here ends – freely interpreted by me – the official version of my Uncle Max's ill-starred and lifelong love for Susie Siebermann. He married Cousin Lily and in exchange for a single sacrifice on her part (the replacement of her milk teeth necklace by a string of garnets he bought for her), he gave her security, consideration, even affection. Cousin Lily, as is the way of frail, pale, unassuming women, lived an extraordinarily long time. By the time she died, my Uncle Max himself was close on eighty and Susie herself had only a year to live. Throughout his life, however, he visited her on Tuesday evening and on Saturday afternoon. The last time he went to see her she apologised for being no longer any 'use' to him, and then she died.

'It's monstrous,' I had said to my mother, years and years later. Just a week ago, in fact, before I took this flight. 'All his life he loved her and never once could they be openly together.'

My mother had followed me to England and settled in Oxford, first to be near me as a student, later, when I began to roam again, for choice. Now, thirty-odd years away from her native city, she made a gesture which was still infinitely, unmistakably Viennese.

'Rubbish!' she said. (Only what she said was 'Schmarrn'.)

'That old cow, Helene,' I went on. 'Leaving a letter like that. Emotional blackmail of the crudest sort.'

My mother sighed and quoted Schiller. ' "With stupidity even the gods struggle in vain" ' she said. 'You, my poor boy, are an idiot.' She paused, her head on one side. 'Although one must admit you never saw the squirrel.'

I stared at her. Mere senility is always too much to hope for in my mother.

'I went to Susie's apartment once or twice before she died,' she went on. 'Such a clean, fresh, pretty place! And then that awful squirrel. Someone had to have given it to her. Someone she respected too much to throw the thing away.'

'Well?'

'Who collected stuffed animals? Who adored the smelly things? Who filled her house with them?' demanded my mother, twitching at her shawl.

'*Helene*? Helene *knew* Susie? You must be mad!'

My mother raised her eyebrows. In old age and exile she had taken on a patrician, Habsburg haughtiness which went down like a bomb in North Oxford, but not with me.

'I don't *know*,' admitted my mother. 'But taken in conjunction with the gloves. . .'

'All right,' I said, defeated. 'Go on about the gloves.'

'When I was a very small girl they took me to see Aunt Helene in Hitzing. You know how bored children get. When she was out of the room I started playing around with the sofa cushions and I found her sewing basket pushed out of sight. There was a pair of men's grey gloves in it and a pair of scissors. The gloves had been cut, deliberately.'

I stared at her. 'I don't believe it.'

'Why not? I liked Helene. It's not so funny, after all, to fall off a steel cable. If she couldn't make Max happy in that way, I think she might well have found a nice, friendly girl and seen to it that he met her.'

'It's impossible,' I said. And then: 'No, it's just possible. But if she knew all about it and wished Susie well, why did she mess it all up for them? Why did she leave that note about Cousin Lily?'

My mother looked at me and shook her head. 'My poor boy,' she said. 'How many doctorates have they given you? Even you,' she went on, 'must see what Helene gave to those two.'

I was silent for a moment, thinking of my Uncle Max as I had last seen him: small and bandy and very, very old – and of the legend which encircled him.

'A Great Love?' I said.

'Oh, as for that,' said my mother, pulling her shawl closer, 'I don't know. That was extra, I think. A bonus. . .'

And that's all really. A period piece – something from the safely distant past. We manage things better now; more honestly.

Only just for one moment, as the plane came in to land, I wished we didn't. So that one day, perhaps, I might go into a glove shop in the Kärntner Strasse . . . If there still are glove shops in the Kärntner Strasse . . .

If I wore gloves . . .

This Beetroot is not Screaming

It was always rather gratifying, the first day of term. Sitting in the staff-room which faced the pleasant, green-turfed court-yard of Torcastle Agricultural College, we could see them all arrive; mostly men of course, because that's how it is with life, but here and there like sudden gherkins in a jar of unpromising pickle, the girls . . . Wholesome, old-fashioned girls, pros-pective farmers' wives and mushroom growers' daughters whose tiny mini-skirts and simple, bursting sweaters told fashion where it could put its latest kinks.

Not that any of us was seriously at risk. I myself could reckon to lecture to rooms-full of girls – all looking at me with eyes turned by incomprehension of the reticulo-endothelial system into twin pools of despair – without turning a hair. Rescuing their eyelashes from the pancreas of a pickled dogfish, dis-entangling their earrings from stray vertebrae was nothing to me after three years as lecturer in Zoology at Torcastle.

It was not quite so easy for Pringle, who suffered domestic-ally from a 'not-tonight-dear' wife and research-wise from a recalcitrant beetroot supposedly respiring in a tank of CO_2. 'It's the way they keep tossing all that hair back as they walk,' he said, watching a tall brunette glide past the window.

Davies, the nutrition expert, admitted to a more con-ventional, a mammary approach. 'And freckles. . .'

It was left to the vet, Ted Blackwater, to give the tone of the conversation its *coup de grâce*.

'With me,' he said humbly, 'it's simply legs. Legs and legs and legs . . .'

'That's the lot,' I said. And then: 'Oh, my God!'

Trailing up the path like one of those perennial 'wait-for-me' ducklings tucked on to the end of so many otherwise normal broods, came this girl. She wore ancient jeans and a shapeless duffel coat, her tow-coloured village-idiot-looking hair seemed to have tangled with a spray of traveller's joy and her pollen-dusted nose was tilted ecstatically skyward.

'I'll bet she's in my option,' I said gloomily.

And of course I was right.

My first-year Zoology practical class is a strictly academic and orthodox affair, the Principal insists on that. Straightforward dissections of the earthworm, the frog, the afferent and efferent systems of the dogfish, that kind of thing. And although the lab assistant, Potts, is a treasure, everyone – another college rule – prepares their own specimens.

Torcastle is low on student unrest. I entered the lab that first morning to find two dozen earnest heads already bent over their pinned-out earthworms, scalpels flashing, scissors snipping . . .

Except, in the corner of a bench by the window, this kind of anarchic cell, this area of silent nihilism. In short, the tow-coloured duckling girl whose name, it seemed, was Kirstie Hamilton, gazing raptly through the orifices in her nose-length fringe at something held in her cupped hands.

'You haven't begun yet?'

She lifted her head and looked at me. Both her eyes were green, but one was also yellow and the whole thing was not what I was accustomed to.

'Dr Marshall, I'm extremely sorry, but I find myself unable to chloroform this worm.'

At first I didn't take in what she had said and this was because her voice, with its rolling 'R-s' and lilting vowels, let out of the bag my ten-year-old self, the one that had been going to live in a Hebridean croft, befriended by seals, the confidant of shearwaters, world expert on the breeding habits of the cuddy-fish. When I had disposed of him and her words registered, I grew cross.

'Look, this is a scientific department and there's absolutely no room in it for whimsy. If you're one of those anti-vivisectionists–'

'Oh, but I'm not, I'm not!' she cried and the worm, interested, raised up a dozen or so if its anterior segments and laid them across her thumb.

'Of *course* people have to do experiments and test drugs and things. Of course they do!'

'Well, then?' I was getting impatient. All around me I could see butchered seminal vesicles, lacerated cerebral ganglia . . .

'It's just that I *personally* can't kill this worm . . . I can just feel its bristles on my wrist,' she said, and she might have been describing a 'Night of Love' in Acapulco.

Something in me snapped. 'Perhaps you would like to go out and look for a worm that's died of natural causes?'

Clearly, she was not a girl sensitive to sarcasm. 'Oh, thank you, Dr Marshall. What a marvellous idea! Yes, that's what I'll do.'

And with her hand still cupped protectively around her specimen, she left the lab.

The whole thing rattled me. I went to look at my experiment, but what had seemed like a pretty significant breakthrough in endocrine physiology now looked like thirty-eight mice without their ovaries looking less cheerful than thirty-eight mice who still had them. Fortunately the Principal, Dr Peckham, chose that moment to send for me.

'James,' he said excitedly as soon as I entered his study, his bald head and his bi-focals all gleaming with joy. 'I think we're going to make it!'

'No! You mean our Charter?'

Dr Peckham nodded. 'Sir Henry Glissop's coming with the whole Glissop commission. They wouldn't send him unless there was a good chance. Just think of it, James! Us and the Tech. and the Art School all united in the new University of Torcastle!'

Raptly, Dr Peckham made for the open window, seeing I knew, not the pleasant flower gardens of Torcastle Agricultural College, its unpretentious animal houses and white-washed farm but a glittering campus, a towering Science Block and he himself, gowned in scarlet, hurrying from Senate Meeting to Congregation and back again . . .

'It all depends on the research side of course,' he went on. 'How's Pringle's beetroot?'

'Playing up a bit, sir.'

Peckham frowned. 'And Blackwater? That new technique for storing A.I. samples?'

'Well, sir, you know how it is with Hannibal,' I said and Peckham winced, for Hannibal, after fathering some three thousand offspring in all corners of the globe, had suddenly gone cold on the whole thing and lounged about in the North Paddock, a seventeen-hundredweight drop-out from the permissive society, wincing when a heifer even passed his gate.

'But *your* work?' said Peckham hopefully. And then: 'Good heavens, what on earth is that girl doing crawling about in that flower bed?'

I told him. Peckham didn't really like it. He didn't, in fact, like it at all.

Sir Henry's visit was timed for the last week of term and following Peckham's instructions, the college threw itself into a frenzy of scientific activity. The pigs were put into metabolism cages, the turkeys reserved for the staff's Christmas dinner vanished from their shed and reappeared in a pen marked 'Organo-Phosphate Toxicity Trials'. Davies doggedly anaesthetised thirty sheep, stuck tubes into their stomachs and set up an impressive – if statistically dicey – feeding experiment. Blackwater began a systematic attack on Hannibal's failing libido, tramping nightly over to the North Paddock with house-sized syringes of hormone extract, while Pringle (though his wife had taken to covering herself all over with cold cream) set up five more beetroots respiring in a tank.

All in all, it was a surging, forward-looking scene with nothing to indicate that already there was a canker gnawing at its breast.

The Zoology practical class the following week was a straight-forward dissection of the frog. Killing a frog is simple and painless. All the same, it was with a leaden lack of surprise that I walked past the neatly pinned dissections and came, presently, upon this palpably still living frog, its bulging 'cornered-financier' eyes glittering moistly, one webbed foot hanging limply from a space between her fingers.

'Dr Marshall, I'm extremely sorry –'

'Don't tell me,' I said bitterly. 'I know. You personally, just at this minute, find yourself unable to kill this frog.'

She nodded. 'Those spots are really sort of *golden*. . .'

Goodness knows how it would have ended. I walked away and left her and when I came back the black-bearded Welshman who worked next to her had given her his pinned-out specimen and was preparing another for himself. Sex, as they say, is everywhere.

It was certainly at the Agricultural Society's ball held in the College Hall on the following Saturday. The ratio of men to girls at Torcastle is five to one, so I was accustomed to seeing girls dragged round like pieces of mammoth by men still sweating from the chase. The worm-saving Miss Hamilton, however, was being dragged round by an entire rugger scrum, all of whose members seemed certain that time was not on their side.

'That's Kirstie Hamilton, isn't it?' said a voice on my left.

The other student, an Afro-haired agricultural engineer, nodded. 'They say she's absolutely fantastic. Goes out with anyone, no holds barred.'

'Funny, she doesn't look the type.'

'Apparently she's going into a convent or something when she's through here. So she's getting it all in now.'

She was certainly getting it in. Slightly disgusted for some reason, I steered my own piece of mammoth – a succulent dental nurse called Charline – towards the buffet.

By the time I got back to the ballroom, single ownership of Miss Hamilton had definitely been established. Peering closely at the victor, I saw the sallow face and slicked-down hair of our prize student Vernon Hartleypool, winner of the Mortimer-Ponsonby Prize for the best essay on Silage Utilisation and holder, two years running, of the Potterton Scholarship in Egg Production.

Agriculturally, she couldn't have done better. But for a last outburst of sensuality before renouncing the world, her choice struck me as odd. Which was not to say that I didn't by the end of the evening feel extremely sorry for Vernon Hartleypool. For just as the lights grew really dim, the music more and more insistent, I saw Vernon, scowling, leave the ballroom, return with a ladder, climb (among drunken cheers from his class-mates) to the top of the thirty-foot window and release, at last, into the ink-black Torcastle night, a passé and not noticeably grateful turnip moth.

As half-term approached and Sir Henry's visit drew nearer, activity in the college became more and more frenetic. Blackwater increased Hannibal's dosage yet again and it took two men to carry the syringe. Davies added intestinal fistulas to his already gastrically fistulated sheep and Pringle (though his wife had purchased a set of hair-curlers that would have interested the Inquisition) nevertheless added at least two feet of significant glass tubing to his beetroot.

All the same . . .

'Staff all right, James, do you reckon?' asked Peckham, the Principal, putting it into words. 'Not feeling the strain?'

I said no, the staff were fine. What else could I say? That I had encountered Davies, after he'd taken the First Years for animal nutrition, staring haggardly at his fistulated sheep.

'James, this is a *useful* experiment? Worth causing a bit of discomfort for?'

'Of course it is.'

'I mean, they're just sheep. Not happy sheep. Not unhappy sheep. *Sheep*. St Francis just doesn't come *in* to a thing like that.'

Or Blackwater, striding angrily into the staff-room. 'So the Buddha gave up sex at thirty. So he gave it *up*. Is that any reason why I shouldn't inject Hannibal?'

In a way it was Pringle who showed most fight. 'I don't care *what* the new work on plant sensitivity shows,' he said, sitting with teeth clenched over his tank. 'This beetroot is *not screaming*.'

'Look, Kirstie,' I said, using her christian name for the first time and removing from her shoulder the white rat she had personally been unable to chloroform. 'I understand your feelings very well. But why inflict them on us? You don't need a diploma in agriculture to go into a convent.'

'It's not like that, Dr Marshall, honestly. I just *have* to get this diploma. Particularly now that this ghastly thing has come up with Vernon —' She broke off and to my horror, her piebald eyes began to fill with tears. 'Don't be cross, *please*.'

And for some reason I wasn't. Not until I went to tell Potts that we had run out of formalin and found him lost to the world, reading *The Little Flowers of St. Theresa*.

As one would expect from the Ministry's top scientist, Sir Henry's schedule was worked out to the last detail. He was to arrive at Torcastle Station at nine-fifteen, inspect the Technical College and the Art School in the morning, lunch with the Lord Mayor and reach us at two o'clock.

Ten minutes to two on the great day saw us, accordingly, dark-suited and – we hoped – scientific-looking, assembled on the steps to greet Sir Henry's motorcade. Two o'clock struck, two-fifteen, two-thirty . . .

At ten to three the college secretary came running out of her office and whispered something into Peckham's ear.

'Oh *no!*' I heard him say. 'Not today of all days. This really is the end!'

'That was Torcastle police,' he said, coming over to me. 'They've arrested one of our students for kicking a policeman. Get over there quickly, and for God's sake, *hush it up!*'

I was in my car, turning out of the drive, before I realised that I hadn't even bothered to ask who the student was.

'That's marvellous,' I said, storming into the police station an hour later. 'You can't chloroform a worm and you go round kicking innocent policemen.'

'I didn't kick him, Dr Marshall, honestly,' said Kirstie. There was a black smut on her nose and between her green and yellow eyes a purple bruise gleamed fitfully. 'He was stepping on a pigeon.'

'Pigeons,' I said, speaking with care, 'are birds. They don't get stepped on. They can fly, remember?'

'This one couldn't, he had a bad leg. I was sort of keeping an eye on him. There were a whole lot of us guarding this lime tree by the station, you see, stopping it from being cut down, and then the police started making a cordon and one of them stepped back on to this pigeon and I just gave him a little shove. . .'

There was a pause while I wondered just where the breaking point of the average Mother Superior might be expected to lie. 'Well,' I said at last, 'I suppose we should try to get you out of here.'

'Dr Marshall, you've been marvellous and I'm terribly grateful, but I don't feel I should leave here till I find out what's happened to that dear old man they arrested along with me.'

'Look, Kirstie, you're already in trouble enough —'

'But he *helped* me. He jumped out of his car when they started carrying me off in this van. We had such a *marvellous* talk! You've no idea how wise he was, and how *good*. There was nothing he didn't know about. Albert Schweitzer, Lao Tse, the lot!' Suddenly her face crumpled. 'You don't think they're beating him up?'

'For heaven's sake, Kirstie, will you stop drivelling about this old man? Why don't you worry about yourself for a change? You don't seem to realise you're a case of student violence, the kind that has to be nipped in the bud. I'm horribly afraid they're going to chuck you out.'

I was right. By the time we got back, delayed by a blocked petrol pump, Sir Henry's visit was over. Peckham thought it had gone well. Though the unexplained delay at the beginning had made the whole inspection somewhat hurried, he felt that Sir Henry had been pleased. Indeed Sir Henry's secretary had confided to Peckham that he had never seen the great man look so relaxed and peaceful.

For Kirstie, however, there was no reprieve. Peckham sent for her straight away and the look on her face as she came out of his study made me long to go and knock his smug and disciplinarian head against the wall.

'All right,' I said when I found her at last, sitting hunched and wretched under a clump of birch trees beside the ornamental lake. 'Now explain. Why does it matter so much? What's with the convent?'

'I never *said* I was going into a convent. I said I was going where there weren't any *men*.'

'And where's that?'

She sighed. 'I don't suppose you've ever heard of an island called Braesay?'

But there she was wrong. 'I have. It's one of the most beautiful islands in the Hebrides. But you can't get on to it. It belongs to a crusty old —'

'My father,' said Kirstie. 'He doesn't like people all that much.'

I was silent, thinking of Braesay with its grey seals, its white-fringed foreshore, its fabled, bird-hung cliffs . . .

'My father's getting old and I'm the only child. I wanted to learn about agriculture so that I could go on running it after he couldn't. There's an old shepherd, a couple of crofters on the North Shore . . . You can't just sell up and turn people out.'

'Look,' I lied, 'this diploma's just a load of rubbish. All you have to do is marry some nice, competent man and —'

'But I've tried and tried! You've no idea how I've carried on. And I almost had Vernon Hartleypool. He didn't exactly send me, but he was absolutely fantastic about oat smut and rape seed and things. He even knew about digested *sludge*. And then he turned me down because of his *appendix!*'

'His appendix?'

'Well, on Braesay we have to put up flares for a doctor and his appendix grumbles.'

She sighed and a despairing silence fell. After a while her hand, without exactly creeping into mine, somehow indicated that it was *there*. I picked it up, turned it over, passed my thumb to and fro along her wrist. It was not as if I didn't see what that worm had been on about, it was that I didn't *want* to.

'What do you do up there, say, when the seal population builds up and begins to interfere with the fishing?'

Her green and yellow eyes lit up.

'Well, I put the pups in a boat and the mothers swim after us and we take them away to another island.'

'I thought it might be something like that,' I said heavily. 'I just thought it might.'

Six weeks later at the beginning of the spring term, we received notice that our Charter had come through. Peckham was triumphant, but like all men who have battled through and won, he found that victory brought problems.

There was, for example, the sudden, curious decimation of his staff. Davies, who was twenty-six, said he felt he was getting too old for experimental work and left to join his brother on a hill farm in Wales. Blackwater accepted an offer from a firm of strawberry growers, and it was generally understood that I had been called away to do Nature Conservancy work in the Hebrides.

But in a way it was Sir Henry's letter that disconcerted Peckham most. Sir Henry found himself compelled to decline the flattering offer to be Torcastle's first Chancellor. He had, he said, long harboured a great desire to retire from the world and end his days in prayer and meditation, but had forced himself to remain at his post in order to foster those values – respect for life, conservation of the environment and so on – without which mankind was doomed to perish. A recent encounter with one of Peckham's own students, however, had shown him how completely the youth of today could be trusted to carry on just these ideals. He was accordingly leaving to join the ashram of Shri Ramananda in Jaipur and wished the new university every success.

'Must have been Vernon Hartleypool, I suppose,' said Peckham, puzzled. 'He had quite a long chat with him, I know.'

But it is of Pringle that I think, always, when I remember my last days at Torcastle. Pringle the survivor, crouched over his tank, shielding something with his hand.

'I want you to understand, James,' he is saying, 'that this is a *happy* beetroot. A very happy beetroot indeed!'

A ROSE IN AMAZONIA

SHE HAD not expected it to be so beautiful.

In Vienna, in her luxurious villa in Schönbrunn, she had read about the 'Green Hell' of the Amazon. Now, standing by the rails of the steamer on the last day of her thousand-mile voyage up the 'River Sea', she was in a shimmering world in which trees grew from the dusky water only to find themselves in turn embraced by ferns and frònds and brilliantly coloured orchids. An alligator slid from a gleaming sandbar into the leaf-stained shallows; the grey skeleton of a deodar, its roots asphyxiated by the water, was aflame with scarlet ibis.

She was bound for a city which even in the few decades of its existence had become a legend: fabled Manaus with its rococo mansions, its mosaic sidewalks and exquisite shops . . . A city of unbelievable luxury and sophistication thrown up by the wealthy rubber barons in the mazed and watery jungle to rival the capitals of Europe which they had left behind. And in particular – since she was a singer – for the prime jewel in the exotic city's heart: the Opera House, the Teatro Amazonas, the loveliest, they said, in all the Americas.

Only a few years ago her journey would have been a fitting one. Lured by unimaginable fees, Sarah Bernhardt had acted there and Caruso sung before an audience whose jewels would have put Paris and London to shame. But now, in the autumn of 1912, the good times were over. Faced by competition from the East, the 'black gold' that was rubber had crashed as spectacularly as before it had risen. Fortunes were lost overnight; the spoiled and pampered women who had lived like princesses in their riverside *fazendas* returned to the countries from which they came; the men, according to temperament, shot themselves or prepared to begin again. And to the Opera

House there came now only second-rate companies – people who were glad to get an engagement anywhere.

Yet the woman who stood by the rails, her blonde head under the lacy parasol bent in attention to the river, was not – and never could be – second-rate. Nina Berg was an opera singer of distinction and quality who in her native Vienna had been accorded the homage which the Russians reserve for their dancers, the British for their sportsmen and the Austrians for those who sing. 'Is she beautiful?' an eager student had once asked Sternhardt, the famous *régisseur* who directed her. 'At second sight,' the great man had answered, paying tribute to her stillness and the gentle reflection in her blue eyes.

From this hard-working and intelligent woman, youth had stealthily crept away. At first she did not heed its passing: venerable *divas* abound in the opera houses of the world. But now, far too soon, hastened by an unexpected illness and an operation that had gone awry, her voice was going too. And with her voice would go all the rest: the villa, the money, the adulation and protection of men . . . She would become a singing teacher in a little dark courtyard somewhere, one of the tens of thousands of musicians who had never achieved their goal, or passed it, and now watched young girls scrape fiddles or sing arpeggios.

Well, so be it! But why, having accepted her fate, had she decided to come on this trip? Why, when she had been warned of the danger if she sang again, had she decided to appear in this doomed wraith of an opera house? And why, oh why, had Kindinsky chosen *Carmen* – one of the few operas she did not like – for her farewell?

Jacob Kindinsky, sitting sad-eyed and perspiring in a deck-chair, watching her, could have told her why: because Carmen was a part that suited neither her temperament nor her voice and he did not choose to be dismembered by seeing her bring to her last Violetta or Mimi her unique quality of bewilderment at the loss, the inexplicable passing of happiness. It was bad enough, thought Jacob, to have to come to this unspeakable place – seemingly full of boa constrictors and electric eels, not to mention a fish that he dared not even contemplate which entered one's orifices when one was bathing and became, by means of backward-pointing spines, impossible to dislodge . . . Bad enough to be broiled alive and in the end, in all probability, not even *paid*, without having to submit to Nina's devastating empathy with those doomed and great-hearted girls. Whereas in the role of Carmen, singing opposite that Milanese bullock, Padrocci, who was now snoring under the fan in his cabin; keeping abreast of the ludicrous *tempi* which that clown Feuerbach would imagine to be 'South American', she would be compelled into the routine, heel-tapping, fan-clicking performance – and Feuerbach's imbecile crescendos would drown those heartrending breaks in her top notes.

And Jacob, who could hardly bear what was happening to Nina, found himself wondering for the first time in years if they had done right – he, Sternhardt who had become her *régisseur* and Fallheim, the director of the Academy, when they had sent that boy away. Jacob had been with Fallheim at that last interview when they had finally persuaded him that he was harming Nina and standing in her way. He had never forgotten the look in the boy's eyes, but he had forgotten his name. Stefan? Georg? Karl?

The boy's name had been Paul – Paul Varlov – and Nina, now watching with her customary quiet attention, a flock of green and orange parakeets had *not* forgotten it. It was, she could have said (without hysteria, without hyperbole) stamped into the marrow of her bones.

He had been twenty-three – a Russian father, a Hungarian mother, educated by some whim in an English public school and when Nina met him, a student at the University of Vienna. In him, nations and causes bubbled and boiled; just to touch him was to risk burning, he was so terribly alive. With his too large, too dark eyes, his high cheekbones and olive skin, he was an outlandish figure among his phlegmatic classmates, yet everywhere he went he was surrounded by friends who clung to him like puppies, lapping at his obsessions: the novels of Dostoyevsky, the Brotherhood of Man, the fate of the pigeons on the Stefan's Dom . . . He made speeches on Freedom for Hungary, waving his searingly beautiful hands; swam the Danube; discovered the Secessionists, made yoghurt in his landlady's button boots . . .

Then, standing at a Mahler Concert, he found himself next to a girl, golden-haired and gentle, with a sweet wide mouth and tender eyes.

Nina was twenty, studying piano and singing at the

Academy. Paul's friends parted to let her through and closed
again behind her.

She was home.

Her innocence, at that time, was total. She believed herself to
be an indifferent student – seeing in the extra work, the harsher
criticism that her professors handed out to her, only evidence of
her own inadequacy. Everyone else in the Academy knew of her
promise, but not she.

Now, in any case, she forgot her studies; forgot everything
except the glory of being alive and loved by Paul. The
selflessness and modesty that were her hallmark enabled her to
respond completely to his passion. Uniquely, for someone so
young, she never got in the way of her own happiness.

So it was spring in Vienna . . . In the Prater, the violets; on
the slopes of the Wienerwald, the greening larches. And
everywhere, in the cafés, the parks, floating from the windows
of the grey, stone-garlanded houses – music. Sometimes the
friends came, unexacting and affectionate as spaniels; sometimes they were alone. Their love was so immense it spilled over
to embrace the children bowling their hoops in the Tiergarten,
the waiters in restaurants who paused, leaning on their brass
trays, to tell them the stories of their lives. They stood,
marvelling, their fingers interlaced, before the quiet Dürers in
the Albertina, adopted an ageing llama in the Kaiser's zoo,
danced to the open-air bands under the linden trees . . .

One night from a deserted garden in Grinzig, Paul pilfered
for her an early, perfect, snow-white rose. They were the first
roses, he told her, the white ones, sprung from the tears of the
angel who had been compelled to lead Eve from Paradise. He
would find them for her always, he said, and when she laughed
and spoke of winter he said there could be no winter while they
loved. That night she stayed with him. She was a Catholic – it
was mortal sin. For the rest of her life, when she heard the word
'joy', it was to the memory of that sin that she returned.

If Paul had one characteristic above all others, it was a high
intelligence. There was no moment when he did not understand that what was between him and Nina was a God-given
gift, entire, enduring and sublime. And young as he was he
began, without a second's hesitation, to undergo the paperwork
and practicalities which would make possible their marriage. It

was now that the Academy began to sit up and take notice. Nina was sent for and informed of her potentially glorious future as an opera singer. She was surprised and pleased that her voice was good and told them, with her gentle smile, that she was going to marry Paul Varlov and go abroad with him. The Principal, horrified, sent for Sternhardt, the opera's famous *régisseur* who had earmarked both the voice and, when the time was ripe, the woman.

Nina, serene as a golden lotus, stayed firm.

So they turned on Paul. He had not known of the future that awaited her. To be a singer in Vienna is to be a little bit divine. Aware of this, wanting only what was right for her, Paul listened.

And so, into the Eden that those two had created, their elders introduced the poison-apple of self-sacrifice. Benign, experienced, twice his age, they bore down on the boy, keeping their visits secret from Nina – emphasising again and again her promise, her glittering future, the life of an acclaimed and dedicated artist which awaited her and which marriage and childbearing and poverty would put for ever out of reach.

Paul was only twenty-three. The call they made was one to which youth has always rallied: the sacrifice of happiness, of life itself, for a high ideal. After weeks of sleeplessness, he lost his fine perception of the truth and reached out, blind and despairing, for their poisoned fruit.

One day Nina, going to his room, found the friends grouped like figures in a *pieta* – and on the pillow, his last gift to her: a single, long-stemmed, snow-white rose.

She never saw him again.

The clanging of the ship's bell made Nina turn. They had come to one of the sights of Amazonia: the 'Wedding of the Waters' where, at the confluence of the two rivers, the leaf-brown waters of the Amazon flowed, distinct and separate, beside the acid, jet-black waters of the Negro to within sight of Manaus.

Responding to the bell, there now emerged Padrocci, the tenor, in crumpled mauve pyjamas, the ludicrous Feuerbach with his moustache cups, the dishevelled members of the chorus, all to peer over the rails and exclaim.

'Oh, God,' thought Jacob Kindinsky, indifferent as always to the marvels of nature. 'What scum is this that I have brought to sing with Nina?'

But as they steamed up the Negro, past the neglected and once-splendid planters' houses, past sheds where ocelot and jaguar pelts hung out to dry, he heard her draw in her breath.

'Look, Jacob! There it is!'

He looked. A dazzling, soaring dome of blue and green and gold surmounted by the Eagle of Brazil . . . a glimpse of marble pillars, a glittering pink and white façade . . . The Teatro Amazonas would have been lovely anywhere – here in the midst of the steamy, dusky jungle it was staggering.

And the fading opera star, the little Jew who loved her, turned and smiled at each other, for after all there was no disgrace here. This place would make a fitting ending to their pilgrimage.

A few hours before curtain-up, the thing happened which Jacob had known would happen. Nina, unpacking in her sumptuous but already mildewed dressing-room, asked for a white rose.

'Nina, we are in the *Amazon!*' he cried. 'You have *seen* the flowers! They are probably full of dead birds they have eaten for their dinner.'

'Please, Jacob.'

So it ended as it always ended . . . As it had done in Berlin in a blizzard which had cut off all supplies to the city; in Paris with the streets sealed for some visiting dignitary so that Jacob, with an hour to spare, found himself begging for a single bud from a bad-tempered gardener in the Tuileries; in Bucharest where every available rose had been pounded into attar for the tourist trade.

'You cannot wear a *white* rose for Carmen,' Sternhardt had yelled at her years and years ago, when he had at last persuaded her to try the mezzo role. 'Carmen wears red flowers always – scarlet, crimson – she is a *gypsy!*'

But Nina, who stood so patiently while they fitted her costumes, who would put herself out for the most insignificant member of the chorus, only said very quietly that if they wanted her to sing Carmen they would have to find her a white rose. And as with Carmen, so with Violetta (whether or not she was the *Dame aux Camellias*), with Mimi and Gilda and Butterfly.

So now poor Jacob stepped out of the resplendent foyer with its gilded mirrors and corpulent muses, to search among the frangipani, the hibiscus and the voracious orchids in that steam-bath of a city for the flower which alone linked this lovely, deeply weary woman to her youth.

In his ornate gold-leaf and red-plush box next to the stage, a man whose look of extreme distinction even the recent months of strain and agony could not eradicate, waited – entirely without interest – for the curtain to rise.

As usual in these times of slump and mismanagement there had been a muddle about the posters. The company was second-rate, the opera was *Carmen* – that was all he knew and it was enough to have kept him away but for the need to kill time for an evening before the arrival of the tycoon from Sâo Paulo to whom he was selling 'The Dragonfly'. Everything else was sold already: the other boats, the carriages, the antique silver and fine furniture he had shipped out from Europe. Only for Roccella itself had he found no purchaser. Soon now the lovely Palladian yellow-stuccoed house with its blue shutters, its flower-wreathed arcades, its fountains and terraces, would vanish in the murderous embrace of the jungle from which he had wrested it.

'Look, Mother, there's Mr Varlov! So he can't be in prison yet,' said the convent-fresh daughter of a Portuguese customs official, looking raptly at the solitary figure in the box.

'Don't stare, dear,' said her mother, irritably aware that neither disgrace nor bankruptcy would dim the image of this curiously magnetic figure in her daughter's eyes.

But the girl's father did stare, and nodded, for it seemed to him that Varlov had had a raw deal. Though he had been among the wealthiest of the planters and hospitable to a fault, Varlov had not indulged in the pranks of so many of the others –washing their carriage horses in champagne, sending their shirts back to Paris to be laundered. Varlov had built houses for the *serengueiros* who tended his thousands of acres of wild rubber, and schools for their children. It was to save these that he had gone to Rio when the crash came, to raise more money by means which, though he could not have known it at the time, had turned out to be illegal and now left him facing, along with the men he had trusted, a charge of malpractice and fraud.

Leaning back, indifferent to the looks he was attracting, Paul looked round the Opera House that he had helped to bring into being. It was he who had insisted on the best Carrara marble, he who had suggested that de Angelis himself be fetched from Italy to paint the ceilings. He had put thousands of pounds of his own money into this crazy, lovely building and for one reason only. Obsessionally, doggedly, idiotically, Paul had been convinced that one day *she* would come.

Well, she had not come. He had entertained Charetti and her entire company from La Scala to a seven-course banquet on 'The Dragonfly', had taken half a Russian *corps de ballet* stricken with yellow fever back to Roccella to be nursed . . .

But she had not come and never would come now. It was over.

Jacob had found a rose. Feuerbach, twisting his idiot moustache into imagined perfection, went to the conductor's rostrum. Padrocci completed the egg-swallowing and mi-mi-mi-ing routine so beloved of bad tenors all over the world and was eased into the uniform of Don José.

The curtain rose. Soldiers and passers-by, hopelessly sparse on the over-large stage, wandered about. Padrocci made his entrance. He had burst a button on his tunic and was already a quarter-tone flat.

In his box, Paul Varlov yawned.

Carmen appeared on the steps of the cigarette factory, was greeted by the crowd, moved forward, getting into position for her 'Habañera'. A heavy black wig, a flounced skirt, In her hair a rose . . .

In the stage box a man stood up, threw out an arm, spoke some unintelligible words. He was glared at, hushed.

Nina looked up. Across the glare of the footlights, at a distance at which normally she could distinguish nothing, she saw him, understood why she had come – and began to sing.

What happened next was a miracle. Jacob Kindinsky said so, anyway, and he should have known. The kind of miracle that enables a mother to leap across a chasm to rescue a child threatened by fire, or enables a mortally-wounded pilot to land his aircraft safely. For Nina now sang as she had sung at the height of her glory. Her illness, the effect of her operation ceased to exist. 'Sing with your voice, with your heart, with your life', St Augustine had begged, and so now sang Nina Berg, forcing from Padrocci as the opera continued a decent, near-musical performance, from Feuerbach a respect for Bizet's marvellously subtle score.

The first interval found Jacob in tears and Paul Varlov sitting in his box as if carved from stone. 'I *cannot* do it again,' he silently implored the Fates. 'I *cannot!*'

For the first few moments, following the ecstasy and shock of seeing her, hope had soared. Even with the heavy make-up he could see how she had aged. That she was appearing with this appalling company at all seemed to indicate that her career was over. In which case, surely he had a right, even disgraced and bankrupt as he was . . . ? But as she began to sing he knew it was not so. She was exactly what they had foretold: a great and glorious artist. If she was here it was for some chivalrous reason of her own.

The curtain rose again. Padrocci, pawing the white rose with his hot, fat hands, managed the 'Flower Song' and Paul, watching him, smiled crookedly. There was one gift and one gift only that he grudged the encroaching jungle. The greenhouse at Follina with its latticed screens, its fan and ice-machine where, to the puzzlement of his gardeners, he had coaxed and bullied from the black soil of Amazonia a sweetly-scented, snow-white rose.

Carmen read her doom in the cards, sent José away, went forward to her death . . . Right at the end the strain began to tell and Jacob, cowering, waited for the first tell-tale crack in her voice but Feuerbach, scenting the stable, was rampant again and no one noticed.

The curtain fell on an ovation. The audience rose, stamped, roared. Flowers rained on the stage. Nina took curtain call upon curtain call, leading forward the stunned Padrocci, the simpering Feuerbach. She was not at all impatient and hardly glanced at Paul's box. There was all time, all eternity now for them to be together. Even she could not imagine a God so wrathful that he would separate them twice.

The delay before she could escape from the theatre gave Paul his chance. He sent a note round to the stage door and made his way quickly down to the docks. He was selling 'The Dragonfly' fully equipped and his Indian crew had been persuaded to stay on and work for the new owner. If he worked fast it could be done – her own devastating humility would aid him – but he thought it might be the last thing he would do.

Hurriedly he gave his instructions: a perfect intimate dinner for two on deck; the Venetian candlesticks, the best champagne – and no word to Madame, no single word to indicate that 'The Dragonfly' was no longer his.

They nodded, pleased to serve him once again. They would not betray him and spoke, in any case, only their own language and a smattering of Portuguese.

Time, now, to go to the riverside café he had appointed for their rendezvous.

She came as he had asked, alone, in a hansom, telling no one where she was going. As she stepped out and the lamplight shone on her well-remembered face, he felt a moment of rage that time had dared so patently to lay hands on her. Then it was over, for this was Nina. She, in her turn, experienced no such moment, for he was handsomer than ever, the skin taut over those incredible bones, the streaks of silver highlighting his jet-black hair.

'Come,' he said, allowing himself once and once only to touch her hand. 'We're going to have dinner on my yacht.'

'Yes,' she said. 'Yes.'

She followed him like a child. She wanted to go on saying 'yes' to everything: 'yes' to the lapping of the river, 'yes' to the hot night and the cry of the frogs; 'yes' to the future – 'yes' even to the lonely and agonising past because it had led her to this place. So totally, shiveringly happy was she that she made a characteristic gesture, laying a finger sideways across her lips so as not to cry out and Paul, remembering it, stumbled for a moment as he led her aboard.

'What a beautiful yacht, Paul!'

'Yes: she's the fastest on the river. I have four others: a schooner, a motor launch. . .' He began to show off, boring her with tonnages and the luxurious fittings he had installed. Useless. She seemed enchanted at his success; to regard it as absolutely natural that he should boast like a silly boy.

'Oh, I *knew* you'd do well! Tell me everything! Start with *now*. Where do you live?'

A servant had taken her cloak, drawn out a chair at the

snowy candlelit table on the front deck. She took a roll, began to crumble it – then looked up at him to see if he remembered.

Yes, he remembered . . . That they had always kept a handful of crumbs from every meal they ate together and gone afterwards to find a one-legged pigeon who roosted between the feet of a particularly Gothic saint above the west door of the Stefan's Dom. A good life they had given that pigeon, who had abandoned thereafter any efforts to support himself.

Deliberately he looked away, refusing the shared intimacy, and began to describe his house. 'It was built by an Italian over a hundred years ago – it's an exact copy of the *palazzo* in his native village. Roccella, it's called. He didn't live long to enjoy it, poor devil. I got it for a song and I've made a water garden, an arboretum. . .'

Yes, he would do that, thought Nina. She remembered how he had bought a packet of seeds once, mignonette they were, and they had wandered through the courtyards of the Hofburg scattering them in the cracks between the paving stones. She had been surprised and enchanted that someone so wild and masculine should care so much for flowers.

'I've brought in trees from all over Amazonia – there must be five hundred species. And I've made the house into a real show place. The furniture's mostly Louis Quinze shipped out from France, the chandeliers are Bohemian. . .'

He was getting nowhere. To his infantile showing-off she accorded only the lovely, quiet attention that was her hallmark.

'I wish you could see it,' he said.

Ah, that was better. She had made a small movement of the head. Was she not going to see it, then?

'You are happy in the Amazon, Paul? You like it?'

He was silent. Then, forgetting his role, he began to quote the lines that the great Cervantes had written about the new world that was South America: '. . . the refuge of all the poor devils of Spain, the sanctuary of the bankrupt, the safeguard of murderers, the promised land for ladies of easy virtue, a lure and disillusionment for the many . . . and an incomparable remedy for the few.'

Nina had closed her eyes. 'And you?' she said softly. 'Have you found it to be that? An incomparable remedy?'

Paul did not reply. For him there had always been only one 'incomparable remedy'. This woman to whom he had committed himself wholly at their first meeting and whose absence had left him with a lifelong, ever undiminished sense of loss.

So now on with the slaughter, for he saw that like himself she had kept faith. He had only to reach out and she would give it all up – the fame and adulation, the homage of the students who had pulled her carriage through the Prater after her first *Bohème*, the bouquets glittering with diamond drops which besotted Habsburg counts threw for her on stage . . . If he mishandled the next few moments he would doom her to squalor and poverty, waiting for him to come out of prison if the trial went against him, friendless in this vile climate, in danger of every dread disease.

'You gave an incredible performance tonight.'

She waved a hand. 'No . . . no! It was a mistake, Paul. I am —'

He interrupted her. 'But I wondered why you wore a *white* rose? One would expect Carmen to wear *red* flowers, don't you think?'

There. He had done it. He had also, apparently, crushed the stem of his wine-glass.

Nina looked down at her plate. Not to make a fuss, that was what mattered. Women lost their only sons in battle. Children starved. Paul had not loved her. Blindly she groped for her fork, speared a dark, unfocused object and conveyed it, with infinite care, to her mouth.

Even now perhaps she could do it. If she admitted to him that her voice was finished. He was so chivalrous, so kind.

Oh, God, *no!*

Paul's glass had been replaced; the next course brought. His bleeding hand, wrapped in a napkin, was concealed beneath the table. Now to finish it off.

'Have some more wine, Nina. It will give me an excuse to have some. Steffi always fusses when I get drunk.'

'Steffi? Your . . . wife?'

He shrugged. 'We're not actually married – one doesn't bother out here. But she's been with me for a long time.'

'What is she like?' said Nina. She was speaking with great care now, like a small child reciting poetry.

Paul's mind juddered to a halt. What indeed was she like? Had he ever, among the string of girls with whom he had tried to forget Nina, even known a Steffi?

'Well, she's French . . . dark curls . . . a real minx but. . .'

He rambled on, creating an 'ooh-la-la' *soubrette* from a

fifth-rate operetta. ('You cannot believe me, Nina. You *cannot*. Tell me I'm lying; see through this idiot game.')

But she believed him. The modesty and selflessness he'd so much loved in her finished the job he had begun. It was over.

What followed was the worst. Nina lifted her chin and took up, almost visibly, the mantle of prima donna and woman of the world. For exactly the time that politeness demanded she made conversation, speaking amusingly of her travels, telling him bizarre and interesting stories of the stage. Then she rose, gave him her hand to kiss, sent her regards to Steffi.

'Steffi?' said Paul wildly, nearly ruining it all.

But the pain was beginning to take over now; she noticed nothing and holding herself very erect she walked down the gangway to where the hansom cab still waited – and was gone.

The next day, Nina fell ill. Jacob, who knew nothing of what had passed, was convinced that she was dying. He had read about swans who sing gloriously before dying and Nina, lying mute in her hotel room, managing to shiver although the temperature was 95° in the shade, seemed a good candidate for death. He found an understudy, placated the manager of the Opera House, brought a Portuguese doctor who offered him a choice of lethal tropical diseases and suggested he cut the *diva's* waist-length, still golden hair.

Jacob refused, sat with her for three days and nights and remembered for the first time in ages that he had a wife in Linz who ran his leather goods business and made the best *blintzies* in Lower Austria.

Nina, however, did not die. On the fourth day she got up, apologised, kissed Jacob and prepared for the journey home. Neither of them mentioned her voice, for both knew that she would never sing again.

So now she stood again by the rail of the steamer, erect and careful but with a new gesture, her arms folded across the bodice of her dress as if to stop the pain escaping and troubling others with its unmannerly intensity. They reached the 'Wedding of the Waters', began to steam down the 'River Sea'
. . .

After a while Jacob came over to stand beside her. He must make her speak, listen, *anything*.

'You never asked where I found your white rose,' he said.

She flinched, but as always answered gently. 'No. Where did you get it?'

'It was quite an adventure,' said Jacob proudly. 'I think perhaps it was the only white rose in Amazonia. I tried everywhere and then I met an Indian who had been employed as a gardener on one of the great estates. The man who owned it had left – he's gone bankrupt and faces a prison charge too, poor devil. But the Indian swore there was a special place there, where the owner used to grow a white rose. Apparently he made a great fuss about doing it – it's very difficult to grow roses here.'

Nina's voice seemed to come from a long way off. 'What was it called, this place?'

'Roccella. An Italian built it after some *palazzo* in —'

He broke off for Nina had clasped his shoulders. She was looking at him as if he were wreathed in unutterable majesty and her eyes were the eyes of a young girl.

'Again, Jacob, please. Tell me again what happened there. *Everything.*'

Not all great loves, faithfully kept, end in tragedy. Nina returned, found Paul hunched and despairing by the riverside, saw his face as he watched her come towards him . . . and knew why she had been born. His prison sentence was minimal. She waited. They returned to Roccella to begin again. Nor had they been in any way mistaken: each found in the other, and was to do so always, the 'incomparable remedy' they had sought.

No, if there was a tragedy, it was that of Jacob Kindinsky who had adored Nina and now returned to Linz. But a passer-by, seeing him on his verandah above the Danube, spooning sour cream on to his *blintzies* and listening to the clink of the till as his wife chatted to the customers in the shop below, might think that as a tragedy it was . . . well, *endurable*. Soon, too, he is going to write a book that will take the operatic world by storm. He has the title ready: *The Diva with a Rose.*

A Little Disagreement

BECAUSE I have been married with great content (and to the same woman) for twenty years, I am often asked questions. Questions which imply that there is some formula for married happiness; a recipe for success. And when this happens and I am forced into an answer, I tell the questioner a story. The story of Tante Wilhelmina Ziegelmayer and her husband Uncle Ferdi, in Vienna, before the war.

And I begin at the end. With Tante Wilhelmina's death-bed, to be exact, which took place on a Tuesday evening during that socially grey period when the Opera Ball is over for another year, the holy statues wear their Lenten shrouds and a wind straight from the plains of Hungary bites eastward into the city.

On a dull, cold Tuesday in early March, then, Tante Wilhelmina (who actually was no relation to me at all; I was the housekeeper's son and still a child) clutched her heart, shrieked, turned purple – and sent for the hairdresser.

In life, Tante Wilhelmina, prematurely retired from the chorus of the Opera, took little interest in her appearance. Death, however, was a different matter. Now, as she lay gasping on her pillows in a nightdress of lilac crêpe de Chine, she nevertheless managed to give precise instructions to Herr Kugelheim.

'You will, of course, make absolutely certain that I am dead. You know how to do this?'

Herr Kugelheim, ancient, bandy-legged and servile, clutched his curling-tongs and muttered something about mirrors.

'Then two low curls on the forehead. Low, and a plaited chignon in the nape. Have you got that?'

I, meanwhile, had been sent to fetch the cats. Wotan and

Parsifal presented no problems. Huge, neutered tom-cats, they were perfectly prepared to finish their cream at the foot of Tante Wilhelmina's bed. Siegfried, however, was another matter. Siegfried's operation had not been a success and he was absent on the tiles.

By the time I had returned from an unsuccessful search, most of the relatives sent for by my mother had arrived, and in hushed whispers were assembling in the bedroom. It is naturally with hindsight that I see the grouping as having the weight and dignity of a Delacroix or Titian. In the centre, of course, lay Tante Wilhelmina, the lamp falling on her ravaged features and heaving breast. Behind her, the hairdresser; across her feet, the cats. At the back of the room, in shadow, a respectfully doleful row of servants. Leaning against the wardrobe, a creaking cousin, male, from Plotz . . .

Kneeling by the bed itself, hiccuping with grief, was Tante Wilhelmina's adopted daughter, Steffi; a blonde, kind, silly woman, her trusting sea-cow eyes brimming with tears. By the window Steffi's husband, Victor Goldmann, a Jewish violinist from the Philharmonic, surveyed the scene like a flayed, El Greco martyr.

Tante Wilhelmina stirred and groaned. Silence fell. A waiting silence.

As though on a cue that only she could hear, my mother now stepped forward.

'*Gnädige Frau,*' she said, leaning over Tante Wilhelmina, 'if you will forgive the impertinence, I think the Herr Professor should be sent for. I think your husband should be here.'

Then: 'If you . . . insist,' said Tante Wilhelmina, speaking with great difficulty. 'I . . . don't wish it . . . personally. But if . . . you insist.'

A sigh of relief seemed to pass round the room. Tante Wilhelmina stretched out a failing arm and reached for the note-pad on her bedside table. 'I AM DYING,' she wrote in indelible pencil and underlined each word.

My mother tore off the paper and handed the message to me. At a nod from her, I ran downstairs and knocked on the door of Uncle Ferdi's study.

Uncle Ferdi had been sitting there quietly, his bald head gleaming in the lamplight. Now he peered at the note through gold pince-nez, blew softly through his moustache, sighed, nodded – and followed me upstairs . . .

And if all this seems a little odd, the explanation is very simple. Tante Wilhelmina and Uncle Ferdi had been married for thirty years. And for twenty-nine of these, they had not exchanged a single word.

No one knew what Uncle Ferdi had done, only that it was very, very bad. That somehow he had hurt and humiliated Tante Wilhelmina to such an extent that she had never been able to forgive him. There had been no scandal, no break-up. They lived under the same roof and when she wanted anything she sent him notes, first through Steffi (adopted from an orphanage mainly for the purpose), later through me. But from that day to this no word had passed between them.

And now, with Uncle Ferdi sitting sadly in the big carved chair which had been placed in readiness for him, the death-bed could begin.

I was ten years old and very nervous. A bit ghoulish, too, as I leant against my mother's skirts. What would happen? Would she scream or gasp or . . . *rattle?* Would there be blood?

Well, what happened was that Tante Wilhelmina *forgave* people.

She forgave everybody. She forgave the maids for not dusting behind the piano and she forgave the creaky cousin for doing her out of a barrel of rollmops during the First World War. She forgave her sister-in-law for filching her recipe for *lungenbeuschel* and she forgave my mother for not appreciating Wagner. She even (and this took some time) forgave me.

After that came Steffi.

What she forgave Steffi for was not marrying a Jew, for in those days Hitler was just a faint, foul cloud on the horizon. What she forgave Steffi for was getting it all so *wrong*. And it is true that the intricacies of Jewish orthodoxy seemed to be quite beyond poor Steffi, who cooked *gefilte* fish on days of strictest fasting and was once seen trying to remove her husband's hat on the way to synagogue.

And then Tante Wilhelmina turned and fixed her suffering, other-worldly eyes on Uncle Ferdi.

With a superhuman effort, the dying woman struggled up from her pillows. My mother on one side, Steffi on the other managed to support her heaving, swaying form into an upright position. An arm in lilac crêpe de Chine crept out towards her mournful, waiting husband.

It was going to be all right. She was going to forgive him. The great wrong he had done her almost thirty years ago was now expiated. In death they would be reconciled.

'F . . . Fer. . .' Gasping, choking, Tante Wilhelmina tried to say her husband's name. Then with an unutterably awful cry she fell backwards on to the pillows.

A choking rattle followed. Silence.

Uncle Ferdi, grief-stricken, huddled back in his chair. The hairdresser stepped forward tentatively, a mirror in his hand . . .

And jumped back like a scalded cat as Tante Wilhelmina, exhausted by her labours, gave vent to yet another enormous and room-shattering snore.

'You mean she *often* does it?' I said to my mother a few days later. 'Often has a death-bed?'

My mother was folding table linen, her square deft hands flicking the damask. Now she looked up at me and sighed. 'Fairly often. About twice a year. You were too young before; I always sent you away.'

'But why?' I said. '*Why?*'

My mother frowned. 'I think . . . I don't know really . . . but I think perhaps she wants very much to forgive him. To make up the quarrel. Only her pride won't let her. The death-beds are a way of . . . forcing her own hand. But then in the end, she can't quite make it.'

I only partly understood. But: 'Poor Tante Wilhelmina,' I said, and my mother smiled and touched my hair as though I had said something to please her.

It was then that I plucked up courage to ask something I had wanted to ask for years. 'What was the quarrel *about?* What was it that Uncle Ferdi did to her?'

The smile left my mother's face. 'Never ask me that, Karl,' she said, turning back to the linen.

During the next few years the death-beds came thick and fast. By the time I was twelve, I could have organised one almost as well as my mother. Long before Herr Kugelheim arrived with his curling tongs, I'd have caught Wotan and Parsifal, arranged the big chair for Uncle Ferdi, helped to round up the maids, the cousins and Steffi . . . Always Tante Wilhelmina forgave the rest of us and always, just before she could forgive her husband, she fell back, apparently lifeless, on the pillows. 'I SEEM TO HAVE BEEN SPARED' she would write to him next day. And everything would go on exactly as before.

Then, when I was about thirteen, came a death-bed which I shall never forget because what happened there set the pattern for the rest of my life.

I wish I could think of better and less hackneyed words to use, but I cannot. So I only state that I fell – and it really was a falling – in love.

I knew, of course, that Steffi and Victor Goldmann had a daughter. But while I normally had the freedom of the house, when visitors or relations came my mother kept me strictly in the servants' quarters. So it was not until she was old enough to attend her first death-bed that I saw Ruth.

It was an autumn death-bed, I remember. The chestnuts in the square outside were dropping golden fingers on to the Archduke somebody-or-other who rode out there for ever. I remember this because Ruth's hair was the colour of those leaves and so were her eyes – her father's wise, El Greco eyes – but hair and eyes, both, were lightened, gold-flecked, because of silly, blonde, incurably Aryan Steffi.

I don't think anything happened, except that I had an overwhelming longing to cross the room and stand beside her on the other side of Tante Wilhelmina's bed, but didn't because she was 'family' and I was the housekeeper's son. But after that we met secretly after school wherever and whenever we could; in the Volksgarten, on the steps of the Karls Kirche, by the Mozart memorial . . . And if I say I was happier then than I have ever been, I don't want to imply some childish mock-romantic idyll. It was with absolute seriousness that Ruth and I, trailing our satchels through the streets of Vienna, discussed our future life together, planning everything from the kind of dog we would breed on our farm near Salzburg to the portion of our income we would donate to the poor.

And then came the last death-bed. The one at which death, which had been mocked so long, was mocked no longer.

It began exactly like the others. The hairdresser came, the cats were caught. Even Siegfried, temporarily sated, was present for once – and Ruth had a blue ribbon in her hair.

Tante Wilhelmina forgave the maids, the rollmops cousin, Steffi, me . . .

And finally struggled into a sitting position to stare, her arm extended, at Uncle Ferdi.

Uncle Ferdi had aged a lot recently. His eyes behind the gold pince-nez had lost their piercing blue; his moustache drooped; even his bald head no longer shone bravely in the lamplight and I remember praying that this time it really would happen. That this time, at last, she really would forgive him.

'F . . . Fer. . .' began Tante Wilhelmina. And then suddenly, her whole face crumpled into a look of agony and disbelief.

While slowly, very slowly, Uncle Ferdi slipped from his chair on to the floor and lay there, very peaceful looking and quite, quite still.

What I remember most vividly is not Tante Wilhelmina's racking sobs, nor even Ruth Goldmann's gold-flecked eyes as they widened to take in the shock and pain, but the baffled, bewildered look on old Kugelheim's face as he stepped forward, clutching his curling-tongs, and stood looking down at Uncle Ferdi's totally bald head . . .

After Uncle Ferdi's death, Tante Wilhelmina went to pieces. She grieved as though their marriage had been the most fantastic idyll. She lost two stones in weight, dressed totally in black, saw no one.

I was shocked by what seemed to me to be the most appalling hypocrisy, 'Why does she carry on like that?' I said to my mother. 'She can't have loved him.'

My mother didn't say anything. She just looked at me. Later, people often looked at me as though they envied me my youth, but that day I saw my youth profoundly pitied.

It was Steffi, adopted on a whim from an orphanage, silly, undervalued Steffi who now took charge of Tante Wilhelmina, carrying the broken old woman off to Berlin where Victor had a new job in the Conservatoire, comforting her, caring. The house was sold; my mother went to work in a shop; we moved to a little flat in the suburbs. There were no more death-beds. And no more Ruth.

As though Uncle Ferdi, sitting sadly in his study, had kept the old world together, his death seemed to unleash chaos. Chaos in the outside world as Hitler seized power in Germany and the conflict and cruelty began to seep across the border to smug and sleepy Austria. Chaos within as the loss of Ruth unleashed in me all the squalor and confusion of adolescence.

Politically, my mother and I were almost simpletons. So that when a year later Ruth Goldmann wrote to me from England, I wasn't relieved for her safety, I was appalled. England, that grey and foggy land of horsemen and ham-and-eggs; what was Ruth doing there? How would I ever get to her again?

'It is good here,' Ruth wrote, 'because no one minds that Father is a Jew and they don't spit at us in the street. When we arrived, Mother said the prayer of thanksgiving for the deliverance of the tribes of Israel, but Father said it was the prayer to make married people have children. . .'

It was a long letter and it ended: 'I would like it very much if you remembered me.'

Well, I remembered her. I remembered her through the *Anschluss* and the war in which, by then, I was old enough to fight. I remembered her through three years of imprisonment by the Russians and I remembered her when, sick and verminous and sullen, I was released.

But by then the continent was adrift in chaos and I lost her. Physically. Literally. No letters reached her in England, none came to me.

All the same, within a year of the war's end, I managed to get myself to London on a language course. I went, of course, to look for Ruth. Anyone less naïve would have known how hopeless it was. Each evening, when I finished at the language school, I rang up another couple of dozen Goldmanns, trudged round the refugee organisations, the Emigration Office . . . Nothing . . .

And yet in the end, quite by chance, I did find someone.

I was walking, on a warm evening in May, from Swiss Cottage tube station towards the room in which I lodged. My way led through streets of large Victorian terrace houses, many of them knocked together to make a hostel or hotel.

In front of one of these I used to linger and eavesdrop. It was a kind of old people's home – though a pretty classy one – run by a Viennese woman and filled with the elderly relatives of refugees whose matriarchal 'Momma' or embarrassingly proletarian 'Poppa' had not fitted into the new prosperity of the house in Golders Green or Finchley. From this hotel the smell of good Austrian cooking used to drift out, plus plaintive comments in German or Polish or broken English.

'No,' I heard on this particular day. 'I go absolutely not to the death-bed of that old *schickse*. I am sensitive, me, and my nerves cannot hold out such nonsense.'

A pleading murmur, softer, in English. A resigned: 'Once more, then; once more only, I go,' from an old gentleman.

And an arm in a white overall, scooping up a huge, reluctant cat . . .

'Excuse me, but do you have anyone staying here by the name of Ziegelmayer? Wilhelmina Ziegelmayer?'

The flustered maid looked at me with relief. 'Oh yes, we were expecting one of the relatives. I'll take you up.'

I followed her upstairs, opened the door.

On the pillows, in a nightdress of the austerest post-war cotton, lay Tante Wilhelmina. Where Herr Kugelheim had stood with his curling-tongs sat the matron, looking resigned and holding in a vice-like grip a large and displeased cat. And in a circle round the bed, creaking with visible reluctance, sat an assortment of elderly ladies and gentlemen.

Tante Wilhelmina was forgiving them. She forgave Frau Feldmann for taking the last of the sauerkraut at luncheon; she forgave Madame Kollinsky for always hogging the best arm-chair in the lounge. She forgave Herr Doktor Zellman for the extraordinarily unappetising way he left the bathroom.

And then Tante Wilhelmina saw me.

Really, I mean, saw *me*. She broke off, struggled up on her pillows, stretched out a hand. A spasm shook her and then over her silly, self-indulgent face there came a look that I had never seen on it before: a look of pure and unmistakable happiness.

'*Ferdi*,' she said, loud and clear, 'Ferdi! I forgive you, Ferdi; I forgive you *everything*.'

Then she fell back on the pillows. Her breathing changed. Behind me I heard light footsteps, a door opening; someone begin softly to weep. It was only then that I realised that Tante Wilhelmina had made it at last, that she was dead. And I turned round and there was Ruth . . .

'I'm so glad,' said Ruth later. 'Oh, God, I'm so glad she had the chance to forgive him.'

I don't know where we were then. Hampstead Heath, perhaps. We had walked about for hours, holding each other's hands like greedy children, and now it was quiet and green.

'I'm glad, too. But I don't understand, really. Why did she think I was Uncle Ferdi suddenly? She seemed quite sane.'

Ruth turned to me, surprised. 'I forgot you didn't know,' she said. Then she opened her handbag, took out a mirror and held it up to me.

I looked at myself. Blue eyes; fair hair; shrapnel scar on the temple. Just a face.

'Try a moustache,' said Ruth. 'And gold pince-nez.'

'No,' I said. '*No.*'

Ruth nodded. 'He was very lonely. And your mother was a sweet woman. You're very like him.'

'Good God! So that was the sin Tante Wilhelmina couldn't forgive him! An affair with the housekeeper. To be made a fool of in her own house!'

Ruth smiled, but her gold-flecked eyes were sad. 'No,' she said. 'That was a *big* thing and it was years after. Tante Wilhelmina was awfully good about it. You know what a pet she made of you.'

'But what, then? What *had* he done?'

So then Ruth lay back in the grass and I took her in my arms and she told me.

And if our marriage is exceptionally happy, if really we *don't* seem to quarrel over trifles, perhaps it is because we both remember an old woman – locked in loneliness and silence because thirty years earlier, her new young husband, in a careless moment, had told her that her fresh-baked *apfelstrudel* tasted like a boot . . .

TANGLE OF SEAWEED

SHE WAS always reading, Nell. Well, when she wasn't stroking the sooty London leaves of plane trees or laying her cheeks against cool window-panes or loving – ecstatically – unsuitable young men. You could have given her a Chinese couplet from any part of the Golden Dynasty of T'ang and she'd have finished it for you. Dostoyevsky was her brother, Victorian children's books her passion and though she lived, when in funds, mainly on avocado pears, she took her bath each night with a different cookery book.

But somehow Freud, that great psychologist had passed her by. His theory, for example, that we forget what we want to forget, lose what we want to lose, had hardly crossed her mind.

So when she woke up and couldn't at once find her engagement ring beside the bed, her panic, though intense, had no particular overtones. Sleep-drugged, she blundered round the room, picking things up, feeling the sweat collect on the nape of her neck. Larissa and Kay, with whom she shared the flat, wandered in and, their eyes half-shut still, began groping for it too. Looking for the ring Harold had given Nell had become second nature to them by now.

Nell found it herself, on the bathroom shelf next to the indigestion tablets which she'd bought because everyone knew that being engaged made you tense and gave you stomach cramps, and even before she'd cleaned her teeth she put it on and it was like putting on Harold. She felt safe, controlled, calm.

Harold . . . She was so grateful to Harold for so much. For being *called* Harold in the first place, when no one really was any more. For having a mother whom he not only loved but was taking that very afternoon to the Zoo. The idea of Harold steering his mother from the baboons to the sea lions, from the coypu pond to the zebra house, pulling her gently out of the way of supercilious camels with sticky children on their backs was, to Nell, infinitely touching. A guarantee, too, of the changes that would take place in her own life when she was married to Harold. She would stop drifting, taking any old job like this one she was doing now, for example. She would learn to say, 'No'. 'No, I will not lend you my last fiver.' 'No,' (to the men who were never called Harold) 'you cannot take me to Hampstead Heath to hear the nightingales, to St Tropez in your string vest of a car. . .'

She looked down at the ring. Two diamonds flanking a very reasonably sized ruby. Harold hadn't actually said that it wouldn't collect dust but he'd implied it because he was an Expert. A Time and Motion Expert, and this, too, Nell found moving. He would make things work for her. She would catch buses, water her house plants correctly from *underneath*, stop singeing her eyebrows on the geyser . . .

'Half past,' called Larissa from the kitchen, and Nell shot into violent action. Her hair, that was the most important thing. Today it *had* to stay tidy. After all, it was a sort of lab she worked in, it was science . . . She brushed it out: green-gold, plumb-straight; hair she washed as often and as carelessly as her face, and began to fasten it on to her head. A rubber band, two clips, a pin . . .

And now, suddenly, as happened every morning, she was frantically late.

'Oh God, let me catch my bus,' she prayed, and threw the *Tibetan Book of the Dead* and the indigestion tablets into a straw basket, and swallowing a mouthful of *brioche* ran out into the street.

At once, she was blinded by summer. The tarmac shimmered, the pavement bit her feet; the street cat lay like a spent Ingres courtesan across the steps.

Nell shut her eyes, pierced by a desperate longing for her childhood summers. For the smell of decaying weed along the tide line (which, whatever people said, really *was* ozone). For the voluptuousness of sand between her toes; for rose-coloured cowries mysteriously special in a handful of common shells. For a man she could see coming out of the water (but this was hardly childhood?) shaking back his hair and laughing as he uncoiled the strands of seaweed round his feet. A man she hoped so much was Harold. Only, would Harold have *allowed* the seaweed to tangle round his feet? Wouldn't he, being an Expert, have seen and avoided it?

'Oh no, my *bus*,' yelled Nell, and, too late, began to run, clutching her diamond ring with her free thumb and feeling already the first dreaded slither of what would soon be the waterfall of her descending hair . . .

On the other side of London, hemmed in between fifteen volumes of a decomposing German dictionary and something called *Wissenschaftliche Pädagogie*, sat Toby Sandford, bent over his dissertation on Animal Symbolism in Sanskrit Literature and trying to extract from his pocket, in total silence, a vinegar-flavoured potato crisp.

The college library was all-enveloping, silent, fusty, with marble busts of surprisingly unclad scholars placed at intervals between the tomes, but Toby wasn't fooled. This was one of those rare days when all the rules were broken and the whole country ran riot with summer.

He extracted a crisp, closed his eyes and gave himself over to an emotion for which he was really rather young: intense and violent nostalgia. He saw the sea as it had been on the limitless, empty beaches of his native Northumberland, not blue but a cool and pearly grey; saw the entrancing pink legs of oyster catchers glint in the sun, saw a girl (but this was moving out of childhood) come out of the water, letting a skein of seaweed trail in her hand. Now she was bending down, biting with delicate pleasure the bladders of wrack between her teeth. Girls always bit into seaweed . . .

Or did they? He played the last reel through again in his mind, hoping against hope that the girl was Margaret, with whom he had what was generally termed a relationship. But would Margaret have *bitten* into a piece of seaweed? Wouldn't she even there, coming out of the sea in the swimsuit whose straps would not have worked loose, been carrying her dissecting scissors, her scalpel?

'Overwork,' said Toby to himself. He'd been determined to finish the thesis for his doctorate before he went away, and usually an English summer was easy enough to ignore. But today . . .

Suddenly he closed his book, bundled up his papers. He'd

take a day off, take Margaret out. To the Zoo? To the Aquarium! And immediately an explosion of images ran through his brain. 'Sabrina fair . . . under the glassy, cool, translucent wave. . .' 'Full fathom five thy father lies. . .' He saw ferns and fronds and fins and was suddenly and devastatingly happy.

Margaret, when he ran her to ground in the Zoology lab, saw only an interruption to a sensibly planned day. She sat in her white lab coat, bent over the hepatic portal system of an extremely pickled dog fish, lifting with calm forceps the fragile threads of empty arteries, snipping unruffled among clusters of organs as delicate as Lilliputian grapes. Like Toby, she was doing post-graduate research. Unlike him, she never felt as he did, even after he took a First at Oxford, that the research was doing *him*.

In the end, however, she took off her overall, resigned, composed, because he was nothing but a child, really, and needed humouring, and went to fetch the large, cool, plastic handbag which had in it all the things that Toby never had – clean handkerchiefs, door keys that really fitted doors – and still smelling slightly but impressively of formalin, agreed to go with him to the Aquarium . . .

There was nothing impulsive about the visit of Harold, with his mother, to the Zoo. It had been carefully planned for days and the route they were to follow memorized from Harold's map. So far all had gone well, but it was with a certain amount of relief that Harold went up the steps to the Aquarium. The llamas, overcome by the unusual heat, had shown a disconcerting amorousness and the baboons – well, baboons were *like* that. But it was his pride to spare Mother, who lived alone in Teddington, the least unpleasantness, and there was always something calmingly ethereal about fish.

After the heat outside, the dark, columned halls of the Aquarium were marvellously cool. Margaret and Toby were proceeding tank by tank along its length, for Margaret was above all a systematic girl. A fleet of bass floated motionless in a forest of bamboo. Flounders performed strange and dreamy acrobatics with their bulging eyes. Dust-speckled bubble stars illumined a black heaven beneath which a deeply placid carp smiled as he swam.

'In a cool curving world he lies and ripples with dark ecstasies,' said Toby happily, and Margaret, who was beginning to despair of ever curing him of quoting pointless bits of poetry, sighed.

'Actually,' she said, 'they have an interesting reproductive system,' and told him serious things about whitish tubercules and elongated papillae.

'Oh,' said Toby, unaccountably cast down, and moved on. An octopus with rows of suckers like milky pearls, gave them an *enfant terrible* grin from a Stonehenge of sea-washed rocks.

'Their pancreas is excretory, did you know?' said Margaret, and elaborated.

'Well, I don't like it,' said a sharp, elderly voice beside them, and Toby, who didn't either, who wanted the octopus entire and lovable, turned round in sympathy. But the woman, who appeared even on this burning summer day to be clutching a plastic raincoat, was suffering from a different obsession. 'Nothing will make me believe that the girl will settle down and make you a good wife. I tell you, I heard her talking to my begonias when you brought her to tea. No self control, she said they had. And always barefoot with those straw baskets. An invitation to thieves.'

'She is very willing to learn,' said Harold calmly, and looked down at the luminous dial of his watch, pleased to observe that they were comfortably within schedule.

'Oh!' said Toby, suddenly and deeply harrowed. In front of them a hopelessly narcissistic lung fish alone in its tank floated constantly upwards to kiss its own reflection in the moment that it broke.

'That's tragedy,' said Toby, 'to be in love with yourself because there's no one else.'

Margaret, who disliked him to be fanciful, had moved on to a tank of bewigged anemones like infant dish mops. She was explaining something about interlamellar junctions.

'And then she's always losing things,' came the querulous voice as the woman with the plastic raincoat caught up with them. 'Even her *ring*.'

'I shall help her,' said the man's voice calmly. 'I shall draw up a routine for her.'

As though the word 'routine' was a beautiful image now to be permanently shattered, thirty-odd children – a school party from Bracken Hill Secondary Modern – erupted into the dark and vaulted halls of the Aquarium. At once, like molecules of effervescent gas, they filled every corner, emitting shocked 'coos' and admiring 'cors', finding everything either terribly funny or marvellously beautiful.

Only one boy, by far the smallest, stood silent, aloof from the rest in the shelter of a pillar. His knee socks had hopelessly descended, the lenses of his goggle glasses threw back weak glimmers of light from a tank of guppies and he was shivering with fear.

One could have been forgiven for not recognizing him for what he was: a *deus ex machina*, a messenger of the capricious gods whose name – because things are so seldom what they seem – was Johnnie Biggs . . .

Toby and Margaret had reached the angel fish, so celestially slender that their organs could be seen pulsating winsomely inside them.

'And you'll see, she's not one to hold down this job,' said the elderly woman, raising her voice against the oncoming children, 'and that's menial enough for a girl with her background.'

'Look, Toby,' said Margaret from the next tank. 'Come here a minute. Interesting spermatophore development.'

But Toby didn't come – quite simply couldn't come. His scalp tingled and the delighted shrieks of the schoolchildren discovering the horrors of the electric eel reached him as only the faintest of tinklings.

For after all, the strange patch of summer ecstasy he'd been going through, the dreams of childhood seascapes, of long-haired girls rising from the water, had been the prelude only to some particular condition. In short, he was going nuts. Because one minute, without a doubt, the tangled, sea-green strand hanging from the top of the tank had been a coil of seaweed. And the next minute, equally unmistakable, it had turned into a girl's green-gold and streaming hair.

With a desperate effort he tore himself away and followed Margaret, who had reached the turtles. It was no good, he told himself, getting maudlin about turtles. So they cried when they laid their eggs and lumbered back into the water like heart-sick tanks. There was nothing one could do.

And then it happened again. Up there, among the bubbles of silver which defined the turtles' sky, something floated. But not a fish, a plant . . . A *wrist?* A girl's slender, blue-veined wrist with something hearbreakingly frantic in the way it broke the water.

'Margaret,' Toby tried to say, very calm, very matter-of-fact, 'I think there's a drowned girl in this tank.'

But Margaret had moved on to a tank of tropicals in which ferocious dragons, seductive geishas, idiot clowns, all masqueraded temporarily as fish.

And inside which, beside the serrated, gaping mouth of a great conch, pale fingers – surely *human* fingers? – desperately searched.

'Do you *see* anything, Margaret?' said Toby frantically.

'Well, naturally,' said Margaret, and told him what she saw, which was a Schomburgk's Leaf-fish with a fungus infection on its caudal fin.

'Not a drowned girl?' said Toby. 'Not a drowned girl with sea-green hair?'

'Harold, my feet are killing me,' said Harold's mother, and for a time said nothing more.

Because suddenly there was a strange, curiously unnerving thud and almost at once smoke began to snake in evil choking clouds through the hall. The schoolchildren began to cough, then to scream and run in a stampede to the door, and still the smoke came, blotting out sight, making each drawn breath an agony.

'Margaret?' called Toby, groping his way back into the hall, 'Margaret?' and getting no reply felt his way blindly towards a half-remembered door. 'Margaret?' he croaked again.

Then he reached it and here at last was Margaret blundering into him. He put out an arm and felt with relief the cold plastic of her sensible handbag before she fell, smoke-blind, against him. To his relief he found he could lift her somewhat solid bulk quite easily and stumbling between the storage vats and water pipes which made up this looking-glass world behind the tanks, came out at last into the open and laid Margaret down on a patch of grass.

Except that it wasn't Margaret . . .

Meanwhile Harold, tying a clean handkerchief about his mouth and keeping extremely calm, extremely steady, began to sidle along the hand rails, one arm extended in a filial search for Mother.

'Mother?' called Harold. 'Mother, where are you?'

And: 'Here, *here*, Harold,' called Harold's mother. 'Harold, I'm choking, I can't *see*.'

Harold couldn't either, but he bravely abandoned the hand-rail, ignored the stumbling children running for the exit and at last, with untold relief felt the cool slither of Mother's unnecessary raincoat beneath his hand.

'It's all right,' he said, putting a protective arm round her, and steered her, coughing and moaning a little, towards safety and daylight. 'It's all right, dear,' said Harold, setting her down on the steps and managing in spite of the pain of his inflamed and swollen eyes to pat her soothingly upon the back. 'We're safe now, Mother. Everything's perfectly all right.'

Which in fact it was. Except that the person he was patting so soothingly wasn't Mother.

Out of sight, on the other side of the Aquarium, Toby stared at the girl who lay stretched out before him on the grass. He should have known that Margaret, who was a hockey blue, would not have hung so lightly from his shoulders. This girl was slender, her long, blonde hair was soaking wet and she smelt movingly of fish. Moreover, the handbag which had bumped so coldly against him was not in fact a handbag. The object which the girl, half faint still, was nevertheless desperately clutching, was a large polythene bag filled with water, inside which swam, slowly and majestically, a large, grey fish.

'You saved a *fish*?' said Toby, awed. 'Wouldn't he have been quite safe in all that water?'

She said nothing, but her eyes, sea-green like her hair, brimmed, overflowed and made tentative runnels of pink on her smoke-blackened cheeks.

'Perhaps he's special?' suggested Toby, finding her silent grief unbearable. 'A reincarnated Buddhist prince,' he suggested, caught by a look of deep serenity somewhere round its nostrils, 'with bliss-bestowing fins?'

She tried to smile through her tears, but almost at once she drooped again and ran desperate fingers through her soaking hair.

'He's swallowed it,' she said in a choking voice. 'At least I think it was him. I dropped it in the tank. I kept looking and *looking*. I work in there, you see, in the Aquarium. I'm a sort of lab girl.'

Of course. He saw it now. The seaweed-floating hair, the frenzied searching . . .

'What did he swallow?' said Toby, watching the fish – a tench, possibly – for signs of gastric tension.

'My ring! My engagement ring. I *always* lose it. Harold'll be so angry. He said if I lost it once more, we were through. It was two diamonds and a ruby and it didn't collect the dust,' she said wildly.

Harold. Toby remembered the voices in the Aquarium and everything fell into place.

'I get it all so wrong. I'm supposed to *clean* the tanks, not fall into them. I'm sure to get the sack after this and I'm so *worried* about the tench. They were terribly *hard* diamonds.'

Toby leaned forward and took her narrow, smoke-black hand. 'Ah, don't,' he said tenderly. '*Don't*. He'll be all right, I promise you. Diamonds for tenches are like grit for pigeons. Roughage, you know.'

And as she turned to him, believing it, radiant with relief, Toby felt, quite distinctly, the earth shiver beneath his feet . . .

Harold's consternation on finding that he was soothingly patting a totally unknown and very personable female with a handsome figure and a pretty profile, was absolute.

'I *beg* your pardon,' he said, 'I thought you were my mother.'

'Well, I'm not,' said Margaret, but she spoke sensibly and without rancour, as was her wont.

'I mistook your handbag for her mackintosh,' said Harold. 'I felt it in the dark,' and blushed, for it had to be admitted that he had felt other things also.

A couple of keepers came out of the Aquarium and Harold inquired for Mother. 'Everyone's safely out now,' they assured him. 'Your old lady'll be along at the First Aid Post with the schoolkids, I dare say. A case of smoke without fire.'

'I must go and look for my friend,' said Margaret, knowing how little Toby was to be trusted.

This was the kind of problem Harold enjoyed. 'You don't, of

course, propose to search round the Zoo at random?'

'Indeed not,' said Margaret. 'A system is obviously necessary.'

'Might I suggest ever-narrowing concentric circles,' suggested Harold, 'as if looking for a ball lost in a field?'

Margaret nodded. 'You don't happen to have a map?'

'I have,' said Harold, and Margaret sighed with approval because Toby never had anything except vinegar-flavoured potato crisps and stray pebbles whose veined markings he expected her to rave about. 'However, if you will allow me, having ascertained that Mother is quite comfortable, I will accompany you. . .'

'If I take him back, and explain, Harold'll want him killed,' said Nell, looking down at the fish who, no longer Buddhistically calm, was growing noticeably short of oxygen.

'And Margaret will dissect him for you beautifully,' said Toby.

They looked at each other. Then without a word they got up and walked together towards the Regent's Park canal.

'Cor!' said the boy, walking beside Johnnie Biggs in the crocodile. 'Did you see that?'

The Bracken Hill School party had re-formed and the children, now savouring in retrospect their narrow escape from death, were going home across the bridge. 'It was a bloomin' great fish jumped in the water.'

But Johnnie Biggs, the *deus ex machina* who had changed four lives, was not remotely interested in fish. Johnnie was in a state of exaltation far beyond speech. He'd done it. He'd done what the gang said. He'd let off the smoke canister they'd nicked from the army dump and he hadn't been caught, so now they'd *have* to let him join. And Johnnie, whose father was in prison, whose mother had given up the struggle long ago, walked from the Zoo that strange, hot summer's day filled with one of mankind's oldest enchantments: the prospect of *belonging* . . .

Toby had explained to Nell gently, interestingly, the ideas of the great psychologist, Freud: that we forget what we want to forget, lose what we want to lose. Now they sat on the banks of the canal into whose green and muddy waters they had launched two hundred and twenty-five pounds' worth of diamonds and in a sense, too, a great deal of well-designed Scandinavian furniture and a split-level oven which cleaned itself.

'I didn't really want any of it?' inquired Nell.

'No,' said Toby.

'Not even Harold?'

'Particularly not Harold.'

'I get afraid when I'm alone,' said Nell. 'All that ecstasy, all that despair. . .'

'I hadn't thought of you being alone,' said Toby, shocked. 'I hadn't thought of that at all.'

And as they turned to each other, not quite believing, yet, that dreams and reality could meet so unconflictingly, Harold, not seeing them, appeared on the other bank. His arm was through Margaret's and though it must have become clear to both of them that Toby, unlike a ball lost in a field, was indulging in purposeless and confusing movements of his own, they continued – so pleased were they with each other's company – to move gravely past the camel house, the zebras, the antelopes, searching, in ever-narrowing concentric circles, the emptying Zoo . . .

SIDI

THE SILKEN, sky-blue curtains of the luxurious fitting booth in London's most famous department store parted and the young bride stepped out. Her dress of snowy muslin was tight-waisted, wickedly full-skirted, ankle-length: a paean to the 'New Look' which Dior had launched, in a sunburst of ruched and tuckered extravagance to banish, in this spring of 1947, the austerities of the war.

But it was not at the dress that the bride's erstwhile governess was staring, but at the look in the girl's eyes. For here was radiance and serenity and a shining, unmistakable joy. No, this could be no marriage of convenience. In marrying John West, whoever he was, Sidi, with banners flying, was going home.

Well, why not? Why this ridiculous sense of disappointment, of betrayal? Had she herself not told Sidi, years and years ago in Berlin, about Lot's wife and the uselessness of looking back? Did she really expect this child who, above all others, deserved her happiness, to remember a place that was now a heap of rubble, a country that was despoiled, dismembered and unreachable?

It was nine years since she had last seen Sidi, who had spent the war in America, evacuated with her English boarding-school within a year of reaching Britain. Sidi's excited voice on the phone, tracking her down in her Berkshire cottage to tell her of this wedding, had been their first contact since then.

'You *must* come, Hoggy,' Sidi had said, her voice still retaining beneath the New England burr she had acquired in the States the traces of her European origins. 'I need you most *particularly*.'

And Miss Hogg had agreed to come not only to the wedding

but to this fitting, for of all the children she had looked after only Sidi, that strange little Continental waif, had stayed in her memory. Yet as the dressmakers surged forward and Sidi's glamorous mother, now in her third marriage to a wealthy stockbroker, issued her instructions, she longed to push them all aside and say to this illumined, joyous bride: 'Don't you *remember*, Sidi? Don't you remember Vlodz?'

She had been named, among other things, for the woman who had loved and succoured the great German poet, Wolfgang von Goethe: Sidonie Ulrike Charlotte Hoffmansburg. But she was a small child with worried dark eyes, the frail, squashed-looking features of an orphaned poodle and soft, straight hair which was cut to lap her eyebrows but never quite made it to her ears, and 'Sidi' was as much of her name as she could manage.

This small girl traversed, four times a year, the great plains and forests of Central Europe – from her mother's elegant apartments in Berlin or Dresden to her father's estate in Hungary, sent 'like a paper parcel', she said to herself, backwards and forwards, forwards and back.

The year was 1935, divorce less common, less civilised. The little girl, the victim of her parents' inability to endure each other, bled internally. All she hoped for as she climbed on to the train at the Friedrich Strasse Bahnhof, already pale with indigestion from consuming the sugared almonds and *langues de chats* pressed on her by her mother's latest lover, was that her father would say one kind word about her mother. All she prayed for as she mounted the train in Budapest, clutching the doll in Hungarian peasant costume hastily procured by her father's current mistress, was that her mother would at least ask how her father was. A simple wish, but one that in all her life was never granted.

This was the time of the great *trains de luxe*, beasts of power and personality which raced across the Continent. The *Train Bleu*, the *Ahlberg-Orient*, the *Süd Express* . . . Sidi travelled in immense comfort, gallantly swallowing five-course dinners in the restaurant car of the wagons-lits, retiring to snowy bed-linen in her damask-lined first-class sleeper with its gleaming basin and pink-shaded lamps. Yet her eyes, as she looked out over the heaths and birch forests, the great fields of maize and rye, seldom lost their sad, bewildered look. Who wanted her?

where did she belong?

Sidi's mother was an actress, the ravishing Sybilla Berger whose silken peroxide-blonde hair, plucked ethereal eyebrows and high cheekbones concealed the constitution of an ox and the single-mindedness of a column of driver ants.

Marriage to a minor Austro-Hungarian landowner without influence or brains was a mistake she quickly rectified. After three years of domesticity in Vienna she divorced him, moved to Berlin, broke into films . . . 'Home' for Sidi with her mother was a series of suites in 'Grand Hotels' from which the little girl was exercised by the hotel porter along with the dachshunds and schnautzers of the guests and 'listened for' at night by suitably tipped chambermaids. Sometimes taxis would call for her and she would be taken to film studios, patted by directors, kissed by actresses – and then forgotten, sometimes for hours. She played under café tables and, in the corners of frowsty dressing-rooms; made pebble houses in the courtyards of restaurants, looking up occasionally to trace through the clouds of cigarette smoke the face of her loved and unattainable mother.

Then suddenly there would be a spate of clothes-and-present buying to impress the other parent, an affecting scene at the station as Sybilla, surrounded by admirers, took leave of her little girl . . . and the long journey to the moated Wasserburg at Malazka to see if perhaps it was her tall, good-natured father with his easy laugh who really loved and wanted her – and to watch the tumbrils cross the cobbled courtyard with the piled corpses and blood-stained antlers of the deer which her father spent his days in killing as he killed, with seasonal enthusiasm, his pheasants and water-fowl and boars.

Sometimes, when her parents tired of their tug-of-war, other pieces were thrown on the board: a grandmother in Prague, a trio of maiden aunts in Paris – and Sidi, the small pawn in their machinations, was put on to yet another great train with some hastily assembled travelling companion.

Thus Sidi, at nine years of age, was a child to whom one could not give a present without her passing it on within minutes to some recipent from whom she might buy even a momentary affection; a child who, if you played her at halma, would wrinkle her abortive nose, trying and trying to lose so that the winner might be pleased and care for her. A child at whose feet the waters of Babylon inexorably lapped.

At which point there entered Miss Hogg.

Miss Hogg was English, a governess, imported with Frau Hoffmansburg's marmalade and riding boots. A stout red-headed lady, she proceeded to bring order and routine into Sidi's life – but not love. Love was a commodity in which Miss Hogg no longer dealt.

Once it had been different. Once, long ago, Miss Hogg had been the Vicar's Sarah-Ellen with a bridge of freckles across her upturned nose and waist-length tresses that struck fire from the sun. Once she had had an adored twin brother, two ginger-haired boy cousins with a penchant for dreadful practical jokes and a fiancé called Hughie who could melt her bones just by entering the room. On her nineteenth birthday her brother and the twins and Hughie had taken her in a punt down the river with hampers and bottles of champagne and a gramophone that played ragtime. A year later, not one of the four young men was still alive. When the last of the telegrams came, the one that told her of Hughie's death on the Somme, Sarah-Ellen had excised her heart, gone to a training college and become, eventually, a governess.

Miss Hogg's twin brother, however, had been a train fanatic. Consulting the Baedecker for Central Europe, she found that it was not necessary, when travelling from Berlin to Herr Hoffmansburg's estate on the edge of the Carpathian hills, to go through Budapest. One could, instead, take the express to Bucharest and, by arrangement with the guard, be set down at an obscure railway station in the middle of nowhere from which, some three hours later, one could catch a stopping train which meandered southwards into Hungary.

And the name of this station was Vlodz.

One could look for a long time at the map of Central Europe and not find Vlodz. It is not quite in Romania, not really in Czechoslovakia, more or less in Poland. The rivers Wistok, Klodza and Itzanka are not far away, nor is the town of Jaroslaw. But since this helps most people very little, it is easier to say that the station was very like a thousand others in that vast European plain: the platform riding high over a sea of Indian corn, sunflowers leaning their enormous heads against the low, white-painted building, geese perambulating on the tracks . . . A Fiddler-on-the-Roof station, a station over which the painter Chagall might have floated a blue-green, dreaming poet . . . A station to the like of which Tolstoy had come in old age to die.

And yet Vlodz was not quite like other stations. To begin with, to those in the know – as was Miss Hogg – it was a junction. Because of this there was a proper waiting-room with a picture of Marshal Pilsudski on the wall, a curly iron stove and wooden benches. There was a real booking office, a place for registering parcels . . . And to accommodate all these, the station-master's house had been detached and built elsewhere, in a meadow just across the earthen road.

Over certain houses there seems to hang a kind of rightness, almost a seal of approval bestowed by a divine hand leaning down with a fatherly pat from the sky. This is the kind of house that children will draw for you with their new Christmas crayons; the kind of house to which storks will return year after year, winging their way from Egypt. The station-master's house was built of aspen wood with a sheen that was almost silver; hearts and roses were carved into its shutters, and into the window-boxes in which petunias and French marigolds grew with the neat abundance which is the hallmark of careful husbandry. Each part of the garden was cultivated and cross-cultivated, a palimpsest of lettuce and kohlrabi, of onions and mignonette, of sweet peppers and raspberry canes and mint. The pig in its pen seemed a little cleaner and fatter than the pigs kept by a thousand station-masters between Cracow and Kiev, the ducks livelier, the bantams more brightly-coloured and audacious.

In this house there lived the station-master, Mr Wasilewski and his wife, Hannah, who had learnt in the practice of a daily kindliness the secret of a happy marriage. There lived also a complacent and not very feline marmalade cat, a dog called Joseph, a canary . . .

And a boy . . .

A boy who, sitting in his attic from which he could look over the road, the station, the great sea of ripening maize which led to Abyssinia, heard the signal clank downwards, closed his school-books and ran downstairs.

For it was very seldom that the Berlin Express deigned to stop at Vlodz. There might, just once, really be treasure trove: an explorer in a topee who wanted his luggage carried to the inn; a wild bear in a crate . . .

His father was ready, his tunic buttoned, his cap straight. Once it had been the boy's greatest joy to be allowed to blow the horn which hung on a chain round his father's neck, to unfurl and wave the green flag. But he was eleven now, no longer a child, and he waited quietly, perched on a trolley, his arms clasped round his knees. He could make out the black dot of the engine now, hear the imperative whistle with which it signalled its intention to stop – and seconds later it was there, blotting out the sky, hissing, enveloping him in its hot breath.

Somewhere at the far end of the platform a door opened and at the same time a great cloud of steam billowed out from under the carriage, obscuring everything.

Almost at once, the door slammed shut again, Mr Wasilewski waved his flag. The train began to move, to gather speed.

The steam cloud lifted.

No treasure trove . . . Only, standing alone, surrounded by her luggage, a little girl.

Miss Hogg had gone into the building to reconnoitre. 'Wait here,' she had said to Sidi and Sidi waited. She had hurt her fingers, trapped them in the twisted, heavy leather strap when the guard pulled down the window, but there was no blood so as an injury it didn't count. No blood, no tears – everyone knew that.

She glanced up. A boy had appeared as if from nowhere. He had cropped fair hair, very blue eyes, leather trousers and bare feet . . . A peasant boy who would despise her, shout things, perhaps throw stones.

She bit her lip, waited as the boy came closer, staring. He had never in his life seen such an elegant and burnished little girl. She wore a white sailor suit, a blue beret set back on her narrow head, snowy knee-socks, gleaming black shoes with silver buckles. Nothing was crumpled even after hours in the train – nothing except her face.

'Have you hurt yourself?' he asked.

He had rejected his native tongue, spoken in German. He could have managed, also, a little French. The village schoolmaster – a saint – had picked him out for university and, given a little luck, the premiership of Poland.

She looked at him in amazement. 'It was my fault,' she stammered.

To his own intense surprise, he reached out, took her creased, bruised fingers, blew on them . . . And was suddenly, blindingly pierced – rent – no word is too apocalyptic – by an all-consuming, earth-shaking tenderness.

Somewhere, two hundred miles or so to the south-west, in the beautiful grey and gold city of Vienna, the great Sigmund Freud was at that moment propounding to a world destined to be entirely transformed by his doctrines, his theories of infant and pre-pubertal sexuality. But the Professor, if present at Vlodz station, would have been wide of the mark. This was the other thing.

Wonderingly, Sidi took back her hand. The waters of Babylon receded. Ruth when exiled amid the alien corn had wept. Sidi, who very much resembled her, standing above a rustling sea of maize, now lifted her head and tentatively, experimentally, smiled.

Miss Hogg was to look back on the afternoon she spent in the station-master's house mostly as somewhere it had been possible to sit and knit comfortably and at the proper speed. After the last of the telegrams came, the one that said that Hughie too was dead, she had been what she later referred to as 'a little bit silly'. She had, in short, thrust her arms through the belt of her summer dress and jumped into the Thames. Rescued by an unnoticed fisherman she had, in the hospital, been advised to take up knitting, the therapeutic properties of which the doctor was much inclined to praise.

Miss Hogg had obeyed and in her subsequent career as a governess, been glad of it. It was the intricacies of a turned heel on an extremely complicated Fair Isle pattern sock that had prevented her from getting up and hitting Frau Hoffmansburg when she referred to Sidi's father, in the child's presence, as a Magyar runt with the sexual appetites of a ferret. It was the need to insert a cable needle, precise as a catheter, into the sleeve of an Arran sweater, that had enabled her to keep silent when Herr Hoffmansburg informed his daughter that her mother had the soul of a Jewish pawnbroker and had embezzled the family pearls. But at Vlodz, sitting on the carved rocker, a glass of tea beside her, protected by her monumental ignorance of Polish from the rigours of conversation, she knitted contentedly and in peace.

But Sidi . . . Sidi, from the moment that the boy opened the white-painted gate that led into his garden, entered upon her heritage.

She had known, really, that somewhere there had to be such a house. A house that smelled of vanilla and cinnamon and fresh-baked bread . . . A house with embroidered cushions tied to each carved pine chair and a canary as yellow as butter that sang and sang and sang. She had known too that such a house would have a cat with whiskers like cello strings which jumped on to your knee the moment you sat down, and that she would not be banished to the parlour but allowed to help at once, given a straw basket to go into the garden and pick raspberries for tea. She had known, without quite knowing that she knew it, that somewhere in the world there had to be a couple like the Wasilewskis who smiled at each other as they passed, touched each other on the shoulder or the arm.

But the amazing thing, the thing she had been quite unable to envisage, was the boy.

For the boy was *hers*; she had known this at once. She had no words for what she saw in his steady blue eyes, but she was compelled to understand it. He was older than she was, tall, strong and very brave. She saw how fearlessly he shooed away the hissing gander that barred their path, how skilfully he whittled a stick with a wicked knife. Yet he wanted to be where she was. If she moved away, even a few steps, he followed. It was incredible, yet unmistakable. She *pleased* him.

The boy meanwhile had been pondering, his forehead creased. Now he seemed to have made up his mind.

'Come outside,' he said – and at once she pushed back her glass of milk and got up from the table.

'Where are we going?' she asked, trotting after him, her shining shoes whitening in the dust from the road.

'Into the field,' he said – but he could as well have said, 'into the sea', for it was like the sea, that limitless field of Indian corn, stretching as far as the eye could see, rustling, murmuring, brushed by cats-paws of wind as was the sea itself.

He led her across the railway track, down the embankment and into a kind of tunnel he had made between the stalks and she crawled after him into a small, circular patch that he had cleared – a nest, a cave in which one was invisible from the house, the station, everyone.

'I come here to think,' he said.

She nodded, for she had already understood that he was a person who thought. Characteristically, she was looking not upwards at the sky but downwards at a scurrying golden beetle. About to commit to her his life, the boy – studying the hollows in her appallingly vulnerable neck – nevertheless felt a momentary sense of grievance. She was going to be very little *use* in Abyssinia.

'Your house is lovely,' she said shyly. 'It's the most beautiful house I've ever seen.'

He frowned, surprised. Like all happy children, he took his home for granted. But she had given him a lead.

'Actually,' he said, 'I shan't be in it much longer. As soon as I'm old enough I'm going away. To Abyssinia.'

'Oh.' Desolation overwhelmed her. She had been entirely mistaken, then.

'Abyssinia is in Africa,' he explained. 'It is a country ruled by a lion . . . the Lion of Judah. . .'

He began to speak, his voice strong and full of joy and as he spoke she saw the great, fair-minded beast watching over its weaker brethren, its gentle eyes gazing benevolently at the grazing deer, the lambs skipping among the flowers, the monkeys swinging by their tails from trees heavy with fruit . . .

'That's what they call the Emperor,' said the boy. 'He has a bodyguard of warriors who are seven feet tall and can run like an ostrich and he wears a crown and is enormously brave. And there are mountains full of gold and very old men because the air is so good that no one ever gets ill, and lakes bursting with fish, and forests. . .'

His dream began to stir in her. She saw that he would have to go and tried, with frantic gallantry, to rise to his need.

'Where will you live?'

'I shall cut down trees and train elephants to carry the logs and build a house. We shall need a house because—'

'We?' came Sidi's voice, small as a cricket's, beside him.

He turned. 'I want you to come.' And as she was silent, more urgently: 'Will you come?'

Still she did not speak. Then, as he watched, he saw her become slowly, utterly transformed as she allowed happiness to smoothe her crumpled little face, straighten her frail shoulders, lift her head . . .

'Yes,' she said. 'Oh, yes.'

She had been right, then. She *was* going to live in the station-master's house. For she knew now that he would – with the aid of elephants – build it for her there, by a blue Abyssinian lake. A house with carved shutters and a flower-filled balcony from which she would emerge in a red-checked, braided apron like Mrs Wasilewski's, to call, from the encroaching jungle, her children in to tea.

'What was the name of the boy?' Miss Hogg asked later that afternoon, when Sidi had stopped waving at last and Vlodz station was just a tiny dot on the vast landscape.

'Jan,' said Sidi, still grave-eyed from the parting.

But to herself she went on calling him 'the boy' as though there was no other in the world.

Sidi went to the moated Wasserburg where her father continued to dismember stags by day and to assert, at night, his dominion over a series of apparently identical blondes. But she was stronger, she looked sometimes at the sky. She also became an expert on African affairs, browsing in her father's deserted library and surprising his house guests by a familiarity with Ethiopian kinship systems and the population of Addis Ababa.

When they came to Vlodz again, en route for Berlin, it was early autumn. This time it was already a homecoming. Miss Hogg had a crochet pattern for Mrs Wasilewski. There was frothy milk and gingerbread and a kitten that Jan had saved from drowning for her. But the last hour before the train came belonged to the children alone and they spent it in the maize field, now head-high and ready for reaping.

They had laid down the blueprint for their lives, but there was something to be done and the knowledge weighed heavily on the boy.

'I have to kiss you,' he said abruptly, breaking into her happy prattle. 'I have to.'

The panic that even he could not entirely still in her leapt to her eyes. Their noses would bump; she would fail him.

'I have to,' he repeated, for he knew what belonged to Abyssinia: the passports, the documents, the marriage . . . But as she knelt up and offered her bleak little face as to a feared yet trusted dentist, his heart smote him. Under his brutishness she would wilt, would die.

He bent his head, kissed her soap-scented cheek and then, fleetingly, her mouth.

Her eyes flew open and something danced in them.
Then: 'Do it again,' said Sidi.

It was after this that they began to write letters. From Berlin to
Vlodz, from Dresden to Vlodz when Sidi's mother went to film
there; from Vlodz to Paris when she was sent to her aunts.
Socrates, who said that an unexamined life is worthless, would
have been pleased with them as they began to draw out of their
daily lives something that would please or amuse the other. For
Sidi, the letter-box became the point of reference in whatever
town she alighted; she navigated by it as mariners navigate by
the stars. At Vlodz, the old postman with his warty face became
the Grail-Bearer, the Rosenkavalier.

In November, Sybilla Berger scored a success in a play based
on the life of the ill-fated Elisabeth of Austria and as a result,
Korda sent for her to make a film test in London. Christmas
had been heavily disputed between the parents. Now, Herr
Hoffmansburg was told that he could have the child.

'You'll manage the journey, Hoggy, won't you?' said Frau
Hoffmansburg, and departed on the *Nord Express*.

'I'll manage,' said Miss Hogg. She was only too pleased to
leave Berlin, for her initial reaction to Herr Hitler – that the
poor man could not last long with that ridiculous moustache –
was fast giving way to serious misgiving. She consulted the
timetable, cooked the books, sent telegrams.

Thus Sidi and Miss Hogg 'lost' a day and spent it in the
station-master's house at Vlodz.

It was not quite Christmas, but for Sidi there was never any
other. They were given the best bedroom with the blue-and-
white-tiled stove, the goosefeather bed and the samovar that
had belonged to Mr Wasilewski's grandmother, and the house
smelled of roasting pork and apples and mulled wine. The days
when Sidi had passed her presents on as soon as she received
them were gone. She had kept everything: scent and chocolates
and silk scarves from the women who aspired to be her
stepmother; crystallized fruit and musical boxes and fountain
pens from her mother's suitors – and all these she now emptied
joyfully on to the scrubbed pine table.

But when, an hour before sunset, the boy rose from his stool and said: 'Come,' not one of the Wasilewski's seasonal visitors disputed his right. For the people of Vlodz were under no illusions about Jan. He was the woodcutter's third son, the one who answered the riddles, and the exotic foreign little girl was no whit too good for him.

Outside, the snow was king. Under its blanket, their maize field slept; the shrouded station was muffled and still.

'Where are we going?' asked Sidi.

'You'll see.'

He led her into a shed behind the house where there was a high, carved sledge and a bearskin rug in which he wrapped her so that only her bright face showed. But as he began to pull her along the white road towards the rim of fir trees standing out darkly against the orange sky of sunset, his eyes were anxious. It was strictly forbidden to cut down trees in Vlodz. The forest was a private one, planted by the squire centuries ago for his hunting in this country of open plains. And even Jan's parents had not understood how important it was that Sidi should miss nothing that belonged, in her own life, to Christmas. He had had to contrive, beg, pilfer and even then, rising at dawn, been at the mercy of a sudden blizzard.

By the gate which led into the wood, he stopped the sledge.

'Wait,' he said to Sidi, sitting bright-eyed inside her furs. 'And don't look. Shut your eyes.'

It was dusk now; the firs, in their white mantles, stood in dark and solemn ranks.

All except one . . . a small tree standing a little apart from the others, whose needles had been freed from snow. A tree garlanded in gold and silver, hung with rosy apples, with gingerbread hearts and brightly painted toys . . . A star-crowned tree whose array of candles Jan now set carefully alight.

'You can look now,' he called.

Sidi took her knuckles from her eyes, climbed down from the sledge – and saw, shining from the darkness of the winter forest, the living glory that was Jan's tree.

'Oh,' she said. '*Oh!*'

And for her, this moment was for ever Christmas and was for ever love.

That summer, they lost Abyssinia. 'That beast, Mussolini,'

wrote Sidi from Berlin, knowing the blow that Jan had sustained over the Lion of Judah, now exiled and playing croquet on an English lawn.

'It doesn't matter,' the boy wrote back. 'We'll go to Madagascar – or the Gold Coast, maybe.'

But when they met again, they went on speaking of Abyssinia for it is not easy to rename a country of the heart.

They were growing up fast. The lost look was seldom seen, now, in Sidi's eyes. The boy was her secret, her philosopher's stone, her talisman against the confusions and betrayals of her life. As for Jan, it seemed to his teachers and his family that there was nothing he could not do.

Then, in the autumn of 1937, a minor actress who coveted Sybilla Berger's roles unveiled a secret. Frau Hoffmansburg's father, a blond, amiable Professor of Botany in the University of Trubingen was, by birth, a Jew. The massive deportations had not yet begun, but Frau Hoffmansburg wasted no time. She collected her jewels, her latest lover and (partly to annoy her husband) her daughter – and prepared to leave for England.

'But we can't go! We *can't!*' cried Sidi, and broke into a storm of weeping.

'What on earth's the matter with the child?' asked Frau Hoffmansburg.

Miss Hogg, decreasing for the armholes of an angora cardigan, did not enlighten her.

They went to London. Miss Hogg was dismissed, went to stay with a cousin in Berkshire and after three months of boredom, took a job with a family in New Zealand. Sidi trailed after her mother from hotel room to borrowed apartment, writing, writing, printing her changing addresses on the outsides of envelopes, the insides, always and only terrified that she would lose touch with Jan. He wrote back bravely, hearteningly. He had found a Scottish lady in the market town and was learning English. He was learning it *quickly*, she had praised his accent and very soon now he would come. 'And wherever we are, Sidi, wherever we go,' he wrote, old enough now for metaphor and poetry, 'we'll *make* it Abyssinia.'

Sybilla, meanwhile, devoutly navigating the tricky shoals of the casting couch, was finding her nearly adolescent daughter distinctly in the way. She jettisoned her lover, acquired a rich protector and sent Sidi to an exclusive boarding-school in Kent.

When Jan's first letter came, Sidi was sent for and told that letters from boys were not allowed. She smuggled her own letters out, gave him the address of the village post office, was caught and sent for again. When it happened a third time, Frau Hoffmansburg was informed and expulsion threatened. It was only when Sybilla swore to make trouble for Jan's parents that Sidi gave in.

Six months later, Hitler invaded Poland – and the waters of Babylon closed over her head.

Miss Hogg, who had not been rated very highly by the ushers, was in the back pew. She had, after all, not managed to have tea with Sidi after the fitting, but as she was dragged away by Sybilla, Sidi had once again implored her governess to, 'Please, oh please be there!'

So Miss Hogg *was* there, in the flower-bedecked private chapel on Sidi's stepfather's estate, beside a lady in a magenta toque with veiling who now said:

'Of course it's been a great disappointment to Sybilla. She had such hopes for Sidi.'

'What's wrong with the young man?' asked her neighbour, who had patriotically retrimmed her pre-war Ascot hat with cherries. 'He's supposed to be terribly clever and I gather he did some fearfully brave cloak-and-dagger thing in the war.'

'Well, my dear, a foreigner and an absolute nobody it seems.'

'A foreigner? With a name like John West?'

'Oh, the Intelligence people re-christened him in the war. They did that quite often with Jews and Poles and things when they dropped them back into Europe. The Nazis did such awful things to them if they were caught. He wanted to change back, I believe, but his firm persuaded him not to.'

'Well, I must say I think he looks rather sweet.'

The bridegroom had reached the chancel steps. Miss Hogg fumbled for her spectacles, then gave up, for the organ had burst into a glorious Bach chorale. The bride entered, paused to give her erstwhile governess a smile of complicity and utter joy – and walked to where the boy stood waiting.

Miss Hogg, at this point, wept. But somewhere in the forests of Abyssinia, a lion, golden-eyed and gentle, lifted his great, majestic head . . . and roared.

A DARK-HAIRED DAUGHTER

WHEN JULIE HOWARD came to tea and burst into tears over my flapjacks, I rejected, quite quickly, a number of possibilities. That she had 'Fallen in Love with Another', for example. I lived opposite the Howards in a cottage I had bought after my retirement from the village school, and only the broadmindedness acquired by dealing for thirty years with what went on behind the Infant lavatories enabled me to view, unblushingly, the physical enthusiasm of Julie for her husband and his for her. Similarly I rejected bankruptcy (Donald was the local doctor and doing very nicely), petty crime and illness. Julie looked fine.

Or did she?

'You're pregnant again?' I hazarded and quickly poured another cup of tea.

She nodded, sniffed. 'It's so awful, Mouncey, I don't know *what* to do! It isn't just the guilt, though that's dreadful. I mean, did you know that all the people in the world can't stand together on the Isle of Wight any more? Perhaps on one toe, that's all! But quite apart from that, I just don't feel I can *bear* it!'

'I suppose you couldn't. . .' I began – and stopped.

My first memory of Julie was of a huge-eyed and duskyheaded five-year-old, tottering in tear-stained from break with a waterlogged earthworm hanging in a swoon from her small, pink hand. As a destroyer of life, born or unborn, Julie Howard was clearly a non-starter.

'There's only one way I can bear it,' she said. 'If it's a girl. A dark-haired little girl, very small and gentle. I could bear that. Maybe she'd love music and I could play the piano to her, or she'd want to go to ballet classes. Of course I wouldn't *pressurise* her; if she wanted to be an engineer or an aviator I'd back her up. Naturally. But you know what I mean?'

I did know.

Julie already had three little boys. I myself had watched them – alike as peas, terrible as an army with banners – grow from bald and bullet-headed babies chronically crimsoned with hunger and rage, to flaxen-headed, blue-eyed replicas of their father who spent their days ricocheting off the furniture, whooping from upturned wheelbarrows or falling out of the few trees in the Howards' garden which had survived their coming. 'Julie's Juggernauts' was how Angus, Jamie and Guy were known in East Moreton, and if Julie felt she could face only a gentle, dark-haired daughter, no living soul could blame her.

'Girls are more likely later in marriage; I read it somewhere,' I said. 'It'll be all right, you'll see.'

News of the baby spreading through East Moreton found the village sharply divided. There were optimists like Mrs Hicks, the grocer's wife, who cited cases of daughters born to men with as many as seven sons, and there were others, such as Ben Farrer at The Feathers, who said darkly that Dr Howard's genes were not of the kind that gave way suddenly. What everyone was agreed on was that if the baby was another boy, Julie – already worn out by the other three and never allowed, being a doctor's wife, to be ill – would crack up and crack up badly.

I like to think that my own efforts had something to do with the growth of confidence in Moreton as Julie's pregnancy advanced. After all, a retired headmistress has a certain standing. Certainly by the late spring, anyone who dared to suggest that the Howards' new baby might be a boy was regarded as unpatriotic, defeatist or just plain nasty.

Meanwhile, over snatched cups of coffee in my cottage, Julie and I played the name game. Sometimes it was a grave and dedicated little girl out of a Russian ballet school that we conjured up:

'What about Natasha, do you like that? Or Tatiana?'

Sometimes we felt old-fashioned and Victorian.

'Tabitha's nice, don't you think? Or Griselda? Do you remember *The Cuckoo Clock*?'

Or we would draw out of the ether a peat-eyed, barefooted little Celt as we toyed with Kirsty or Mhairi or Catriona.

Once – I had neuralgia and wasn't quite myself – I said

stupidly: 'And if it's a boy?'

Julie's face clouded over. 'Oh, don't, Mouncey. Please don't even *talk* about it!'

As the months passed, the support of the village grew steadily. Mrs Hicks said Julie was carrying high and that was a girl for sure; old Mrs Elmhirst, who dabbled in astrology, said that nothing could be more favourable than the way Jupiter was carrying on with Mars; and the Vicar, when questioned, closed his eyes and intoned: '. . . *all shall be well and all shall be well and all manner of things shall be well.*'

Nevertheless, in secret I worried about Julie. As her pregnancy advanced she looked more and more exhausted and once, when I found her crying over the ironing board, she said, 'Oh, Mouncey, I had such a ghastly dream! The midwife was holding up the baby – all bald and bullet-headed, you know, with ears like handlebars – and saying, "It's a boy!" and when I put out my arms to take him he punched me on the jaw.' She began to cry again. 'I'm so tired, Mouncey, I can't *take* any more males!'

Two weeks before the baby was due, my widowed sister rang from London. She had to have a minor operation and asked if I could possibly come up for a few days to help.

It was a beautiful summer afternoon when I returned. Stepping down on to the platform I saw Mrs Hicks on the other side, waiting for the 3.47 to town.

She saw me and waved. 'The baby's come, Miss Mouncefield!' she shouted – and then her train drew in and I could hear no more.

Well, no matter. The cottage hospital was not far out of my way and I only had a little case. I set off down the High Street.

It was a heartening and friendly place, the maternity wing. Glistening lino, fresh-painted walls . . .

'May I see Mrs Howard? I know it's not visiting time, but I've just come from town.'

The Sister nodded. 'Room 23. She's on her own, being a doctor's wife.'

My hand was shaking as I opened the door. Suddenly I felt I could not bear it if Julie had not got her heart's desire.

It was all right! More than all right! Julie was sitting up in bed, her cheeks glowing and her eyes blazing with joy.

I went over and kissed her. 'I haven't brought any flowers yet, pet, I just came off the train.'

'I don't need flowers,' said Julie ecstatically. 'I don't need *anything*! Look!'

She pointed to the cot from which soft snuffling noises came. I went over, peered inside – and almost recoiled.

Pugilistic, steaming with uncontrollable life, bald and bullet-headed, with ears like handlebars, the latest Howard chewed with cannibalistic fervour at his own wrist.

'Isn't he *gorgeous*, Mouncey? Isn't he the most beautiful baby you ever saw?' said Julie, and the look on her face made my heart turn over. 'I'm so happy! So incredibly happy! I must be the happiest person in the world!'

This Year's Winner

THERE ARE not many girls left nowadays who care deeply about the fate of the anchovy, but Gussie MacLeod was such a girl.

It was not anchovies, however – dangerously over-fished and threatened though they were – that were occupying her attention on the morning that the summons came, but turtles, infant ones, some one hundred and fifty of which she was escorting, under a large golfing umbrella, from the fringes of the white sand beach down to the azure Pacific.

Augusta had spent all of her twenty years on the Toto Islands where her father was the doctor, and escorting things took up a good deal of her time. She escorted orphans to the clinic, lepers to film shows of *The Red Shoes*, displaced boobies back to their nests . . . And now, the baby turtles whose tragic odyssey after hatching, menaced by vultures and frigate birds, by iguanas and ghost crabs and dessication, Gussie could not allow to proceed without her help.

She had reached the water's edge and was shoving off an inane and tank-like parent who seemed on course to flatten the entire brood, when she heard a sharp whistle and looked up to see a little native boy beckoning to her.

'You're wanted,' he said. 'By the fire-engine shed, straight away. With a bathing costume.'

'Oh no! What is it, do you know?'

The boy shook his head. 'It's important, though.'

Gussie sighed. Another shark drill, probably. And planting her umbrella in the sand she plunged into the shade of the seaward-leaning palms, making her way towards the bungalow where, since the death of her native mother, she and her father had lived alone.

She collected her bathing costume, from which a nesting

weaver bird had removed a sizable chunk and wandered down to the village square. There, in front of the fire-engine shed, a number of planks had been laid over packing-cases, producing a kind of ramp around which half a dozen girls were standing.

'I hope it's not injections,' said Manai, whose father kept the liquor store.

'Or head lice,' said Tepee, who was still at school.

But it was neither. It was, for some mysterious reason, a beauty competition and one in which Gussie, in deference to her father's status and the high esteem in which the MacLeods were held, came third.

An hour later, taking tea with her lepers on Fara atoll, she had forgotten the whole thing. The lepers were disgruntled. Long since cured, they had led under Gussie's guidance a peaceful existence stringing shells into necklaces which they sold to cowed tourists on the twice-monthly boat from Samoa. But the previous week an occupational therapist, newly trained in Brisbane, had flown out and opened up for them a whole new world of raffia mats, cane baskets and poker-work fire screens – a veritable hive of organised handicraft in which they, the lepers of Toto, would play a leading part. Then, as is the way of visiting experts, she had gone away again, leaving Gussie to take the rap. For Toto was short on raffia, poor on cane and practically devoid of pokers.

Gussie had just begun to soothe them by reading aloud for the fifteenth time the last chapter of *Love Story*, when the silence of the lagoon was broken by the chug of a motor-boat from which there presently emerged Gussie's father and the Mayor himself, a corpulent copra grower, now ripe with importance and almost fully dressed.

And the news that this dignitary brought was that Gussie, as a result of the morning's competition, had been selected as Miss Toto Islands to represent the newly independent federation at the Miss Galaxy Contest to be held in London in July.

'But that's ridiculous!' wailed Gussie. 'I didn't even win. Manai did.'

A few words from her father informed Gussie that Manai was pregnant and that the runner-up had been removed by her irate father to the safety of the interior.

'I *can't* go. People will die laughing if they see me in a Beauty Contest!'

The Mayor demurred politely, but he saw her point. In

Gussie MacLeod the genes had not so much mingled as tangled. Her father's bright red hair, cropped to a cockatoo's crest, topped her native mother's large, dark eyes; freckles rampaged across the bridge of her sawn-off khaki nose; she was so thin that the beating of her heart seemed likely to displace her rib-cage altogether. And he sighed, for he would have liked to do better for the Toto Islands.

'I think you should go, Puss,' said Dr MacLeod. 'London's not like Inverness, of course, but there must be some good things left . . . fish and chips and the Wren churches and the Turners at the Tate. You might even like it enough to stay,' he added, turning away his face, for the thought of life without his daughter was almost unendurable.

But it was a gnarled and fierce old lady, stepping out of the circle of interested lepers, who settled Gussie's fate.

'In London,' she said firmly, 'will be raffia. And pokers for making the works.'

Dr Richard Whittacker's reaction to being told by the president of the Galaxy Chemical Company that he was to organise the Miss Galaxy Contest was the same as Gussie's. He was convinced that he was the victim of an uninspired and tasteless joke.

He had been summoned from the Research Laboratories of which, though absurdly young for such a responsibility, he was the head, and whisked by private lift to the thirtieth floor from which, flanked by picture windows, Mexican breadfruit plants and tropical aquaria, the 'Old Man' ruled the most powerful chemical combine in Britain.

'But I can't do that, sir! I'm a *chemist*,' said Richard, whose response to girls in bathing costumes and high heels was to turn the television off – and fast.

The Old Man looked at him. Young Whittacker had come to them after getting the best First in Biochemistry which Cambridge had produced for twenty years. Even his Ph.D. had thrown out some enormously interesting angles on the isomorphism of oxonium compounds. Since then he had done extremely well for Galaxy and the tragic ending of his marriage, regrettable though it might be in itself, had produced an output of work that was remarkable by any standard. The way to the thirtieth floor and a place on the board was undoubtedly open to young Whittacker. If, that was, his academic background did not conceal an inability to deal with the seamier side of things: with pressmen and pressure groups and the lunatic fringe. Ordeal by fire commonly faced those seeking the higher path. Ordeal by beauty competition, as the Old Man proceeded to make clear, now faced Richard en route for the board room.

'Might I ask, sir, why Galaxy is organising this contest? What benefit do we propose to derive from it?'

'Benefit?' The Old Man looked shocked. 'This, dear boy, is strictly a matter of charity. Of course, it's true that Galaxy Cosmetics have lapsed a little behind our other interests. I don't know if you've seen the figures. . .' He became technical. 'But that's by the way. Now here is all the information you need,' he went on, handing over a massive folder. 'I know I can rely on you. And remember the motto that has always sustained us at Galaxy: "Everything clean. Everything fair" '.

'Yes, sir,' said Richard dully – and was dismissed.

Three months later it had all been done. Richard had commandeered the Woodward Hotel, organised the trips down the river, the visit to Marlborough House and the ballet, the charity banquets and kissing of babies in suitably selected orphanages – all the events which were to occupy the girls until the actual contest in the Albert Hall.

Now, flanked by assistants and chaperones and some more than usually foul-mouthed pressmen, he waited at Heathrow to welcome the last of the arrivals. Already bedded down in the Woodward were Miss USA, a charming and curvaceous blonde so pretty and friendly that it was generally agreed she had no chance of even being placed and Miss Rumania whose awe-inspiring bosom seethed with contempt for the Western world. He had obtained study facilities for Miss Germany, who was finishing a thesis on 'Schiller's Nature Imagery' and arranged for Miss Canada, a motherly brunette, to share a room with Miss Papua New Guinea who seemed to be allergic to something or other and had come out in bumps.

He had also welcomed to the opulence of the Woodward this year's hotly tipped favourite, Miss United Kingdom.

Miss United Kingdom was a raven-haired, blue-eyed, dyed-in-the-wool professional who could hold her winsome, girl-next-door smile for twenty minutes flat if there were cameramen around and walked even to the bathroom with the pelvic undulations so characteristic of those who have spent their life on ramps. She was also – and it was this which had brought a frown to Richard's face – a girl called Delma Lasenbury with whom he had tangled briefly during his time at Cambridge.

It had been during his last year there; he was doing postgraduate work and Delma had just arrived at one of those cookery-cum-secretarial colleges which have mushroomed around the older universities, enabling pubescent girls to get a nibble at the flower of British manhood without the strains of scholarship.

Richard's tenure of Delma had been brief and due to the fact that he had scored an unexpected success in an OUDS production of *The Winter's Tale* where, in plum-coloured velvet and a silver wig, he had played Prince Florizel.

For one delirious summer, Delma had been his Perdita. Even then she was beautiful, even then her beauty was for her a kind of creed. Richard's memories were of an almost incessant bodily horticulture, oiling her back in punts, brushing her hair as they picnicked on the Backs. Nevertheless, when she moved on, he was desolate. And then, two days ago she had swept into the Woodward surrounded by publicity men and later, when they were alone, made it quite clear that she remembered him. To find that the organiser of a contest she was hell-bent on winning was an old flame was almost too good to be true. What is more, Richard had found himself responding just a little. That summer on the river had been very sweet – a time of lost innocence before the agony that had ended his ill-starred marriage.

'Everything clean, everything fair,' he reminded himself – and went forward to disentangle the newly-arrived Miss Denmark from the attentions of a bunch of women's libbers protesting (with some justice, he could not help feeling) against the degradation of the contest.

He despatched in taxis a series of dusky beauties whose names bore witness to the rapid rearrangement of the African continent, found the succulent Miss New Zealand obscured by luggage and lusting cameramen – and was scanning his list to see if he could call it a day when he felt a tug at his arm and saw a thin girl with vestigial amounts of bright red hair looking up at him.

'Excuse me,' she said, 'but I was told to get in touch with you. It's about the Miss Galaxy Contest.'

Richard nodded. 'Yes, well . . . I'm sorry, but I have all the secretaries I need – there really aren't any jobs left at all.'

'Actually, it isn't that,' said the girl, talking for some reason in the softest of Highland accents. 'I'm . . . sort of supposed to take part. I'm something called Miss Toto Islands.'

Richard's look of amazement lasted just too long before he changed it to a smile of welcome.

'I know, it's absolutely ridiculous,' she said, grinning. 'It was all a mistake, really – there were only six of us and some were pregnant and so on. I won't be a nuisance to you, honestly. What I really want is some golfing umbrellas for the turtles and a really good pipe for my father and some raffia for the lepers. . .'

'Raffia?' said Richard dazedly. 'Isn't there plenty of that where you come from?'

Gussie shook her head. 'It's the wrong kind. The best raffia comes from Madagascar and of course the lepers feel—' She broke off. 'Oh, look, a proper English pigeon! But surely he shouldn't be *inside* the airport? Couldn't we take him out?'

'He's all right, honestly,' said Richard, watching out of the corner of his eye a reporter approaching. 'They get plenty to eat, I promise you. Is that all the luggage you've got?'

Gussie nodded and let herself be fed into a taxi from which, in the intervals of comforting Miss Trinidad and Tobago who wanted her mother, she hung ecstatically, commenting on the extreme Englishness of the razor-blade factories, leaden skies and rickety hoardings of the approach to London.

She was still exclaiming when, in the foyer of the Woodward, Richard's chief assistant, on the look-out for sacrificial victims, informed her that she was to have the honour of sharing a room with no other person than Great Britain's own contestant, Miss United Kingdom herself.

Delma Lasenbury was lying on the bed, almost totally obscured by fruit. Strips of avocado closed her eyelids, slices of cucumber adhered to her cheeks; her throat and shoulders frothed bloodily with egg-white and crushed strawberry. But she opened her eyes when Gussie entered.

'Good God. Don't tell me you're a contestant!'

Once more, Gussie explained.

'Well, well! And what are *your* measurements, I wonder,' said Miss United Kingdom nastily. And then: 'Pass me a towel, will you?'

Gussie passed the towel and, subsequently, a hair switch like a compressed Pekingese, a massage vibrator and a packet of eyelashes with which one could have towed the *Titanic*, deeply honoured to assist in the creation of the impeccable product that was Delma Lasenbury.

'You're sure to win,' she said admiringly. 'Only . . . I mean, are you sure you *want* to? Wouldn't it be rather awful, kind of wandering about like the Flying Dutchman, opening things and closing them and never being able to go home?'

Delma's pansy-blue eyes stared at her with contempt. 'You bet I want to. It's five thousand quid for a start and a lot more where that came from. And with Richard on the committee—' She broke off, biting her lip.

'Is that Dr Whittacker? He's awfully nice, isn't he?'

Delma nodded. 'Quite a dish,' she said, languorously establishing ownership.

But Miss Toto Islands was frowning. Gussie, that arch-escorter of turtles, orphans and booby birds, would greatly have liked to escort Dr Whittacker from whatever it was that made him look the way he did.

It was not only Delma, however, who took up Gussie's time. Herded together at the Woodward the bewildered girls, like the turtles of Toto, seemed to be constantly at risk. Miss Isle of Man's left breast, due to some defect in the silicone, subsided dramatically, sending the poor girl off into understandable hysterics. Miss Iceland, a majestic 36–26–38 who could hardly have sunk even into the maw of one of her native geysers, had a phobia about plug-holes and had to be removed to a room with a shower, and Miss Trinidad and Tobago, still awash with homesickness, had attached herself to Gussie like a hatched duckling and refused to leave her side.

But it was Miss Korea, a tiny dental student tottering about on six-inch heels, clutching a textbook with pictures of horribly carietic molars, who tore most at Gussie's heartstrings. For within half an hour of her arrival, one of Miss Korea's contact lenses had fallen into the depths of the fountain in the Palm Lounge, leaving the bereaved contestant to face the shame of representing her fatherland in horn-rims.

On the first evening, the girls were invited to a reception in the Woodward itself – a formal affair for the Lord Mayor, members of the organising committee, the BBC . . . Standing beside the Old Man, Richard thought how stunning Delma looked in a black dress high at the throat but slashed to an impressive décolleté around the armpits. None of the others had her assurance and panache. Delma would win all right.

It was a while before he noticed that many of the girls, instead of circulating among the grey-suited dignitaries, were bunched together in the centre of the room from which there emanated an excited, multi-lingual twitter.

He moved across and reluctantly they parted to let him through.

The fountain was deep, chlorinated and heavily fringed with ferns. Then, even as Richard stared, there emerged a figure which already seemed strangely familiar: a girl, thin to the point of emaciation, freckled, dripping from every pore – but radiating now an air of unmistakable triumph.

'I've found it!' cried Gussie exultantly. 'It was a miracle, but look!'

And as she held out the tiny glass object to the delightedly hopping Miss Korea, the cameramen converged.

The picture of Gussie emerging from the fountain, made the front page of almost every newspaper the following day. If Delma was furious, Gussie's fellow contestants reacted differently. Rising from the breakfast table, Gussie was waylaid by Miss Canada from whose arm half-a-dozen bathing costumes dangled.

'We had a whip-round, Gussie,' she said. 'Because quite honestly, yours just won't do.'

'I mended the hole,' said Gussie, a little hurt. But she accepted the offer in the spirit in which it was intended and even allowed Miss Holland to substitute a white silk sheath for the pink taffeta evening dress with puffed sleeves and heart-shaped neckline which – in order not to cause expense to her father – she had borrowed from one of his laboratory technicians.

Even so, she ran into trouble over her national costume at the afternoon's dress rehearsal in the main lounge.

'What on earth is *that*?' sneered Delma as Gussie emerged

from the changing-room in a single strip of bleached cotton which fell from her arm-pits to just below her knees.

'It's a lana,' said Gussie. 'It's what they wear on Toto – at least, they used to.'

'Oh my God!' said Delma.

Gussie looked at her. Delma was wearing that well-known British national costume of skin-tight Union Jack, white thigh-boots and diamanté trident. Next to her, Miss Finland dazzled the eye in a head-dress made of that most Scandinavian of birds, the ostrich . . .

Once again, Gussie's growing band of friends came to her rescue. Miss Trinidad and Tobago stripped herself of a plastic hibiscus *lei* and hung it round Gussie's neck. Miss India culled five of her ankle bracelets, Miss Guam contributed part of a cardboard palm – and Richard, arriving to take stock, was just in time to see Gussie's resigned and acquiescent head sink beneath an enormous, solitary pineapple.

The national costume of the Toto Islands had been born.

There now began the five-day cultural jamboree which pre-çeded the serious business of the contest. Richard had brought to the planning of this the same meticulous care that he gave his research and he made it a point of honour always to be present. For Gussie, the days were a delight: the sight of London's skyline from her river; *Swan Lake* at Covent Garden; the Tower looking so marvellously like pictures of itself – and always Dr Whittacker's humour and intelligence highlighting the experience.

On the day before they were to start serious rehearsals, Gussie decided to go shopping. Accordingly, she put on jeans and a raincoat and went downstairs.

'Hey, hinny,' said the security guard, an ex-heavyweight boxer from Tyneside. 'You're not allowed out without your chaperone.'

'How do you know I'm a contestant?' said Gussie. 'How do you know I'm not one of the maids?'

'Saw your picture in the paper, coming out of the fountain. And the one where you were taking the stray cat out of the Lord Mayor's Banquet. You're Miss Toto Islands.'

'Gussie's the name,' said Gussie sadly. 'The thing is, I *have* to go out and I share a chaperone with Miss United Kingdom and she—'

'Oh, aye. Heard of her. A proper Tartar. She'll win, mind. I've got a fiver on her.'

'Have you?' Gussie's eyes lit up. 'You wouldn't put some money on for me, would you?'

The guard nodded and added his views on the likely order of the runners-up. Then he said, 'Well, I suppose you won't come to any harm. I'll turn my back for a moment – but don't be out long, mind.'

Gussie thanked him and set off for the shops. The raffia proved surprisingly difficult, the golfing umbrellas amazingly expensive. But in that Mecca of pipe smokers, Dunhills, she found for her father a briar pipe as strong and finely made as any Stradivarius. This done, she wandered delightedly along Piccadilly, flattening her nose with indiscriminate enthusiasm against windows displaying exotic cheeses, necklaces plucked from Egyptian mummies or gentlemen's shirts. And found herself standing entranced by the gates of a little churchyard with an ancient, propped catalpa tree, a fountain flanked by greening cherubs, squares of lovingly framed grass . . .

She went in. An old woman sat on a bench, knitting. A quiet-faced statue held out an olive branch. The church, graceful and simple, was by Wren.

Suddenly she stopped, amazed. The only man she knew in England was standing with bent head, looking at a plaque set in the sooty wall.

He turned. 'Oh!' said Gussie. 'I'm so sorry.'

Richard managed a smile. 'It's all right. It's not private, this place.'

'It's so beautiful. As though . . . everything that makes up London is compressed into it. You know, like in that poem: "A box where sweets compacted lie".'

'Yes.' There was a pause. Then he said, 'My wife loved it. We met here. A pick-up. She was drawing the catalpa.'

Gussie looked past him at the plaque in the wall: 'In Memory of Caroline Whittacker'. No inscription. No date.

'I killed her,' said Richard.

Gussie was silent, became part of the leaning tree, the sooty wall, scarcely breathed.

'I was driving. They said it wasn't my fault – the man who hit us was drunk. But *I* was driving. And I didn't have a scratch. Not a single scratch.'

Gussie looked up, saw his face. Then, without really meaning to, she began to cry.

Two nights before the actual contest, Gussie went to bed early. She had swopped beds with Delma who had discovered a draught from the window by the fire escape, washed out five pairs of Miss United Kingdom's tights and now, leaving her room-mate locked in some mysterious ritual in the bathroom, composed herself for sleep.

She was just drifting off when she heard the window slide softly open and, lifting her head, saw the curtains parted by a black-gloved hand. But even as she tried to cry out, the masked man had reached her, was pressing something down over her face . . . and everything went dark.

The kidnap of Miss Toto Islands from the Woodward Hotel produced a furore in the press. Pictures of what everybody hoped was the Toto Islands appeared in all the papers, along with speculations about the island's importance as a source of uranium, oil or foreign agents. The girls who had befriended Gussie (which seemed to be almost all of them) were interviewed; Miss Trinidad and Tobago went into a decline.

'It's me they were after, Richard, you do realise that, don't you?' said Delma furiously. 'It was *me*! I changed beds with Gussie.'

'Yes, the police know all that,' said Richard absently. He had neither eaten nor slept since Gussie had vanished, rushing between Scotland Yard, the Woodward and Galaxy.

'You do seem in a state,' said Delma. 'Why, you hardly know the girl.'

Richard smiled crookedly. 'Don't I?' he said – and was gone.

Gussie woke in a bare room with drawn blinds. She was lying on a pile of blankets and two men were standing over her looking extremely sick.

'Oh, my Gawd!' said the elder, poking Gussie with his shoe.

'Well, it wasn't my fault. She was where you said, on the bed by the window. How do you know it's the wrong one?'

'Look, England may be in a bad way but we 'aven't got so as

we're sending something like that in for Miss Galaxy. The one we wanted 'ad boobs like melons and she's the floozy of that guy in Galaxy who's in charge of it all.'

'You said—'

'Aw, shut up, will yer?' He stared down at Gussie again. 'Who the hell's going to give us a quarter of a million quid for *that*? Not Galaxy. Not anyone.'

Gussie closed her eyes again. So Galaxy was going to be in trouble because of her – and Galaxy meant Richard. Richard who loved Delma but had been so wonderfully kind. Surely – oh, surely – there had to be something she could do?

The show, however, had to go on. The girls were herded into the Albert Hall, paraded up and down ramps and told to smile at 'camera one' as though it was their mother. Bookies touted the odds, with Miss United Kingdom still hotly the favourite; technicians hammered, sound engineers with earphones called to each other like courting kittiwakes. The judges, a panel of eight celebrities, were assembled. Police were everywhere, reporters hid in the dressing-rooms. The kidnap of Miss Toto Islands had sent interest in the contest soaring sky-high and thirty million viewers were expected in Great Britain alone.

Richard, in charge, continued to look like a man on the rack. Galaxy had had a ransom note for a quarter of a million and the Old Man was moving like a snail.

In the Albert Hall, now, everything was ready. The red light went on and Miss Australia, in the fringed leather mini-skirt and plunging satin blouse so beloved of the outback, led the procession on to the stage.

Delma, in her skin-tight Union Jack, received the ovation due to the local candidate. The compère's voice-over informed thirty million viewers that she was a fashion model, 34–24–34, with raven hair and dark blue eyes. Miss Uruguay, who followed her, tripped over her shoes.

The girls vanished to change into evening dress. A pop group played, the judges conferred, speculation spread through the audience packed tier upon tier up to the roof.

'Still no news,' said Richard and Miss Trinidad and Tobago, now mercifully eliminated, began to cry.

Fifteen contestants went forward in their swim-suits, then seven . . . Miss United Kingdom, needless to say, was one of them.

The compère moved in for the interview.

Miss Belgium said she was a pedicurist, liked snorkeling and wished to meet Prince Charles.

Miss Sweden was a ski instructress, loved animals and wished to travel.

What Miss Guam wished no one could discern, since she didn't appear to speak anything – not even, within the meaning of the act, Guamese.

Miss United Kingdom now stepped forward, smiled at camera one as though it was her mother and prepared to tell the compère of her desire to relieve the sufferings of the poor.

Only the compère, incredibly enough, was not looking at her. No one was looking at her and the camera crew had gone beserk. So that on TV screens everywhere the viewers saw what the audience in the Albert Hall itself was seeing. Caught in the spotlight, a dishevelled, lightly-blood-stained girl come limping up the aisle towards the stage.

And the audience rose as to a man and roared.

'You won, then?' said Dr MacLeod, leading his incandescent daughter from the air-strip.

Gussie waved to the orphans, school-children and villagers assembled with banners to meet her and rubbed her face against her father's sleeve. 'Oh, yes, I won! Most fantastically and marvellously did I win! There's no winner in the world like me!' She glanced up shyly at her father. 'Richard thinks I wouldn't transplant. He's a research chemist, a first-class one and he's got some money saved. Could you use him for the hospital lab?'

'Could I?' said Dr MacLeod. 'My God, *could* I?' He broke off to stare at the mountainous luggage now emerging from the little plane. 'Good heavens – that must have cost you a bit in excess baggage!'

Gussie beamed. 'It did but Galaxy paid. They reckoned I'd saved them a quarter of a million by jumping out of the window. Not that I needed it, because I'm absolutely rolling; I cleaned up on my bets! A terribly nice security guard put some money on for me and he got them all right: Miss United Kingdom first, Miss Sweden second, Miss Guam third – just like he said. I've got absolute mountains of raffia!'

Dr MacLeod looked at his blissful daughter, opened his

mouth to speak and closed it again. Time enough to tell Gussie
that another expert had flown out from Brisbane and that the
lepers, totally uninterested now in handiwork, were into
creative writing . . . were, in fact, waiting for her to edit a
magazine already entitled *Scream!* . . .

THE GREAT CARP FERDINAND

THIS IS a true story, the story of a Christmas in Vienna in the years before the First World War. Not only is it a true story, it is a most dramatic one, involving love, conflict and (very nearly) death – and this despite the fact that the hero was a fish.

Not any fish, of course: a mighty and formidable fish, the Great Carp Ferdinand. And if you think the story is exaggerated and that no fish, however mighty, could so profoundly affect the lives of a whole family, then you're wrong. Because I have the facts first-hand from one of the participants, the 'littlest niece' in the story, the one whose feet, admittedly, failed to reach even the first rung of the huge leather-backed, silver-buttoned dining-room chairs, but whose eyes cleared the table by a good three inches so that, as she frequently points out, she saw it all. (She came to England, years later, this littlest niece, and became my mother, so I've kept tabs on the story and checked it for accuracy time and again.)

The role the Great Carp Ferdinand was to play in the life of the Mannhaus family was simple, though crucial. He was, to put it plainly, the Christmas dinner. For in Vienna, where they celebrate on Christmas Eve and no one, on Holy Night, would dream of eating meat, they relish nothing so much as a richly-marinated, succulently roasted carp. And it is true that until you have tasted fresh carp with all the symphonic accompaniments (sour cream, braised celeriac, dark plum jam) you have not, gustatorily speaking, really lived.

But the accent is on the word *fresh*. So that when a grateful client with a famous sporting estate in Carinthia presented Onkel Ernst with a live twenty-pounder a week before Christmas, the Mannhaus family was delighted. Onkel Ernst, a small, bandy-legged man whose ironic sympathy enabled him to sustain a flourishing solicitor's practice, was delighted. Tante Gerda, his plump, affectionate wife, was delighted. Graziella, their adorable and adored eighteen-year-old daughter, was delighted, as was Herr Franz von Rittersberg, Graziella's 'intended', who loved his food. Delighted too, were Tante Gerda's three little nieces, already installed with their English governess in readiness for the great Mannhaus Christmas, and delighted were the innumerable poor relations and rich godfathers whom motherly Tante Gerda collected every Christmas Eve to light the candles on the great fir tree, open their presents and eat . . . roast carp.

Accommodation for the fish was not too great a problem. The house in Vienna was massive and the maids, simple country girls accustomed to scrubbing down in wooden tubs, cheerfully surrendered the bathroom previously ascribed to their use.

Here, in a gargantuan mahogany-sided bath with copper taps which gushed like Niagara, the huge, grey fish swam majestically to and fro, fro and to, apparently oblivious both of the glory of his ultimate destiny and the magnificence of his setting. For the bathroom was no ordinary bathroom. French tea roses – marvellous, cabbage-sized blooms – swirled up the wallpaper, were repeated on the huge china wash-bowl and echoed yet again in the vast chamber-pot – a vessel so generously conceived that even the oldest of the little nieces could have sunk in it without a trace.

And here to visit him as the procession of days marched on towards Christmas came the various members of the Mannhaus family.

Onkel Ernst came, sucking his long, black pipe with the porcelain lid. Not a sentimental man, and one addicted to good food, he regarded the carp's ultimate end as thoroughly fitting. And yet, as he looked into the marvellously unrevealing eye of the great, grey fish, admired the gently-undulating whiskers (so much more luxuriant than his own sparse moustache), Onkel Ernst felt a distinct sense of kinship with what was, after all, the only other male in a houseful of women. And as he sat there, drawing on his pipe, listening to the occasional splash as the carp broke water, Onkel Ernst let slip from his shoulders for a while the burden of maintaining the house in Vienna, the villa in Baden-Baden, the chalet on the Wörther See, the dozen or so of Gerda's relatives who had abandoned really rather early, the struggle to support themselves. He forgot even the juggernaut of bills which would follow the festivities. Almost, but not quite, he forgot the little niggle of worry about his daughter, Graziella.

Tante Gerda, too, paid visits to the carp – but briefly, for Christmas was something she could never trust to proceed even for a moment without her. She came hung about with lists, her forehead creased into its headache lines, deep anxieties curdling her brain. Would the tree clear the ceiling – or, worse still, would it be too short? Would Sachers send the meringue and ice-cream swan in time? Should one (really a worry, this) 'send' to the Pfischingers, who had not 'sent' last year but had the year before? Oh, that terrible year when the Steinhauses had sent a basket of crystallized fruit at the very last minute, when all the shops were shut, and she had had to re-wrap the potted azalea the Hellers had given and send it to the Steinhauses – and then spent all Christmas wondering if she had removed the label!

Bending over the fish, Tante Gerda pondered the sauce. Here, too, was anxiety. Celeriac, yes, lemon, yes, onion, yes, peppercorns, ginger, almonds, walnuts – that went without saying. Grated honeycake, of course, thyme, bay, paprika and dark plum jam. But now her sister, writing from Linz, had suggested mace . . . The idea was new, almost revolutionary. The Mannhaus carp, maceless, was a gastronomic talking-point in Vienna. There were the cook's feelings to be considered. And yet . . . even Sacher himself was not afraid to vary a trusted recipe.

The carp's indifference to his culinary environment was somehow calming. She closed her eyes for a second and had a sudden, momentary glimpse of Christmas as existing *behind* all this if only she could reach it. If she could just be sure that Graziella was all right. And she sighed, for she had never meant to love anyone as much as she loved her only daughter.

Franz von Rittersberg also came to see the carp. A golden-haired, blue-eyed, splendid young man, heir to a coal-mine in Silesia, the purpose of his visit was strictly arithmetical. He measured the carp mentally, divided it by the number of people expected to sit down to dinner, estimated that his portion as the future Mannhaus son-in-law was sure to be drawn from the broader, central regions – and left content.

And escaping from the English governess, scuttling and

twittering like mice, white-stockinged, brown-booted, their behinds deliciously humped by layers of petticoat, came the little nieces clutching stolen bread rolls.

'Ferdinand,' whispered the youngest ecstatically, balancing on the upturned, rose-encrusted chamber-pot. Her sisters, who could see over the sides of the bath unaided, stood gravely crumbling bread into the water. The fish was a miracle; unaware of them, yet theirs. *Real.*

Each night, when the nursemaid left them, they tumbled out from under the feather bed and marshalled themselves for systematic prayer. 'Please God, make them give us something that's *alive* for Christmas,' they prayed night after night after night.

But it was Graziella, the daughter of the house, who came most frequently of all. Perched on the side of the bath, her dusky curls rioting among the cabbage roses on the wall, she looked with dark, commiserating eyes at the fish. Yet, though she was by far the loveliest of the visitors, Ferdinand's treatment of her was uncivil. Quite simply, he avoided her. Carp, after all, are *fresh*-water fish, and he had noticed that the drops which fell on him when she was there were most deplorably saline.

She was a girl the gods had truly smiled upon – loving and beloved; gay and kind, and her future as Frau Franz von Rittersberg was rosily assured. And yet each day she seemed to get a little thinner and a little paler, her dark eyes filling with ever-growing bewilderment. For when you have been accustomed all your life to giving, giving, giving, you may wake up one day and find you have given away yourself. And then unless you are a saint (and even, perhaps, if you are) you will spend the nights underneath your pillow, trapped and wretched, licking away the foolish tears.

And so the days drew steadily on, mounting to their climax – Christmas Eve. Snow fell, the tree arrived, the last candle was lit on the Advent ring. The littlest niece, falling from grace, ate the chimney off the gingerbread house. The exchange of hampers became ever more frenzied. The Pfischingers, who still had not sent, invaded Tante Gerda's dreams . . .

It was on the morning of the twenty-third that Onkel Ernst

and his future son-in-law assembled to perform the sacrificial rites on the Great Carp Ferdinand.

The little nieces had been bundled into coats and leggings and taken to the Prater. Graziella, notoriously tender-hearted, had been sent to Rumpelmayers on an errand. Now, at the foot of the stairs stood the cook, holding a gargantuan earthenware baking dish – to the left of her the housemaids, to the right the kitchen staff. On the landing upstairs, Tante Gerda girded her men – a long-bladed kitchen knife, a seven-pound sledgehammer, an old and slightly rusty sword of the Kaiser's Imperial Army which someone had left behind at dinner . . .

In the bathroom, Onkel Ernst looked at the fish and the fish looked at Onkel Ernst. A very slight sensation, a whisper of premonition, nothing more, assailed Onkel Ernst, who felt as though his liver was performing a very small *entrechat*.

'You shoo him down this end,' ordered Franz, splendidly off-hand. 'Then, when he's up against the end of the bath, I'll wham him.'

Onkel Ernst shooed. The carp swam. Franz – swinging the hammer over his head – whammed.

The noise was incredible. Chips of enamel flew upwards.

'Ow, my eye, my *eye!*' yelled Franz, dropping the hammer. 'There's a splinter in it. Get it OUT!'

'Yes,' said Onkel Ernst. 'Yes. . .'

He put down the sword from the Kaiser's Imperial Army and climbed carefully on to the side of the bath. Even then he was only about level with Franz's streaming blue eye. Blindly, Franz thrust his head forward.

The rest really was inevitable. Respectable, middle-aged Viennese solicitors are not acrobats; they don't pretend to be. The carp, swimming languidly between Onkel Ernst's ankles found, as he had expected, nothing even mildly edible.

It was just after lunch that Onkel Ernst, dry once more and wearing his English knickerbockers, received in a mild way guidance from above.

It was all so easy, really. No need for all this crude banging and lunging. Simply, one went upstairs, one pulled out the plug, one went out locking the door behind one. And waited . . .

A few minutes later, perfectly relaxed, Onkel Ernst was back in his study. He was not only holding the newspaper the right way up, he was practically *reading* it.

The house was hushed. Franz, after prolonged ministrations by the women of the family, had gone home. The little nieces were having their afternoon rest. The study, anyway, had baize-lined double doors. Even if there *were* any thuds – thuds such as a great fish lashing in its death agony might make – Onkel Ernst would not hear them.

What he did hear, not very long afterwards, was a scream. A truly fearful scream, the scream of a virtuoso and one he had no difficulty in ascribing to the under-housemaid, whose brother was champion yodeller of Schruns. A second scream joined it and a third. Onkel Ernst dashed out into the hall.

The first impression was that the hall was full of people. His second was that it was wet. Both proved to be correct.

Tante Gerda, trembling on the edge of hysteria, was being soothed by Graziella. The English governess, redoubtable as all her race, had already commandeered a bucket and mop and flung herself into the breach. Maids dabbed and moaned and mopped – and still the water ran steadily down the stairs, past the carved cherubs on the banisters, turning the Turkish carpet into pulp.

The enquiry, when they finally got round to it, was something of a formality since the culprits freely admitted their guilt. There they stood, the little nieces, pale, trembling, terrified – yet somehow not truly repentant-looking. Yes, they had done it. Yes, they had taken the key out from behind the clock; yes, they had unlocked the bathroom door, turned on the taps . . .

Silent, acquiescent, they waited for punishment. Only the suddenly-descending knicker-leg of the youngest spoke of an almost unbearable tension.

Graziella saved them, as she always saved everything.

'Please, Mutti? Please, Vati . . . So near Christmas?'

Midnight struck. In the Mannhaus mansion, silence reigned at last. Worn out, their nightly prayer completed, the little nieces slept. Tante Gerda moaned, dreaming that the Pfischingers had sent a giant hamper full of sauce.

Presently a door opened and Onkel Ernst in his pyjamas crept softly from the smoking room. In his hand was an enormous shotgun – a terrible weapon some thirty years old which had belonged to his father – and in his heart was a bloodlust as violent as it was unexpected.

Relentlessly he climbed the stairs; relentlessly he entered the bathroom and turned the key behind him. Relentlessly he took three paces backwards, peered down the barrel – and then fired.

Graziella, always awake these nights, was the first to reach him.

'Are you all right, Papa? Are you all right?'

Only another fearful volley of groans issued from behind the bolted door. Tante Gerda rushed up, her grey plait swinging. 'Ernst, *Ernst?*' she implored, hammering on the door. '*Say* something, Ernst!'

The English governess arrived in her Jaeger dressing-gown, the cook . . . Together the women strained against the door, but it was hopeless.

'Phone the doctor, the fire brigade. Send for Franz, quickly,' Gerda ordered. 'A man – we need a *man*.'

The governess ran to the telephone. Bur Graziella, desperate, threw her fur cape over her nightdress and ran out into the street.

Thus it was that in the space of half a minute the life of Sebastian Haffner underwent a complete and total revolution. One minute he was free as air, easy-going, a young man devoted to his research work at the University – and seconds later he was a committed, passionate fanatic ready to scale mountains, slay dragons and take out a gigantic mortgage on a house. For no other reason than that Graziella, rushing blindly down the steps into the lamplit street, ran straight into his arms.

Just for a fraction of a second the embrace in which Sebastian held the trembling girl remained protective and fatherly. Then his arms tightened round her and he became not fatherly – not fatherly at all. And Graziella, with snowflakes in her hair, looked up at the stranger's kind, dark, gentle face and could not – simply could not – look away.

Then she remembered and struggled free. 'Oh, please come!' she gabbled, pulling Sebastian by the hand. 'Quickly. It's my father . . . The carp has shot him.'

Instantly Sebastian rearranged his dreams. He would visit

her regularly in the asylum, bring her flowers, read to her. Slowly, through his devotion, she would be cured.

'Hurry, please, please! He was groaning so.'

'The carp?' suggested Sebastian, running with her up the steps.

'My father. Oh, *come!*'

Maids moaned at the foot of the stairs. Tante Gerda sobbed on the landing.

Sebastian was magnificent. Within seconds he had seized a carved oak chair and begun to batter on the door. Quite quickly, the great door splintered and fell. At Sebastian's heels they trooped into the bathroom.

Onkel Ernst sat propped against the side of the bath, now groaning, now swearing, his hand on his shoulder which was caked with blood. Round him were fragments of rose-encrusted china and shattered mirror which the lead shot ricocheting from the sides of the bath and grazing Onkel Ernst's shoulder, had finally shattered. The carp, lurking beneath the water taps, appeared to be asleep.

'Ernst!'' shrieked Tante Gerda and dropped on her knees beside him.

'Bandages, scissors, lint,' ordered Sebastian, and Graziella fled like the wind.

It was only a flesh wound and Sebastian, miracle of miracles, was a doctor, though the kind that worked in a lab. Quite soon Onkel Ernst, indisputably the hero of the hour, was propped on a sofa, courageously swallowing cognac, egg yolk with vanilla, raspberry cordial laced with *kirsch*. The family doctor arrived, pronounced Sebastian's work excellent, stayed for cognac too. The fire brigade, trooping into the kitchen, preferred *slivovitz*.

And upstairs, forgotten, seeing nothing but each other, stood Graziella and Sebastian.

This was it, then, thought Graziella, this wanting to sing and dance and shout and yet feeling so humble and so *good*. This was what she had never felt and so had nearly thrown herself to Franz as one throws a bone to a dog to stop it growling . . . As if in echo to her thoughts, the bell shrilled yet again and Franz von Rittersberg was admitted. His eye was still swollen and his temper not of the best.

'This place is turning into a madhouse,' he said, running up the stairs. 'Do you know what time it is?'

Graziella did not. Time had stopped when she ran into Sebastian's arms and years were to pass before she quite caught up with it again.

'Well, for heaven's sake let's finish off this blasted fish and get back to bed,' he said, shrugging off his coat and taking out a knife and a glass-stoppered bottle. 'I've brought some chloroform.'

'No!'

Graziella's voice startled both men by its intensity. 'In England,' she said breathlessly, 'in England, if you hang someone and it doesn't work . . . if the rope breaks, you let him live.'

'For goodness' sake, Graziella, don't give us the vapours now,' snapped Franz. 'What the devil do you think we're going to eat tomorrow, anyway?'

He strode into the bathroom. 'You can help me,' he threw over his shoulder to Sebastian, who had been standing quietly on the half-lit landing. 'I'll pull the plug out and pour this stuff on him. Then you bang his head on the side of the bath.'

'No,' Sebastian stepped forward into the light. 'If Miss . . . if Graziella does not wish this fish to be killed, then this fish will not be killed.'

Franz put down the bottle. A muscle twitched in his cheek. 'Why you . . . you . . . Who the blazes do you think you are, barging in here and telling me what to do?'

Considering that both men came from good families, the fight which followed was an extraordinarily dirty one. The Queensberry rules, though well-known on the Continent, might never have existed. In a sense of course the outcome was inevitable, for Franz was motivated only by hatred and lust for his Christmas dinner, whereas Sebastian fought for love. But though she was almost certain of Sebastian's victory, Graziella, sprinkling chloroform on to a bath towel, was happily able to make *sure*.

Dawn broke. The bells of the Stephan's Kirche pealed out the challenge and the glory of the birth of Christ.

In the Mannhaus mansion, Graziella slept and smiled and slept again. Onkel Ernst, propped on seven goose-feather pillows, opened an eye, reflected happily that today nothing could be asked of him – no carving, no wobbling on stepladders, no candle-lighting – and closed it again.

But in the kitchen Tante Gerda and the cook, returning from Mass, faced disgrace and ruin. Everything was ready – the chopped herbs (bravely, the cook had agreed to mace), the wine, the cream, the lemon . . . and upstairs, swimming strongly, was the centrepiece, the *raison d'être* for days of planning and contriving, who should have been floating in his marinade for hours already.

As though that was not enough, as they sat down to breakfast there was a message from Franz. He was still unwell and would not be coming to dine with them. It took a full minute for the implication of this to reach Tante Gerda and when it did, she put down her head and groaned. 'Thirteen! We shall be thirteen for dinner! Oh, heavens! Gross-Tante Wilhelmina will never stand for that!'

But fate had not finished with Tante Gerda. The breakfast dishes were scarcely cleared away when the back-door bell rang and the maid returned struggling under a gigantic hamper.

'Oh, no . . . NO!' shrieked Tante Gerda.

But it was true. Now, at the eleventh hour, with everything still to do and the shops closing fast, the Pfischingers had 'sent'.

And now it was here, the moment for which all these weeks had been the preparation. It was dusk. The little nieces boiled and bubbled in their petticoats, pursued by nursemaids with curling-tongs and ribbons. Inside 'the room', Tante Gerda, watched complacently by Onkel Ernst, climbed up and down the step-ladder checking the candles, the fire-bucket, the angle of the silver star. Clucking, murmuring, she ran from pile to pile of the presents spread on the vast white cloth beneath the tree. Graziella's young doctor, summoned from the laboratory, had agreed to come to dinner so that they wouldn't be thirteen. He had even somehow contrived presents for the little nieces – three tiny wooden boxes which Tante Gerda now added to their heaps.

And now all the candles were lit and she rang the sweet-toned Swiss cow-bell which was the signal that they could come in.

Though they had been huddled straining against the door, when it was opened the little nieces came slowly, very slowly into the room, the myriad candles from the tree shining in their eyes. Behind them came Graziella, her head tilted to the glittering star and beside her the young doctor – who had given her only a single rose.

And suddenly Tante Gerda's headache lifted, and she cried a little and knew that somehow, once again, the thing she had struggled for was there. Christmas.

You'd think that was the end of the story, wouldn't you? But my mother, telling it years later, liked to go on just a bit further. To the moment when the little nieces, having politely unwrapped a mountain of costly irrelevancies, suddenly burst into shrieks of ecstasy and fulfilment. For, opening Sebastian's wooden boxes, they found, for each of them, a tiny, pink-eyed, *living* mouse.

Or further still. To the family at table – white damask, crystal goblets, crimson roses in a bowl. To the little nieces (the youngest wobbling fearfully on her pile of cushions), each pocket of each knicker-leg bulgy with a sleepy, smuggled mouse. To Onkel Ernst magnificent in his bandages, and Graziella and Sebastian glowing like comets . . . To the sudden stiffening, knuckles whitening round the heavy spoons, as Tante Gerda brought in the huge silver serving-dish.

And the sigh of released breath, the look of awed greed as she set it down. Egg-garnished, gherkin-bedecked, its translucent depths glittering with exotic fishes and tiny jewelled vegetables, the celebrated concoction quivered gently before them. Lampreys in aspic! Truly – most truly, the Pfischingers had 'sent'.

The littlest niece, when she grew up and became by mother, liked to end the story there. But I always made her go on just a little further. To the day after Christmas. To the house of the Pfischingers on the other side of Vienna. To Herr Doktor Pfischinger, a small, bald, mild little man ascending the stairs to his bathroom. He is carrying a long-bladed knife, a sledge-hammer, a *blunderbuss*. . . .

OSMANDINE

LATER, PEOPLE said she was a witch. A white witch, of course, white as snow, white as camellia blossom, but a witch all the same. Something to do with her name, which was Osmandine, and more still with the way she looked: that mass of red-gold hair right down her back, those glowing amber eyes, that *skin*. There was also the question of Cuthbert. It was perhaps natural to befriend an earthworm who had mistaken 'up' for 'down' but Cuthbert's status was surely more that of a familiar than a simple household pet?

Osmandine had reached Oversea by accident. She was a girl who liked fate to lead her where it willed, and when it had finished willing her into a boutique in London's Fulham Road, a salami factory in Sicily and an agricultural commune in the Hebrides, it had willed her into the Stanislavsky School of Drama attached, though somewhat insecurely, to the new Oversea Civic Theatre.

'I am in mourning for my life,' said Osmandine, on the morning that this story begins, crossing the Market Square on the way from her digs to the acting school. They were studying Chekhov's *The Seagull* and she had been instructed to feel her way into poor Masha.

It was at this point that she encountered Cuthbert who had made this mistake and was lying confused and dangerously dry upon the pavement.

'Oh, you foolish worm!' said Osmandine. She picked him up and looked round for a garden or a patch of earth. Oversea Market Square, however, remained securely paved and solidly cobbled. Only on the far side of the Square, where she had never been, stood a little bay tree outside a chemist's shop.

'Oh,' said Osmandine, walking across and lowering Cuthbert tenderly into the tub of earth, 'what a beautiful shop!'

It was, too. Old-fashioned and bow-fronted with big urns of red and blue liquids, with *real* sponges in real straw baskets and calming cough sweets in tall glass jars.

Inside it was even better. Liquorice sticks, Beecham's Powders, dark drawers with beckoning labels: Flowers of Sulphur, Citric Acid, Borax (Purified).

'I shall buy a toothbrush,' decided Osmandine, who knew that a girl with a toothbrush in her pocket is always safe.

She waited quietly, enjoying the hot-water bottles hanging like ripe fruit upon the hot-water-bottle stand, the yellow nipples on the lemon soap, but no one came. Osmandine was not a rapper on counters, but from her lovely, lubricated throat she dredged up a gentle cough.

It was answered by a groan. A groan of some seriousness coming from the half-open door of the dispensary.

Osmandine pushed it open. Lying on the floor, in an incongruously spotless lab-coat, lay an elderly man. His bald head glistened with sweat, his face was grey and drawn, his spectacles lay broken beside him.

'It's all right,' said Osmandine, kneeling beside him, loosening his collar, 'I'm going to get help at once. You're going to be *all right.*'

'Doctor Lee . . . Don't want anyone else,' whispered Mr Greenfield. 'Number's by the phone.'

Osmandine found the telephone and the number under Dr Lee, John.

'I'll come at once,' he promised. He did, too, driving too fast in his Ferrari, limping from where he had broken his hip the year before because he always came to his patients too quickly in unsuitable Italian cars. A thin man with a beaky nose, horn-rims and a nervous forehead etched into harrowing furrows by the follies of mankind.

'Perforated ulcer,' he said. 'I'll get an ambulance.'

On the telephone he turned and looked at Osmandine, kneeling statue-still because Mr Greenfield had taken a hunk of her hair and was strap-hanging with it on to consciousness. Inside that hair, thought Dr Lee, one could lie safe from the night-splintering telephone, from loneliness, from fear.

Except that one day, when one tottered in half dead from evening surgery there would be this note pinned to the pillow

'St George's?' he said, and gave instructions.

In the corridor of the hospital it was necessary to sever Mr Greenfield almost surgically from Osmandine's hair.

'The shop,' he whispered, grey and anguished on his trolley.

'I'll mind it for you. I'd like to do it.'

Mr Greenfield tried to shake his head. 'Dispensing . . . illegal . . . you mustn't.'

Osmandine bent over him, her amber eyes shining with integrity. 'I'm a fully qualified pharmacist,' she said. 'Honest-ly.'

Believing her, fumbling under his blanket for his bunch of keys, Mr Greenfield, his mind at rest, was wheeled away.

Back in Mr Greenfield's shop, Osmandine rang her acting school, flicked a feather duster over the hair curlers, arranged the face flannels in a more becoming cluster and opened the shop. It was at this point that she noticed Cuthbert still lying passively in his bay-tree tub, unwilling or perhaps unable to submerge himself.

'Oh, well, come on then,' she said, sighing a little, for love is love and the emotional demands of a maladjusted earthworm can weigh as heavily as any other.

She had just placed him in a dampened saucer when her first customer arrived.

It was a man wanting razor blades. Then followed a woman needing hand cream and a girl who bought a packet of hair-dye. Osmandine was just growing complacent when Nemesis overtook her in the form of Mrs Berryman, bearing an undoubted prescription and looking as if she meant business.

'I'd like this made up, please. It's from Dr Lee. For my dyspepsia.'

'Ah,' said Osmandine. 'Yes. . .' She stared at the prescription, which was probably the right way up and looked like Linear B taken down in shorthand by a lunatic secretary. Dr Lee's signature, on the other hand, seemed familiar. She had seen it in that section of her mother's handwriting book devoted to criminals, the emotionally deprived and those whose native tongue was Sanskrit.

'How is he? Dr Lee, I mean,' enquired Osmandine.

Mrs Berryman said Dr Lee was overworking. 'He's never been right since that silly wife of his went off with a poet. Now about this prescription.'

'Yes,' said Osmandine again. 'You see, Mr Greenfield is ill.'

'Oh, dear. Well then, I'd better take it up the road to Ware and Nicholson.'

'No!' Already Osmandine had acquired Mr Greenfield's dislike and fear of the trendy new chemist-cum-beauty-parlour two blocks away. 'No, no, I'll make it up for you. It's just . . . If you could give me a little while. I'm new, you see.'

'All right. Only I'll have to have it. My digestion is terrible. I just can't stand any more of those clunks.'

'Clunks?'

'That's right. In my stomach. First it gets all knotted up and then the knotted bits clunk together.'

'Mine gets like that,' said Osmandine confidingly. 'When I'm worried or sad.'

Mrs Berryman looked at her sharply. 'Mine's got nothing to do with that. I mean, what would I have to get worried about? A good husband, a nice little bungalow. . .' She broke off. 'Goodness, what's that?'

It was Cuthbert, who had left his saucer and was strolling towards the False Eyelashes (Special Offer). Osmandine presented him and waited for Mrs Berryman's recoil. But a very different expression crossed Mrs Berryman's pinkly-powdered face.

'My Phillip was always bringing in things like that,' she said. 'I used to raise the roof but I don't know . . . I mean, they're alive, aren't they, same as us.'

'Where is he now, your Phillip?'

Mrs Berryman's face became totally expressionless. 'I really couldn't say. We never see him, my husband and I. Never want to either, after the things he said to us the last time he came.'

'Have you got any other children?'

'No, he was the only one. It was a difficult birth. A breech, but he turned. What a bouncer he was! They say fat babies don't thrive but you should have seen him! I fed him myself till he was eight months old and. . .'

Osmandine leaned her elbows on the counter and took into her inmost being Mrs Berryman's Phillip's dislike of sieved carrots and his amazing feat in learning to say 'tomato soup' before he could say 'da da'. Pausing only to sell a cake of soap to a passing student, she shared his triumph over the woodwork prize, his first bicycle and the day he heard that he had got into

Cambridge to read mathematics.

'There's me not able to add two and two and there was my Phillip doing calculus and all that,' said Mrs Berryman. 'And then, when he was all set for this marvellous research job, he met this girl. A real hussy. Half Jamaican or something. And what does Phillip do?'

'Get's her pregnant,' said Osmandine.

Mrs Berryman flushed. 'Exactly. And of course he must throw up his fellowship and marry her. We argued and argued and begged him not to. And then his father . . . Well, his father's a good man but a bit hasty and he said one or two things about the girl. And Phillip just slammed out.'

'And you've not seen him since?'

Mrs Berryman shook her head. 'That was nine months ago. Not that it would be any good him coming now. You'll let me have those pills soon, won't you? I don't want another night like last night and it's my birthday tomorrow.'

After Mrs Berryman came a bottle of aspirin, a toilet roll and five tins of baby cereal. Once again, Osmandine grew complacent. And for not recognising peril in the next customer she could be forgiven.

It was a boy of about fourteen wearing a bottle-green blazer with towers on the pocket. His shoulders were hunched under a huge khaki knapsack full of books and his eyes were the eyes of an old, old man.

'I've got a prescription. From Dr Lee. For sleeping pills.'

'Sleeping pills!' The conviction that Dr Lee was not only emotionally deprived and criminal, but mad as well, took hold of Osmandine. 'Why can't you sleep?'

'Well, I suppose it's the exams. I mean, I'm doing nine subjects and they put me in a year early because they thought I was clever, only,' said Jeremy Blakeney, his voice rising dangerously, 'they're wrong.'

'When do you start?'

'In five days. Next Monday. And I haven't done nearly enough work, only it doesn't go in any more. And at night it all jumbles about – sort of Julius Caesar trying to remember the Lead Chamber Process. Goodness, that's a nice worm!'

Osmandine nodded. 'It's Cuthbert. He's sort of lost the con. Can't submerge.'

'He likes you,' said Jeremy admiringly. He smiled at Osmandine who smiled back at him and then suddenly Jeremy burst into tears. He had been longing to do this since the age of seven, when it finally dawned on him that the son of Professor Cyril Blakeney F.R.S. and Dr Alice Blakeney D. Litt. was wasting his time if he cried because there was absolutely no one at home to listen to him.

'Those exams,' said Osmandine, handing him a box of Mr Greenfield's Tissues for Men. 'Useful to you?'

Jeremy said he didn't know. He didn't know what he wanted to do, he only knew he was going to fail miserably and bring disgrace and shame on his family, his teachers and himself.

'Well then, why bother?' said Osmandine casually. 'To take them, I mean. Those poor examiners, marking all that stuff. Why don't you just go off somewhere?'

Jeremy's tears stopped as if axed. 'Run away, do you mean?'

'Well, why not? As long as you don't worry anyone. You've got to leave a proper message for your parents. And of course you've got to find somewhere sensible to go to. I mean, there's no point in lying around in some gutter being a nuisance to people. Do you have any relatives?'

Jeremy said he had a grandmother. His parents thought she was mad because she talked to her chickens and lived miles from anywhere, but Jeremy liked her.

'Well, you think about it,' said Osmandine. 'And there's no point in doing any more work if you aren't going to take the exams, so perhaps you'd be kind enough to go into the park and get some nice wet earth for Cuthbert. That stuff round the bay tree seems a bit acid. Your pills will be ready after lunch.'

Three peaceful and prescriptionless customers followed. But when Mr Kandinsky walked into the shop, Osmandine knew at once that her halcyon interlude was over. Mr Kandinsky looked like a prescription, and a prescription, duly signed by Dr Lee, was exactly what Mr Kandinsky was.

'They're some new tablets for my headaches,' said Mr Kandinsky, looking with black and soulful eyes at Osmandine. He was young and pale and presumably orthodox, for the hard, black hat seemed permanently moored to his head.

'Ah . . . yes,' said Osmandine sighing. On the prescription, everything was as indecipherable as before, nor did John Lee's signature, as the morning surgery advanced, show any decrease in the signs of criminality, emotional deprivation or early Sanskrit influences.

'Why does everyone in this town go to Dr Lee?' asked

Osmandine. 'There must be other doctors.'

Mr Kandinsky said there were, but Dr Lee . . . 'There is no gap,' said Mr Kandinsky. 'You know, the doctor up there who knows and the patient down there on the floor.'

Osmandine nodded. 'He does prescribe a lot, though, doesn't he?' she went on. 'I mean, couldn't you have massage for your head? Let me try,' she said eagerly, looking at the prescription again. 'I'm good at massaging people.'

A look of terror, lightly tinged with ecstasy, passed across Mr Kandinsky's face. Clearly he had read things. 'I think I'd better have the prescription,' he said. 'You see, it's the last time I shall be able to go to Dr Lee. Mama has decided we must change our doctor.'

'Oh?'

Mr Kandinsky nodded. 'Dr Lee was not very kind to Mama when she came about her palpitations. It is true Mama had difficulty in sticking to her diet, but she expected a little sympathy. Mama is a widow, you see.'

Osmandine said she was sorry to hear it.

'Of course Jewish cooking can be a little on the fattening side. And Mama is very fond of sweets.'

'Yes.'

'But she has such an unhappy life.'

'Why?'

'Well, my father is dead. Some fifteen years ago.'

'They were happy?'

Mr Kandinsky frowned. He said it was not certain. His father had died of drink. Alcoholism was rare in Jews and it had made him wonder.

'Do you live alone with your mother?'

Mr Kandinsky nodded. It was his pride, he said, to make up to Mama all she had missed. Only these headaches . . .

'Well, look, if you could just give me a little time,' said Osmandine and explained about Mr Greenfield.

Mr Kandinsky was very concerned. He said she must not hurry, he would call in the evening before she closed the shop. He couldn't come earlier in any case because his mother had organised a little tea-party for him to meet some nice Jewish girls. Emboldened by the look in her eyes, Mr Kandinsky added that he did not at all mind marrying a Jewish girl, he expected to marry a Jewish girl but why did she have to be *nice*?

Osmandine's last prescription that morning was a small, fat

man with kind blue eyes. His name was Mr Beesley and he
suffered from his 'nerves'.

'From Dr Lee,' said Osmandine, holding out her hand for the
prescription. It was not really a question but Mr Beesley
answered it.

'Oh, yes. I wouldn't go to anyone else. Mind you, that man's
going to have a breakdown if he goes on like that. It was losing
the little girl, of course. He was really nuts about that kid.'

'Oh. Did she . . . die?'

'No, no, that witless wife of his took her when she went. He
could have got her back, I reckon, but he wouldn't play tug-of-
war for the child's sake. Now about these tranquillisers. . .'

At one o'clock Osmandine shut up the shop, dampened
Cuthbert, helped herself to two liquorice sticks and a lump of
horehound candy and went into the dispensary with her
prescriptions.

First she opened some of Mr Greenfield's bottles, smelled
them, and closed them again. Then she dug about in his
wooden drawers and found, eventually, what seemed to be an
old-fashioned pill-making machine, a thing for stuffing cachets
and – hidden behind an old pharmacopoeia – a silver tablet
maker. 'For it is clear,' said Osmandine, furrowed up over the
instructions, 'that a pill is not a tablet. Nor is a tablet a cachet.
And as for a pessary. . .'

Frowning with concentration, sucking deeply on her
liquorice stick, Osmandine got to work.

At two o'clock she opened the shop again. Jeremy was the
first to return. He looked quite different, his hair blown by the
wind, his cheeks pink.

'Here's some earth for Cuthbert,' he said. 'And I've rung my
grandmother. She says the same as you. Not to bother with the
old exams if I don't want to. She says I can come right away.
Only maybe my parents will fetch me back?'

Osmandine leant over the counter. 'Tell you what,' she said.
'Just tell me where your parents live and I'll sort of explain
things to them. I promise I won't upset them and I promise
they won't fetch you back.'

'*Would* you? Oh, God, you are. . .' Words failed Jeremy.
'They're Professor and Dr Blakeney, 15 Osmore Gardens.'

'Fine! Now just forget about everything. Have you got
enough money?'

Jeremy nodded.

'Great. Well, here are your sleeping pills.'

'Goodness!' said Jeremy, impressed. 'They're . . . sort of unusual looking, aren't they? I like the way they're all . . . a bit different. I mean, mostly pills are so dull.'

It was in the lull after Jeremy's departure that Osmandine rang Interflora and ordered a dozen red roses to be sent to an address in Oversea. Her instructions were clear, her voice crisp and her soul untroubled, for though she liked truth she liked kindness even more.

Mr Beesley was the next one of her 'prescriptions' to return.

'They're not like the last ones I had,' he said doubtfully, peering at his bottle which seemed to be inhabited by a litter of premature baby mice.

'It's because they're hand-made,' said Osmandine earnestly. 'Dr Lee wanted you to have something very special. Have you spoken to your mother-in-law?'

Mr Beesley's round face lit up. 'I have. And you were quite right. She's been missing the country like anything. But, you won't believe it, she thought she had to go on staying with us because she was helping us financially. Well, she has been. I mean, no one can say she's mean even if she does say: "Is it a nice cackle fruit for breakfast?" every morning of her life. So we've worked out this plan. . .'

A peaceful hour followed and then Mrs Berryman returned. She was flushed and excited-looking and accepted her livid, oozing capsules with scarcely a second glance. 'You know I told you about my boy, Phillip? Well, just now there was a ring at the door and then this huge bunch of flowers. Red roses. From my Phillip. For my birthday.'

'How lovely! I'm so glad.'

'So I'm going right back now to write him a long letter. And I don't care what his father says, a son's a son and his wife is welcome in my house. I'll send it to his college, but they'll know where he is.'

'Which leaves,' said Osmandine to Cuthbert, 'the question of Mr Kandinsky. You know, Cuthbert, I think Mr Kandinsky ought to emigrate to Israel. Did you notice his hands – sort of square-tipped and practical? I'm sure he'd be happy in a kibbutz. Mama could follow later and go and live with a cousin in Tel Aviv. There's sure to be a cousin in Tel Aviv. If only I can convince him that emigrating is a duty. . .'

At five-thirty, Osmandine shut up the shop and went to visit

Mr Greenfield. He had had his operation and she was allowed only a minute in which she told him that everything was fine. After which she went to see Professor and Dr Blakeney.

'Are you trying to tell me that you *encouraged* Jeremy to run away to his grandmother?' said Dr Blakeney.

Osmandine said she had not just encouraged him to run away, she had practically forced him to do it. A boy of fourteen with a bottle of sleeping tablets before a major exam was something she wouldn't care to take responsibility for. 'I am speaking,' said Osmandine grandly, 'as a pharmacist.'

At the door, however, she took pity on the frustrated academic pair. 'Actually,' she said on her way out, 'it would be wise to have everything ready for Monday; his pens, pencils, exam cards and so on. Because I think he'll probably come back and take the silly things. Once he knows it doesn't matter.'

Osmandine was right. On the following Monday Jeremy came back, said he supposed he might as well have a go and came out of his first exam saying that as a matter of fact the questions were just the ones his teachers had said they would get. But by this time, though she did not know it, fate was closing in on Osmandine. What proved to be her undoing was the rather special two-way relationship which existed between Dr Lee and his patients.

It was a while before Mrs Berryman, bustling round in a delightful tizzy owing to the sudden visit of her son, Phillip, with his wife and baby, noticed that Dr Lee's marvellous new tablets had quite cleared up her stomach clunks. When she did, however, she did not fail to ring up Dr Lee and thank him.

Then Mr Beesley, whose mother-in-law was house hunting, wrote a note of gratitude for the pills which had cured his 'tension' and a girl called Helen Arbuttle, on whose failing love life Osmandine had laid a healing hand, told him that his prescription had at last cured her dizzy spells.

But it was Mr Kandinsky who provided the *coup de grâce*. En route for the Israeli Embassy in London, he had called at the surgery and actually brought the miracle pills which had cured his frightful and incessant headaches.

So that Osmandine, chatting up Cuthbert during an unaccustomed lull in business, found the shop door violently opened, the bell sent jangling – and an irate and limping figure striding towards the counter.

'Would you mind telling me,' said Dr Lee furiously, holding

out a small, round box, 'what these are supposed to be?'

Osmandine peered with interest at the tiny, misshapen objects. 'I think,' she said, 'that those are Mr Kandinsky's headache pills.'

'I know they're Mr Kandinsky's headache pills,' yelled Dr Lee. 'What I want to know is, what's in them? Because I'm darned certain it isn't what I prescribed. Don't you realise you're breaking the law dispensing dangerous drugs with-out—'

'But I *didn't*!'

'What do you mean, you didn't? I've been trying to get on top of Mr Kandinsky's headaches for ten years. Whatever you used must have been dynamite. What *is* it?'

Osmandine frowned. 'I'm almost sure it's icing sugar and rose water. Or was that Jeremy? No, Jeremy's were peppermint essence and cornflour. And Mrs Berryman had powdered liquorice and coffee extract in hers. So I think Mr Kandinsky's must have been—'

Dr Lee sat down. 'Perhaps,' he said, 'you'd be kind enough to fill me in?'

'It's your fault,' said Osmandine, looking into his eyes. 'You prescribe so. They're like snow in a Russian ballet, your prescriptions. Can't you find out what's really wrong and help people?'

Dr Lee's mouth curled into its accustomed lines of self-disgust. 'I'm hardly in a position to offer instant advice to others. So I prescribe.'

He was interrupted by the shop bell. But the men who strode in were not customers. Two smooth-looking men in trendy suits and behind them, looking uncomfortable, a uniformed policeman.

'My name is Ware,' said the older and smoother of the two, addressing himself to Osmandine. 'This is my partner, Mr Nicholson. We represent the new pharmacy in Station Road. And we are here because we have reason to believe that you have practised a serious fraud on a member of the public.'

'No,' said Osmandine. But she moved closer to Cuthbert and also, it so happened, to Dr Lee.

'Yes,' said Mr Ware unpleasantly. 'You see, one of our customers came into the shop yesterday and asked for tablets like these.' He held out a box containing two rapidly dis-integrating brownish blobs. 'Apparently you dispensed these for a friend of hers from a prescription of Dr Lee's. Her friend seemed to have found them highly beneficial for her rheumatic pains.'

Osmandine's brow cleared. 'Oh, yes, Miss Frinton. Well, you see, she had this sister whom she really loved and then the sister died and—'

'I'm afraid Miss Frinton's life history does not concern us,' interrupted Mr Ware. 'What does concern us is that on analysis these tablets were found to contain rice flour, suet and vanilla essence! In other words, you have been tampering with the prescription of a registered medical practitioner and as such are liable to prosecution under—'

'I beg your pardon,' said a quiet voice beside her, and Osmandine suddenly realised why, in spite of his impossible forehead, his Italian cars and his limp, the people of Oversea flocked to his surgery. 'You refer to a prescription of mine. It so happens that rice flour, suet and . . . er, vanilla essence were exactly what I prescribed for Miss Frinton.'

The two men stared and the constable, relieved, stepped back a pace.

'You are perhaps not aware,' Dr Lee went on smoothly, 'of the immense strides made lately in the treatment of rheumatic diseases. I need only quote the work of Zwimmerman and Finkelstein on the catalytic action of vanilla on intracellular respiration. And of course the recent findings of Pringle and Pepper. . .'

'Why did you do it?' said Osmandine when the men had shuffled out.

Dr Lee moved forward to tell her, caught sight of his reflection in a bottle of cough syrup – and recoiled.

'All the same,' he said, 'you must get a proper locum for Mr Greenfield. At once.'

'Yes,' said Osmandine. 'I know. Anyway, I must get back. I am,' she said experimentally, 'in mourning for my life.'

And as she looked at Dr Lee, grounded like a storm-tossed kestrel between the sponge-bags and the after-shave, she thought it was probably true. But she had long since understood that love and suffering are one, and pushing Cuthbert to one side she went forward bravely to her fate.

The Brides of Tula

I suppose for everybody there is a country of the heart, a place where it all comes together: devotion and delight, intensity and awareness – the feeling of being the kind of person one was meant to be.

For the lucky ones it comes with marriage and parenthood: a sunlit pleasance, well-weeded, guarded from trespassers and those we trespass against. For others it is a dark place, a night country of station waiting-rooms, hotel bedrooms and the torture of the silent telephone, Some, I suppose, never find it – Brooke's 'wanderers in the middle mist' – or cannot reach it, lost in a thicket of words like 'honour' and 'duty', which no one any longer understands, but which fasten themselves, nonetheless, like barbed wire round the spirit.

But what if there are two countries? What if there is no bridge?

I was twenty when I married John and straight away I knew it was going to be all right. Oh, it was rough sometimes on the surface; he was on a research grant at a west country university, working on animal behaviour, and when Vanessa was born and then Daniel two years later we were very hard up. But all through the sex-and-money rows, the battles to adjust my manic sociability with his need for solitude, we were all right, our roots steadily twisting together down beneath it all. John was gentle and considerate, yet in no way soft. He supported me, encouraged my work (I was just starting as a freelance writer) and laughed at me. As for our children – ah, glory, there were never children like ours!

We lived in a flat in a shabby terrace of Georgian houses that faced south over the city. There was a wisteria snaking from the basement to support the narrow balcony where I sat on summer afternoons telling stories to my blonde and giggly daughter, my dreamy, green-eyed son. We had friends too, real ones who allowed us to walk in and out of their lives and whose dramas and crises became our own.

A good life, you see. No excuses for what happened. No alibi.

We had been married nearly seven years when a great-uncle of mine died and left me five hundred pounds. That September John had a conference in Vienna. My widowed mother was always glad to take the children, so I went abroad by myself and I went – I never thought of any other place – to Russia.

I had signed on with an Art Lovers' Tour and I struck lucky. They were nice, the Art Lovers: amiable, outgoing Canadians festooned with cameras, north-country schoolteachers who *knew* things . . . We flew to Moscow and in the shabby Intourist bus assigned to us were conveyed to Prince Yussupoff's palace at Archangel, gazed reverently at Pushkin's portrait in the Tretyakorskaya gallery, marvelled at the icons in the Novo-devichy Convent.

Then, on the third day . . .

We had done a sprint through the Kremlin Armoury (the turquoise and tourmaline throne of Boris Godunov, the saddle of lapis lazuli that Catherine the Great gave to Potemkin . . .) and were crossing Red Square, making for the row of buses parked by the Spassky Gate.

There were tourists everywhere. A party of Chinese businessmen hissed with despair as a fat German housewife walked – at the instant of camera-click – into their carefully posed group photograph; a gaggle of Swedish women gymnasts bayed for their courier and in the middle of the square, a tragic figure in a sea of cobbles – an elderly, blue-rinsed American – threw back her head and wailed: 'Oh, gee, I've lost my tour!'

Pausing to comfort her, I all but lost my own. The Art Lovers had reached the row of buses and climbed aboard. And the bus was about the start.

I ran, jumped onto the steps and was pulled aboard by a man with arms of steel. Increasing speed, the bus lurched forward and I fell with a crash on to my rescuer.

It was one of my more ethnic periods. Disentangling him

from my Aztec beads, my Peruvian saddle-bag, I found that my hair (long and thick and fair – my *only* beauty) was caught in the button of his jacket. I began simultaneously to apologise and tug.

'Wait!'

He bent his head and began patiently to extricate the strands. High cheekbones, green eyes, brown hair already thinning a little. I noticed most his hands, which seemed to me very beautiful, and his concentration. He was doing this thing and this thing only.

'There.'

I could look up now. The bus was full of dark-suited, serious men with a briefcase air. Not an Art Lover in sight.

'You could, I suppose, be a hitherto undiscovered Bursting Disc Expert?' His voice was amused and already far too tender. 'On the other hand you *could* be on the wrong bus.'

They were a delegation of marine engineers on a trade mission, now on a day's sightseeing trip to Yasnaya Polyana, Tolstoy's country estate three hours' drive away from Moscow.

'Oh!' I was enchanted. Anything to do with Tolstoy was Shangri-la to me. 'But I must get back to the Art Lovers. They'll be worried.'

And his voice beside me, very quiet.

'No!'

What rubbish they talk about love at first sight. Where is it, all that ecstasy, the singing and the gold? It's terrifying when it happens – a kind of relentless, metallurgical process, some dark *thing* being forged at unimaginable temperatures in some subterranean furnace of the soul.

We exchanged names: Stefan Grant, Helen Gresham.

Neither of us smiled.

It was at Tula that we first saw the brides. It's the provincial capital of the district, the city closest to Tolstoy's estate and the brides were queuing up outside the town hall, rows of them, waiting to get married. The men, stocky with set faces, wore their ordinary, shabby suits but the brides – all of them – were dressed in white. And each one carried a bunch of shaggy, identical flowers – the only flowers to be had, it seemed, in this vast, impoverished land.

'*Asters*,' I said. 'Look, they're all carrying asters.'

Stefan turned, smiled.

'And you,' he said, touching too briefly the gold band on my left hand. 'What did you carry on your wedding day?'

'Oh, roses and stephanotis, much too stiffly wired. Then someone rushed up and said it was unlucky – the red and the white, I mean, and a kind lady gave me her pink carnation and we stuck it in the back. And it was all right, I *was* lucky.'

'My wife didn't carry anything,' he said. 'Me, nearly. I had a dreadful hangover.'

We had exchanged marriages. Happy ones. Feeling suddenly safe, we turned to each other and began to talk.

'Yasnaya Polyana' means 'Luminous Meadows' and it's a good name. As we spilled out of the bus and began walking up the drive, the meadows really did shimmer with light; the poplars and asters trembled. And the birches . . . But I'll come again to the birches.

'I never thought I'd see it,' I said. 'I used . . . oh, to *be* Natasha for years and years and years.'

Stefan was beside me. Naturally. Already what I had learnt about him on the bus was ground into my bones. An Austrian mother, a Scottish father . . . a childhood in a white house by a white strand in the Hebrides. Then the shock of an English boarding-school . . . one of those maths-and-music brains shunted into engineering. He spoke of his wife, Claire, with pride: a practical, blessedly un-neurotic girl; of his daughter, Toussia, with sensuous delight like someone describing flowers or fruit.

We walked together through the great man's house: the bentwood chairs, the samovar, the tiny study with *The Brothers Karamazov* open at the page he had been reading on the day he fled his house to die.

'A guy who asked the right questions,' said Stefan. 'Maybe the answers were wrong, but the questions were right.'

'He could never bear to wake anyone from sleep,' I said.

The narrow iron bed, the peasant smock on the coat-stand . . . and outside now into the grounds to visit Tolstoy's grave.

And now we came to the birches. In Russia birches are not the slender, inconsequential things they are with us; they're as tall as redwoods and they grow packed together in shining forests, miles upon hundreds of miles of them, and the Russians are mad about them: crazy. So Tolstoy, naturally, had asked to be buried beneath his birches. A simple grassy mound; no headstone, no inscription.

To this grave, converging from the criss-crossing paths, there came other pilgrims: groups of foreigners with Intourist guides, Russian families on an outing from Moscow, Tatars from Samarkand . . .

And, then, in the midst of the sightseers, there they were again, white and grave and unmistakable, the Brides of Tula – dozens of them, walking beside their newly-wedded husbands and coming forward one by one to lay their tousled asters on the great man's grave.

It really got me: the sunlight filtering through the birches, the devout girls, the flowers which we would not, at home, have bothered to pick off a rubbish heap.

'My mother was drowned,' said Stefan suddenly, 'crewing for friends in the Bahamas. I used to think a grave would have helped. I'd have burned the things on it that she loved, as the Chinese do.'

'The Chinese?'

He nodded. 'One day a year. Their New Year. They have a feast on the grave of their dead. They burn . . . oh, paper money for a miser . . . toys for a child.'

'What would you have burned for her?'

'A bottle of Je Reviens . . . the score of a Mozart concerto . . . a Schiaparelli scarf.'

'And for your wife?'

He grinned. 'A packet of seeds . . . a hoe . . . a novel with a happy ending.'

We were silent, standing too close, looking down at the quiet mound of earth beneath its tousled flowers.

'And you?' said Stefan. 'What about your husband? What would you burn for him?'

It was my turn to smile. 'A year's subscription to *Ecology*; a home-brewing kit: the spare parts of a vintage Riley. . .'

The Engineers had drifted back to the waiting bus. The brides had gone. Then: 'On my grave,' said Stefan very quietly, 'they would have to make a pyre, I think, and burn. . .'

He paused, trying not to say it.

If I had kept still; if I had only kept absolutely still. But I moved towards him and he had to finish.

'You,' he said. 'They shall burn you.'

So it began.

Moscow is an ugly city: no props for lovers – no intimate cafés, no cosy bars and at night the hotel corridors guarded by grim females sullenly handing out keys.

None of it mattered. We saw *Swan Lake* at the Bolshoi and the fat, middle-aged women in the audience held crumpled asters as the brides had done and threw them, at curtain call, on to the stage. We went to the circus and saw a dozen snow-white yaks dancing a saraband, and to a four-hour opera about the love life of an unidentifiable and deeply crazy czar. When Stefan had to join his delegation I waited, shivering like a kitten, in some public park and each time he walked towards me with his quick, predatory gait, I felt a happiness so violent, so idiotically *pure* that I could not speak but clung to his hand like someone saved from drowning.

On the fifth day after our meeting, the Art Lovers took off for Leningrad. There was no way Stefan could cut the red tape and follow me, but he followed me. It was with him that I stood breathless before the Scythian gold in the Hermitage, with him that I ran through the crazy fountains of Peter the Great's Summer Palace, with his hand in mine that I heard the Cossacks singing at the Kirov.

Then we flew back to London. One more snatched day. We spent it mostly in the bedroom of a crummy hotel near King's Cross, talking, talking . . . frantically garnering the most trivial piece of knowledge against the coming drought. ('Did you have mumps when you were little? Do you like Dvòrák? Modigliani? Gorgonzola cheese?')

Then he took me to the station and put me on the train. There's a sort of anaesthesia about a parting like that. One behaves well because it's so obvious that it's not going to happen.

Only it happened. We parted. I went home.

John was waiting, relaxed and loving. The children ran shrieking into my arms. My friends phoned and said: 'Thank God you're back.' I took possession of my life, incredibly thankful that I had done no harm, that my hostages were safe.

But . . . 'Take it,' said God. 'Take it and pay for it.'

I began to pay.

We had decided not to call each other, not to write. It seemed to me that battles could be won, ships built with the force I expended on dragging myself past the telephone, on destroying the letters that I scrawled on the edges of shopping lists, the margins of newspapers, making them illegible almost on purpose so as to hide the naked words not from John but from myself.

It will pass, I said. Everyone knows that it passes. Hold on. Grind it into the ground. You will forget.

Only I didn't.

It's a lonely thing, a passionate love. Boring, too. If you want to know why Isolde killed herself, I'll tell you. She killed herself because when she woke up on the three hundred and ninety-seventh morning of her life with Tristan's name still on her lips, she said to herself, right this one I've *had*.

The months passed, half a year, more . . . Then one day there was a letter. In his clear, looped, unfamiliar hand. Stefan wrote of the dearth, the greyness, the sense of a spring running dry. 'I will do anything you wish, Helen. I have no answers. Only, can it be right to live so joylessly in a world where, perhaps, joy is a kind of duty?'

It was the letter of a man frightened, as I was, by what had been done.

It was now, driven by longing, by guilt, faced once more with a choice, that I went to see Kirsty.

Kirsty was a painter who had a studio converted from an old chapel a few miles out of town. She worked all day but about five she surfaced, drank enormous quantities of tea, went to find her marvellously independent son and (if she had one at the time) her current lover and began to assemble, like a Braque still life, the ingredients for her evening meal. It was at this witching time that I found her, preparing a gigantic Salade Niçoise to the sound of Bartok on the hi-fi, the last of the evening light streaming through the huge windows on to her russet hair and beautifully faded smock.

I took the chopping-board from her and reached for the onions. Thus covered for impending tears (Daniel and Vanessa were outside playing with Kirsty's Shaun) I began to tell her about Stefan.

'Oh, Helen, you poor old thing! Mind you, I've been expecting something like this. You've had that sort of *look*. And you've lost your smugness.'

'Was I smug?'

'Oh, well, a very little. Just a touch of "I can't see what all the fuss is about" when other people came unstuck. Not much of the divine discontent.'

I reached for another onion. 'Well, there's plenty now,' I said, dabbing at my face.

'What's he like?'

I said I didn't really know any more. He had green eyes and said his 'Rs' in a funny way because his mother had been Viennese and when we went out to dinner he buttered my roll. Then, reaching new heights of originality I said that without him I was probably going to die.

Kirsty poured out a tumbler of wine and pushed it over. 'It's pretty disgusting. I was going to marinate something.'

I drank it down. A mistake. Experiencing suddenly total recall, I began to describe Stefan, gabbling like a mad nun reciting a litany.

When I had finished, Kirsty put down her knife and said; 'If it's like that, then you must go to him.'

I stared at her. The Bartok was finished. The children's voices came from outside.

'You're mad, Kirsty. I can't leave John. I can't break up our marriage. And the *children*. . .'

Kirsty looked at me. 'It's tough, I know. But you're living a lie, aren't you? Lying beside one man and pining for another. It's disgusting, that. Children make out. Husbands, too. You should have seen Chris when I left him and within six months he was having a fantastic time with Sarah. And look at Shaun –he's all right, isn't he? It's lies that kill, Helen. Anyone can stand a bit of pain, but there *has* to be truth.'

I felt suddenly sick with terror.

'We're all right, John and I. We're *good*.'

'If you're all right,' said Kirsty sternly, 'why are you here, howling into my marinade? Why have you lost half a stone since you came back from Russia? Don't lie, Helen, not to anyone. Lying's the end.'

I went home, my head ringing with Kirsty's words. She was

right. I had been smug. I *did* lack courage.

Stefan! If I was brave enough I could be with Stefan.

Four days after my visit to Kirsty, John came home with a little clump of primroses. 'They're the first ones. I found them on the bank at Dundry.' He put them gently into my hand. 'I'll bring back a pot tonight. They'll grow all right, you'll see.'

I knew then that I would never leave him.

So Stefan's letter remained unanswered and the dearth began again. I stood it for a couple of weeks and then I went to see Elaine.

Elaine was married to a businessman. She lived in a Regency house filled with Famille Rose china, potted orange trees and exotic *au pairs* whose emotional disasters were our staple gossip. Her taste, her flair for clothes were a byword. She also handled, with competence and warmth, three sturdy little boys and a jet-setting husband too handsome for his own good.

I usually went to see Elaine on a Sunday morning when Tony went sailing and she sat on a chaise-longue in a series of devastating kaftans, combing her snow-white Shi-Tzu, manicuring her nails and swearing to give up alcohol, dinner parties and sex.

'Helen, how lovely! I'll get Concepción to make us some coffee.'

I shook my head. 'I've just had some. Elaine, I'm in such a mess, I *have* to talk to you.'

And I began it again, my wail, my litany. 'I feel so empty and awful without him, as though everything had dried up inside. It seems so *wrong* to turn your back on something like that.'

'Oh, I know, darling, it's quite, quite dreadful loving someone like that, but really rather marvellous too, and in a way it's what you *need*.'

I stared at her. 'What is?'

'An affair, of course. A bit of fun and excitement. I know you and John are very good and of course it would be *madness* to leave him, he adores you and he's such a pet. But with a little spunk and intelligence. . .'

'Elaine, I don't think I *could*. Even now when I lie to John about something quite unimportant I feel physically sick.'

Elaine twisted the rubber band neatly round the Shi-Tzu's topknot and set him down. 'I'm afraid feeling sick's part of the job, honey. Not sleeping, too. You must make sure you have plenty of sleeping pills, because they do *notice* if you don't sleep and being noticed is the unforgivable thing.'

'It sounds like an illness,' I said.

'I suppose it is in a way.' She smiled. 'But a *lovely* one. People are so stupid – all that about loving only one man.'

'Can you really sort of plough it back into your marriage? The happiness you get from someone else? Like manure?'

'Heavens, *yes*. I reckon some of the best times Tony and I have had have been because I felt as guilty as sin.'

'You make it sound fun,' I said wistfully.

'Oh, Helen it *is*, I can't tell you what fun. Only you don't get anything for nothing. You just have to take all the beastly scheming and plotting on the chin. It's the blabbers that are the criminals – the ones that run to their husbands and confess when the going gets tough.'

I left Elaine's walking on air. How stupid I had been! It was so easy really. I was going to see Stefan and love him dementedly and everyone would be better for it – *everyone*!

In three weeks the children broke up. I would send them to my mother. Then I would tell John that I was going to stay with my cousin, Laura, in Lancaster and spend a whole week with Stefan.

No, not Laura. Laura was coming to stay in the summer and she was terribly fond of John. I couldn't burden her with a secret like that.

Well, then, I would tell him I needed a week to research a novel. Then I'd have to *write* a novel, of course, but that did not matter. I'd say it had a Scottish background and then—

And then he would offer to go with me. John had always wanted us to go to Scotland on our own.

Perhaps we'd better just take a weekend first, Stefan and I.

'John, I thought I'd go up to London for a weekend and see that Islamic Exhibition. Could you cope with the children?'

'Of course, lovey. Do you good to get away; you've been looking a bit peaked. I'll have something in the oven for you on Sunday night. And how about getting yourself a new coat? I've got my examiner's fee coming for that Ph.D.'

'But you wanted that for some new binoculars.'

'Oh, the old ones are all right. Honestly.'

And as he stood there, his eyes shining with delight at my coming treat, I felt my beautiful, sophisticated affair curl up and die beneath my feet.

If I sought out Trudy, the last of my special friends, it was because I knew exactly what she would say and I needed to hear her say it. She was a bit older than the rest of us, a Quaker who taught in a comprehensive school and still had time to bake her own bread, cope cheerfully with a brood of teenage children and secure for her husband the peace he needed to write his history books.

'Helen, no one can tell another person what to do. But you know what I think. Keeping faith, being truthful, sticking to your bargain – these things weren't meant to be easy. But without them – well, I don't think there's any way forward.'

'I . . . must put him out of my mind?'

Trudy looked at me, a fearful pity on her face. 'Absolutely, love. For ever. No backsliding. Because once you marry and have children you can no longer confine the paying to yourself. Others pay, always, when you grab and cheat. Oh, Helen, don't look like that. Have a bun, love – have a big cream bun.'

I took it and ate it. A bun from Hades, from an Egyptian tomb.

That night I wrote to Stefan and said no, there was nothing for us and we must not write or meet again. At least that's what I meant to say. My 'no' took five desperate pages. Like everything I did concerning him it became, somehow, an act of love. So I tore it up; did nothing.

Well, it was over now. I had stood up to be counted and the reckoning had gone against me. Kirsty's way was no use to me, nor Elaine's, though both were right for them. It was Trudy who spoke for me.

Or was it? One day, waiting on a windy corner for Vanessa to come from school, I remembered my old tutor at college when I went to her with some problem. She was a refugee from Hitler and what she had said was: 'When you get to heaven, Helen, they won't ask you if you've been Moses or Abraham. They'll ask you if you have been *you*.'

Only who was 'I'? It seemed I did not know.

All that summer I went into myself with a pickaxe, trying to cut out cant, hypocrisy, fear ... seeking desperately for a solution which, however tentative, should be my own. Then, at the end of August, I went to a concert. It was Haydn's *The Seasons* and when I came out of the concert hall I knew what I was going to do.

Oh, I know it's a foolish, imperfect answer; I can see a hundred ways in which it might fail. But I'm going to take one day and one day only of every season of the year and spend it with Stefan. It's my pledge (on the heads of my children, I pledge this) not to grab one hour more, not to write or phone in between or lapse into the furtive delight of an affair. But once in every summer, once in autumn, once in winter and once in spring, I'm going to be with him.

Tomorrow is our first day. A year has passed and it's autumn once again. No Russian birches this time, no great man's grave. But I'll buy a bunch of asters at the station and perhaps, somehow, they'll know, the Brides of Tula, and pray for me.

With Love and Swamp Noises

It was the kind of place you go to to get out of the rain or to amuse an ancient relative with a passion for stuffed ptarmigans, assegais and the less important kinds of mummy. A tiny, old-fashioned museum – The Havelock, they called it – tucked away in one of those quiet grey squares between the London Library and St James's.

A place in which one might have expected to meet anything – except one's fate.

It was November – somehow it always seems to be in that part of London – with the bobbles on the plane trees swirling out of the mist and splayed leaves on the pavement. My wife wouldn't come – she had an 'engagement' and because I suspected what that engagement was, it was with the familiar ache gnawing at my stomach that I paid my entrance fee, walked past the bust of William Havelock in his pith helmet and found myself gazing into the placid eyes of an aardvark standing solidly astride his piece of painted veld. A family of white-tailed gnus stared from a glass case, a sea-lion reared its majestic chest from a mahogany plinth. It was very quiet.

I wandered past a case of exotic butterflies, models of outrigger canoes in bark, dice made out of knuckle-bones . . . Havelock clearly had collected everything. Then suddenly out of a door marked 'Private – Staff Only' there erupted a girl . . . A knock-kneed, tangle-haired girl carrying a hippopotamus harpoon, a bell-jar of stuffed willow grouse and a cardboard box.

It was all too much. The cardboard box slipped, fell and a dark and unpleasantly mottled object rolled across the floor. A shrunken head, not in the best state of preservation. I retrieved it. She thanked me, apologised, smiled. Then she put down her load again and said, 'Are you enjoying yourself? Would you like me to show you round?'

I must, I suppose, have said yes. At any rate she showed me round. No, what am I saying? She gave me that museum, she laid it at my feet. I felt she would have torn the exhibits from the walls and put them in my cupped hands, so demented was she to share, to give.

'It's such a lovely place – no one ever comes, but they *should*. Look, that's a naked sea slug – they're very rare in Britain – don't you like those purple tentacles? And those silk moths are descended directly from the ones belonging to the Emperor Wu-Ti – the one who bred the Heavenly Horses, you know – and we have the best collection of East Indian sea-shells in the world; a dear little professor sent them from Kuala Lumpur. Did you know that some shells are whorled sinistrally and some dextrally? I didn't until I came to work here.'

Her hand hovered above my sleeve; her heart too no doubt – on mine, on anybody's . . . A cornucopia of a girl who went on talking even on an inward breath. And suddenly I imagined her making love like a football supporter, lurching out into the night afterwards to assault total strangers with her happiness.

'Listen!' she said. We had come to a case of stuffed roe deer: a stag and a hind prancing over some rather wilted heather. She pressed a button and suddenly the museum was filled with an extraordinary mournful, honking sound.

'They're roe deer rutting noises,' she said, her plum-coloured eyes glistening with pride. 'Mr Henry had them put in. He was our last director, he's just retired. We've got some swamp noises too, in the other room, to go with the dinosaur bones. Would you like to hear them?'

But at swamp noises I stalled and excused myself. It wasn't until I let myself into the flat and my stomach-ache returned that I realised it had disappeared during the last few hours. And yet who could I blame? I had wanted to get married, not Vivian. She had warned me all along that she couldn't bear to be tied. 'If you start being jealous, Paul, it's the end,' she had said. So I wasn't jealous. There was just this incessant pain in my guts. I suppose that's all jealousy is. Just pain.

The next day I went back to the Havelock with my new bunch of master keys and let myself in at the back, walking down corridors cluttered with specimen cabinets, old wall charts and piles of skins towards the director's office. Though it was early, I was surprised to see a number of people already at work. A gorgeously dressed and rather pregnant Arabian lady was sorting osprey eggs, an ancient, bald little man assembling ichythosaurus bones, a boy in tattered jeans hammering at a display case . . .

In the director's office I began to search for a list of employees. My brief when I got the job had been to streamline the place, reduce expenses, modernise – or else. It looked as though some pretty heavy staff cuts would be first on the list. But in installing roe deer rutting noises, Mr Henry seemed to have shot his bolt. I could find nothing relevant.

In the end I went to see my second-in-command, Mr Biggers, the taxidermist. I had met him at my interview and knew him to be a level-headed and sensible sort of bloke.

'Mr Biggers, I'm a bit puzzled about the number of people working here,' I said. 'I thought we only employed four full-time members of staff.'

Mr Biggers pushed aside a dodo-head cast, dropped a pickled skin back into its barrel and drew out a stool for me.

'Ah, yes,' he said. 'Well, a lot of people *do* work here, but they're not exactly members of staff. They're voluntary, as you might say.' There was a pause, then he added, 'They're by way of being friends of Flossie's.'

'Who's Flossie?' I asked. But I was only playing for time; I knew of course. In this situation, the imprint of the football supporter was writ large and clear.

'Miss French. The assistant curator. Her name,' said Mr Biggers, 'is Florence.' He sighed and I loved him for it. 'Flossie has this odd sixth sense. If someone comes into the museum who is sad or in trouble in some way, she always seems to know. Then she charges out front and shows them round.'

I scowled. This was a bit close to the bone.

'She's very fond of this place. You might say her enthusiasm is contagious. People start regarding it as home.'

'But this is impossible! These people are handling highly valuable articles. Look, would you ask Miss French to come to my room straight away.'

She came, saw me and flinched. 'Oh! You should have told me you were the new director. Letting me *show* you things. . .'

'It was my first naked sea slug,' I said briskly. 'Please sit down, Miss French. I want to ask you about these friends of yours who've taken to working here. The Asian lady for example?'

'Oh, that's Mrs Rahman,' she said, her face glowing with pride in her protégée. 'She's expecting a baby and she's very lonely because her husband is doing a degree or something; they were very scientific with her in the hospital, so she came here to have a cry. She wants to have her baby by the Leboyer method, you see and they wouldn't—'

'By the *what*?' Vivian didn't want children and the whole scene was one I had blotted out.

'Oh, it's lovely! You have the baby in the dark with beautiful music and you don't thump it and it smiles when it's born. There's a lot about massage too and warm oil and putting it on the mother's stomach when—'

Too late I regretted my question. 'So she came in here to cry. And what then?'

'Well, I took her to my room for a cup of tea and now she's sorting out the Hartington Egg collection. It's been lying around since 1890 all in boxes, because no one's had time to do it and she's found some amazing—'

'But is she *qualified*? Does she know what she's doing?'

Flossie frowned. 'I suppose she isn't qualified on paper, but she has the gentlest hands I've ever seen – like the antennae of butterflies, they are. I can't imagine her ever breaking anything and she's so patient. Also she's terribly generous. She buys all the coffee and sugar and biscuits for break – she insists – and the petty cash is absolutely *flourishing*!'

I was liking this less and less. 'And the little old man?'

'Uncle Laszlo, do you mean? Well, I found him in the back one day, sort of rootling among the ichthyosaurus bones; he'd got lost, I think. It's sad because he's retired and lives in this awful hotel with no one to care for him – all his people stayed behind in Hungary in 1956. He must have been some sort of professor, I reckon. His hands are a bit shaky now, but he's absolutely brilliant with bones.'

'Oh, my God!' I could see it all: medical disasters, insurance scandals, enquiries . . . 'And that guy in jeans doing the carpentry?' Obscurely, he had annoyed me most. 'Your boy friend?'

She flushed. 'No,' she said shortly. 'Matt's American. He went through the drug scene when he was still in nappies and

he's been through some bad times. As a matter of fact, I found
him kind of passed-out behind the stuffed bison in that alcove
where Brian sleeps.'

'Brian?'

'Only in the winter.' She was on the defensive at last. 'He's a
pavement artist and in the summer he likes to sleep in the park.
He's very careful – it was because of him that we found the leak
in the dark-room roof.'

I picked up one of Mr Henry's treasures – a specimen tube
simply and coyly labelled 'cyst' and turned it over in my hands.

'They'll have to go, Miss French. Every one of them.'

She stood there, knock-kneed as ever, taking it.

'Look,' I said. 'I don't know if Mr Henry told you, but this
museum is financially on the rocks. Our endowment's been
reduced to nothing by the inflation and unless we can get a
grant from the Natural History Commission we're finished.'

'We'll have to *close*, do you mean?'

I nodded. 'Just so. And the first thing Sir Godfrey Peters and
his Commission are going to ask me is why this museum is full
of geriatrics and pregnant women and tramps.'

A pause. Then she said gently, 'Could . . . they just finish
what they're doing? They've all worked so hard.'

I frowned, calculating. 'The Commission's due in mid-
February. That's three months from now. All right, they can
finish the jobs in hand but that's *all*. Do you understand?'

'Yes, Mr Bellingham. I understand.'

There followed some of the most exhausting weeks of my life.
Three months was not nearly long enough for what needed to
be done. Havelock had had connections all over the world and
hardly a week passed but some ancient general or intrepid lady
entomologist died and left us their collection of Peruvian
rhinoceros beetles or a tin trunk of mysterious shards. It
seemed to me that unless we could make some kind of order out
of the muddle and get some of the stuff on display, the
Commission would make short work of us.

So we set to work. And I have to say here and now that
rancour was not one of the football supporter's vices. She kept
her lame dogs out of my way in her room and turned herself into
a kind of sloe-eyed helpmeet out of the Old Testament,
contantly at my side. We staggered about with drawers and

specimen boxes, we sorted, we classified. We turned out rusty tins labelled 'Henderson's Breast Developer' or 'Colman's Original Mustard' and found now a valuable effigy, now a collection of mouldering pupae which crumbled at our touch. And always, even at the end of the most gruelling day, covered in dust and tottering with exhaustion, her demented enthusiasm remained undimmed.

Three weeks after my arrival she knocked at the door of my office as I sat in solitary state, drinking my coffee with the CYST.

'Uncle Laszlo's finished the ichthyosaurus. He was wondering if you'd like to see it?'

I followed her into her room. The old man had on his hat and coat; scrupulously he was getting ready to leave now that his task was done. I thought how tired he looked, how old.

The ichthyosaurus took up two trestle tables and so far as I could see he had made a flawless job of it.

'Thank you. That will make a most valuable exhibit.'

Uncle Laszlo took up his briefcase. 'There are some pterosaur bones in the cupboard in Mr Bigger's room,' he said. 'I think they are complete. If they could be assembled, they would make an interesting comparison.'

'Are you sure?' I asked sharply.

'That it is a pterosaur, I am sure. That it is complete, I cannot say.'

'Well, you'd better find out,' I said.

Uncle Laszlo looked at me and then quietly he took off his hat and coat. After all, he did not look so very old. It was only when a sort of sigh spread around the room and Flossie lurched radiantly towards me with the second cup of coffee that I realised what I had done.

After that things went downhill rapidly. Flossie appeared next day carrying a swathe of wild silk, priceless stuff the colour of the sea. 'Mrs Rahman's father-in-law sent it from Quittah. Would you mind terribly if we used it to display the Abyssinian pottery on?'

I said no, I didn't mind. Gradually it turned out that I didn't mind Brian, on leave from his pavement, wiring the display cases for concealed lighting, or Matt repainting the frieze in the main hall. Mrs Rahman moving on from the Hartington Egg Collection to the Kashmiri dried ferns was another thing I didn't apparently mind too much. As for Flossie putting in a fourteen-hour day, that had always been all right with me.

Soon I abandoned not only my principles but the CYST, taking coffee with the rest of them in Flossie's room and giving them the benefit of my views on Leboyer, the political situation in Afghanistan and the efficiency of Yoga in licking drugs. It got so that when Flossie vanished one morning, obeying her sixth sense, and came back with a tragically widowed Brigadier, it was I who gave him the Madagascan ivories to sort.

I began to be hopeful. The Havelock, like a woman who is loved, began to glow, to shine.

'They can't close us, Paul, we're so *beautiful*,' said Flossie, gazing entranced at her newly mounted shrunken head. And removing a mother-of-pearl coconut scraper from her tangled hair, I was inclined to agree.

My happiness was the greater because Vivian, for the first time since our marriage, was taking an interest in my work. 'I was thinking, Paul, if the Havelock is in trouble financially we ought to get going on the social side a bit. Have some fund-raising parties and things? I'd need some new clothes, of course. . .'

Gratefully I made over my salary cheque and Vivian, looking unbelievably stunning, sallied forth in search of American philanthropists, captains of industry and eminent scientists who might interest themselves in the Havelock and its fate.

I had it all sorted out in my mind, of course. Sir Godfrey and his Commission were due on February the twelfth. A week before that I was going to clear out the volunteers, give Flossie a holiday (I saw no way of making that girl into anything that remotely resembled the curator of a natural history museum) and only Mr Biggers, myself and the staid secretary would be there to present accounts and conduct them on a formal tour.

But there I had reckoned without my wife. She had managed – heaven knows how – to get hold of Sir Godfrey socially and to interest him in the Havelock and me.

We were having our coffee break when we heard the sound of purposeful footsteps approaching the director's office, halting and then returning. Then came a knock on the door and a jovial, booming voice – 'Ah, Bellingham, there you are! We've come to look in a bit early, as you see. Thought we might get your case through quicker that way.'

I don't know what I had expected from the chairman of the Natural History Commission. Hardly the Flash Gordon profile, the craggy jaw, the Bermuda tan. Flanked by three steely-eyed, grey-suited experts, Sir Godfrey advanced into the room. As he did so his jovial expression became more fixed, his craggy jaw tightened a little.

On a camp-bed by the window Mrs Rahman was doing her ante-natal breathing, something we insisted upon. Matt, who was deeply into Yoga, was demonstrating the 'Cobra' to Uncle Laszlo. Brian, in the manner of tramps since time immemorial, was stuffing his boots with newspaper . . .

Sir Godfrey came to a halt. He had to since Flossie, who had been on her hands and knees labelling specimens, now reared up in his path. I moved forward to remove a Rhodesian leg ornament which had got caught behind her ear, thought better of it and shook hands with Sir Godfrey.

'Your staff, I take it?' said Sir Godfrey, surveying the room. 'Perhaps you'll introduce me.'

I introduced him. What else could I do?

I must say he was straight with me. Biggers and I showed him round and he asked intelligent questions while his posse took notes. Then we went to my office.

'Look, Bellingham, before we go any further there's one thing I want to make quite clear. Every one of these peculiar volunteers must go and go for good. It's absolutely out of the question that we could award a grant to a place run like . . . a jumble sale. You must know quite well that your exhibits are not insured for handling by unauthorised persons. And what about the medical question? Suppose that extraordinarily pregnant lady should be taken ill and her husband sue you? Or the old man have a fit? You must be as aware as I am of these considerations?'

'Yes,' I said, 'I am.'

'Good. Then I have your word that all these people will be removed immediately?'

'No,' I said.

A flush spread over Sir Godfrey's handsome face.

'I'm sorry,' I said. 'I know exactly how you feel because I felt the same when I first came here. But I find I no longer care to go along with the way things are run nowadays. Friendly old people's homes closed and the residents turned adrift because the fire escape's two inches too narrow. People losing their jobs because they're too old or too young or haven't passed some arbitrary exam. All the goodwill of ordinary people going to waste. Havelock was a tea merchant. Everything he collected, he brought in during his spare time. This museum was built by amateurs and it's only because I've had the help of other amateurs that I've been able to run it. If they go, I go.'

'In that case,' said Sir Godfrey, 'there's nothing more to be said.'

They all knew at once of course. Biggers must have told them and when I came back from lunch they were waiting for me. Mrs Rahman, her doe-eyes wide with concern; Uncle Laszlo, shaking his head; Matt telling me I was silly, that they had always known they wouldn't be allowed to stay.

And Flossie, blaming herself. Flossie putting a hand on my arm and remembering, and turning away with a little gulp . . . Flossie who had lost both her parents in a car crash and to whom the Havelock was home.

The letter refusing the grant came the following week. Vivian was furious with me and I couldn't blame her. After all, Sir Godfrey was her protégé.

'If you would climb down,' she said, 'I'm sure I could get him to change his mind.'

But this I wouldn't do. 'Sometimes you have to stand up and be counted,' I said wearily – and saw her recoil from my priggishness.

Ten days later I came home to find a note on the mantelpiece. Always look for the obvious, they say, in matters of the human heart. But could I have foreseen anything as trite, as banal, as soul-destroying as Vivian and Sir Godfrey? Or that my disgust and bitterness would be so little help in blotting out the pain?

At the Havelock we went on working like lunatics, all of us. You could have eaten your dinner off the floor on the day before we were due to close. That day we had a party. Matt and Brian fixed up a bar between the aardvark and the gnus, Mr Biggers made a speech, Uncle Laszlo and the Brigadier downed the champagne like mother's milk, and to the sound of roe deer rutting noises Flossie and I solemnly waltzed.

Parties poised over an abyss of leave-taking and calamity are generally the best. None of us noticed how late it was, or that Mrs Rahman had long since slipped away. When we did, Flossie went at once to find her.

She returned as pale as death. 'Oh, come quickly, please, *please*! And ring for an ambulance, someone – only I'm afraid it's much too late!'

Flossie was right. Mrs Rahman, that gentle soul, had not cared to spoil our fun. Now she lay on the trestle bed, glistening with sweat and trying between contractions to apologise.

Heaven knows how we did it, but we did. And when it was over and we gave the radiant, exhausted woman her lusty son to hold, I had to hand it to Leboyer. Because I swear to you, the messy, beat-up little thing quite definitely smiled!

It was November again. Bobbles on the plane trees; mist, wet leaves splayed on the pavement. A year had passed since I had first seen the naked sea slug and the football supporter had tottered out of her door, dropping her shrunken head. My decree had just come through and the sense of failure was bad.

I went in past the bust of Sir William in his pith helmet . . . past the aardvark, the gnus . . . Everything was as it had been but a little better, a little more highly polished. A couple of Arab ladies were whispering reverently by the silk moths of the Emperor Wu-Ti. A lot of people came from the Middle East these days: the place was a kind of pilgrimage spot for them. The birth-place of Yusuf Mahomet Abu Rahman, the first healthy male child born to the son of a reigning sheik in the state of Quittah for forty years. Our endowment from the old man, running at one three-hundredth of his annual oil revenue, made the Havelock one of the wealthiest museums in the land.

The door marked 'Staff Only' burst open. Her sixth sense unfailing, out she came.

'Oh, Paul, why did you come in by the front, we've been waiting and waiting for you! Uncle Laszlo's found some new bones which he thinks are——' She broke off, tilted her tangled head. 'Are you sad?'

'Not now.'

She lurched tentatively towards me. I opened my arms and she moved into them. My own personal football supporter. *Mine.* . . .

THE ADULTERY OF JENNY CRAIG

JENNY CRAIG knew that there was no such thing as adultery any more. The women's movement, the new way of thinking had made the word, the whole concept, obsolete. There weren't really 'affairs' any more either; there were just different people relating to each other, taking and giving love, some inside marriage, some out . . . That's what it was like now.

Only, seemingly, not for her. What she was planning to do: to meet a man called Thomas Marsham, to whom she was not married, for a weekend in London, *felt* like adultery. Furthermore the sleeplessness, the indigestion, the tension headaches she had developed as the result of the lies it had been necessary to tell her husband, *felt* like guilt.

Jenny had been married to Philip Craig for twelve years and they had been good ones. All the trouble people had with sex hadn't really come their way. Philip enjoyed it and so did she and when after the first few years they had done all the ordinary things and were perhaps inclined to get a little bit into a rut, they had gone out and bought some books and done slightly less ordinary things. Only, of course, after a while these too got a little bit repetitive, there being only so many things one can expect of the human body; and lately, returning from one of his more exhausting business trips, Philip had been inclined to fall asleep before, rather than after, they had expressed themselves in this particular way.

All of which Jenny understood and didn't in the least mind. As far as she could see, the sex thing was a 'heads you win, tails I lose' situation up to a point, since if you started well you were bound to get caught up in the sheer repetition thing and if you started badly you'd had it anyway. So she was in no way inclined to use this as an alibi for what was about to happen between herself and Thomas Marsham.

She had met Thomas at an adult education class in philosophy run by the local university where he had tried to explain to a group of housewives, retired schoolteachers and weirdos what Wittgenstein had meant by sentences like: 'The World is all that is the case'.

Jenny had not understood Wittgenstein, as she had not really understood Kant or Descartes or the doctrines of logical positivism, but over a cup of coffee in the university canteen she found that she understood Dr Marsham.

He was a few years older than she was, with wild hair already turning grey and short-sighted blue eyes behind thick glasses: an untidy, chain-smoking, neglected-looking man with beautiful hands and a formidable intelligence which he concealed with idiotic jokes, self-denigration and buffoonery. He had married, at Cambridge, a Girtonian with a First in Anthropology whose academic career matched, and now seemed likely to surpass, his own. Between expeditions to the He-He in Basutoland (whose adopted tribe member she was), broadcasts and committee meetings, Professor Marjorie Marsham found life a full and absorbing business and though extremely fond of Thomas, was inclined to communicate with him mostly through little notes propped against the tea-pot informing him how and when to empty the dustbins and roughly what day she could expect her back from Basutoland.

It was therefore with a pleasure whose innocence at first entirely misled him that he looked at Jenny Craig with her snub nose, shining curly brown hair and trusting grey eyes, and listened as she apologised for her lack of education, the fact that she had 'only' been a shorthand typist before her marriage, and confided in him her longing to avoid the 'coffee morning' set-up now that her two children were both at school. With students he was careful, even shy, but this little housewife with her shining cleanliness, her readiness to be impressed by the glory of learning, found him with his defences down.

The first cup of coffee in the canteen after the lecture had been followed by others, as often as not chaperoned by some other member of the class. The way that Jenny looked round the filthy refectory with its plastic cups and garish walls, the wistful look with which she breathed in the 'academic' atmosphere, touched him profoundly. Without realising it, he was starved of comfort, comeliness and grace and these old-fashioned qualities he found in this woman who apologised with every second sentence for her lack of brains.

Inevitably, there came a day when Philip was away on a business trip, Professor Marsham was recording a broadcast in Manchester on the initiation rites of the Wai-Titi and Jenny's mother was staying with her and longed only to put the children to bed undisturbed.

'I suppose. . . you wouldn't care to come to the concert in the City Hall?' asked Thomas hesitantly, and waited – as the nicest men seem to go on doing all their lives – for a rebuff.

'I'd love to,' said Jenny, overcome by the honour of being chosen by the lecturer. 'It's the Brahms Fourth, isn't it? I love that. The bit in the second movement. . .'

So they went to the concert.

A shared love of great music is known to be the greatest aphrodisiac of them all. If it had been Bach, Jenny thought later, perhaps it would have been all right. We might have been uplifted, but not the other thing. Instead, in the second movement, at the exact phrase that always sent her soaring, Thomas turned and smiled at her. After which the thing was done.

They walked home hand in hand through the darkening streets of the industrial city which had suddenly become Elysium. The uncertainty and fear of rebuff were over, the plotting and scheming not yet begun. A halcyon interval; the best, perhaps, in any love affair. They kissed chastely and parted. Thomas had his hair cut, bought a new shirt and gave a series of lectures on 'The Nature of Speech Acts' which left even the stroppiest of his students gasping with admiration. Jenny sang about the house, lingered in her garden to touch the papery calices of her daffodils and bought a new nightdress to take off for Philip when he got back from his trip.

Both of them felt wonderfully happy and very, very *good*.

There followed the next stage, so familiar to all who have trodden this well-worn path: the attempt to open up the friendship, fit it into the quadrilateral of conventional married life. Jenny accordingly gave a little dinner party for Thomas and his wife and the most intellectual of Philip's business friends, a couple who had done PPE at Oxford.

The dinner party was a success. Jenny wore a dark red skirt and a white blouse and cooked *Boeuf Bourguignon* and *Crème brûleé*. There was a great deal to drink. Philip liked Thomas, who was extremely witty about university politics, and Jenny liked Professor Marjorie who made her laugh like anything about the kinship systems of the He-He. By this time, however, it was too late, Thomas and Jenny retaining little from the evening except the look in the other's eye.

It was now that Jenny began to fight. She fought honestly and hard – for her husband, Philip, whom she truly loved; for her own peace of mind and sense of honour, her deep-rooted, uncomplicated belief in an open life; above all for her children, who would pay the price if her indiscretions ricocheted.

She had always turned to the printed word for comfort, so now she removed from her bedside table the women's magazines, biographies and novels with which she usually read herself to sleep and substituted – but gradually, so as not to arouse Philip's suspicions – the great cookery books of religion and ethics wherein the sages of the world have given their recipes for the good life. Thus Jenny borrowed, bought or scrounged the *Tao Te Ching* (which informed her that Desire is Illusion), the *Dhammapada* (which besought her to Straighten her Mind like a Fletcher Straightens his Arrow) and the *Meditations of Marcus Aurelius*, that great Stoic, who regarded it as essential to have nothing in one's mind that could not immediately be spoken aloud to others. She read also a treatise called *The Sovereignty of Good over Other Concepts* and just to keep her options open, she read the *Quiet Corner* of Patience Strong.

The only thing she didn't read was the Bible. She didn't read the Bible because she knew what the Bible had to say on the subject of adultery. The Bible said one should not commit it. As far as she could remember, the Bible did not say *why* one should not commit it, it just said one should not. This struck Jenny as useless and unfair; also old-fashioned in a way which even she, morally stranded as she apparently was in the Middle Ages, regarded as going altogether too far.

She struggled on in this way for several weeks and in his smoke-filled, book-littered room in the university, Thomas Marsham – nominally finishing a thesis on 'The Relationship of Quality to the Objective World' – struggled also. Though more intelligent than Jenny, he was not a great deal wiser, nor did the discipline of his subject greatly aid him for philosophy has never been famous for producing men able to bring the concepts of duty, truth and morality to bear on their private lives.

Philip, throughout this time, remained fond and attentive. Jenny would not in any case have attempted the 'he takes me for granted' routine, since it had always seemed to her that if married people did not grant themselves, each to the other, to take, then marriage was something other than she had supposed.

Term had ended, the lecture course was over. Thomas and Jenny were compelled to meet in secret for occasions referred to as 'only' having lunch or 'only' going for a walk. Perhaps it was the falseness of the word 'only' that made Jenny finally throw in the sponge. Changing her dress three times in order 'only' to meet Thomas for a cup of tea in the refectory, rushing back through the darkening streets with a thumping heart, terrified that the children would be home before her, she experienced such self-loathing at her hypocrisy that for a moment it drowned everything else. That night she packed away the great cookery books of living. The next morning she rang Thomas at the university and in a voice almost inaudible with fright, told him she would meet him in London.

The peace of mind which is supposed to follow any firm decision did not follow. Nor, come to that, did peace of body. But she stuck it out and behaved with efficiency, organising first the confidante so necessary for this kind of enterprise – a warm-hearted, rackety friend called Christine who had divorced her husband and lived a cheerfully promiscuous life somewhere off the Earl's Court Road. Christine sent an eager invitation to an imaginary school reunion; Philip was delighted for her to go; her mother swooped happily on the children and bore them off to her cottage. Jenny threw up in the lavatory, had a hot bath and tottered, light-headed from sleeplessness, on to the 8.57 train.

Thomas was waiting at Euston. He had bought a new jacket and cut himself a little shaving. Meeting, they were suddenly violently shy and embarrassed and in the taxi avoided each other's eyes.

Then, outside the hotel, Jenny suddenly exploded into sophistication, well-being and joy. She felt completely relaxed, wonderfully worldly. There was only one more moment of anxiety and that the worst of all, far transcending any guilt: the terror of not pleasing – and then that, too, was past.

That first time there was mostly relief at having somehow not failed each other, but afterwards they talked in the way that men and women do talk at such a time – perhaps the only time that human speech, being no longer necessary, becomes what it was meant to be. Later they went out to eat and already the alchemy was at work, transforming Thomas from a gauche academic into a courteous and charming host; changing Jenny from a diffident housewife into a subtle and witty woman of the world. When they got back to the hotel they were already old-established friends and lovers and this time found themselves carried by that strange and mysterious act into a place which marvellously mingled gaiety and peace.

Yet when she packed her case the following morning, Jenny thought, well really it wasn't so amazing. No one swung from any chandeliers. We're just people who are fond of each other and wanted to be together. What's all the fuss about? Fidelity . . . adultery . . . all those stupid words. Why do people carry on so? Why did I get in such a state?

They had decided to travel back by separate trains, but Thomas insisted on seeing her off. So once again they stood on the platform at Euston station, smiling at each other, keeping an eye open for acquaintances, thanking each other over and over again.

Then Jenny got on the train and shut the door and lowered the window. And as she felt the door slam between her and Thomas, saw him stand there with his head back, looking at her, his glasses in his hand, she was seized suddenly with an anguish so terrible, so physically overwhelming that she thought she could not bear it. It was as though everything inside her had suddenly imploded – as though each and every organ in her body was collapsing one by one and crumbling into dust – and she cried, 'I can't leave you, I can't, I can't!'

But the train had started; there was only time for a last glimpse of Thomas's face showing the same incomprehensible anguish that was on her own and then they were past the end of the platform, moving between sooty walls and tenements, gathering speed . . .

It was then, standing there in the corridor of the 1.35 to Torchester on a drizzly morning on the twenty-third of June, that Jenny understood about the Bible. She understood why it had said 'Thou shalt not commit adultery' in that stroppy, unequivocal way, and she understood why it had not said *why*. It had not said why because most probably it did not know, or more likely because there were no words for the knowing. But

Jenny, tottering to the buffet car to see if it was yet open and would sell her, so early in the day, a double whisky or perhaps a pint of opium, could have told the Old Testamental gentleman who had penned that bit exactly why. Because to make love is to *make* love and in that plastic hotel behind the British Museum, on a bed most hideously covered in purple candle-wick, she and Dr Thomas Marsham had given birth to this devastating product, had manufactured it as surely and solidly as the Bessemer Process – in the far-off, halcyon corridor of her schooldays – had been supposed to manufacture steel.

There was nothing to be done about it. She had set off on this course and somehow she would work it through and perhaps in the end she would hurt no one, not even herself. But as she travelled homeward, disembowelled and divided, as to a distant, sun-drenched landscape she could never hope to reach, Jenny, drinking whisky and eating hard-boiled eggs (for passion, like pregnancy, most strangely affects the appetite) knew why the Bible carried on the way it did. She wouldn't read it – one didn't any more. But, God, she *knew* . . .

THEATRE STREET

HER NAME was Madame Delsarte. Trained at La Scala, she had danced in all the capitals of Europe, taught with her famous countryman, Cecchetti, in Russia.

Now she was old, the ramrod back held firm against the rigours of arthritis, the dyed hair piled high above a raddled, made-up face. Old, but deeply formidable as she surveyed the intake for the ballet school she now ran in London.

It was a late winter morning in 1931. Pavlova, killed by overwork, had died two months before; Diaghilev too was dead, but they had done their work. Even the English, who prided themselves on being Philistines, wanted their daughters – if not yet their sons – to dance. That morning, over thirty children had been brought to the tall, yellow stucco house in Regent's Park which housed the prestigious Delsarte Academy of Dance. Of these, fifteen had already been rejected. Now, Madame turned her attention to the survivors. They had been weighed and measured, their hearing tested, their ability to sing in tune ascertained. Even so, another five would have to go.

'You can dance now, *mes enfants*,' she said. 'Do anything you wish. Just follow the music.'

The meek little woman at the piano played a Delibes waltz and the children danced. Three revealed themselves immediately as unmusical. There was one boy who was clearly gifted, another who – desperately though she needed boys – would have to go.

But these decisions were made below the level of her consciousness. She was watching only one child.

Someone had taught her and taught her well. There was no precociousness, no dangerous attempt to go up on her toes, yet at nine she had already tasted the control that alone brings freedom. A narrow little face, fawn hair cut in a fringe, large brown eyes. She had been shy at the interview but now she was wholly absorbed. 'Even with her eyelashes, she dances,' thought Madame.

She motioned to the pianist to stop and gave instructions to the two assistant teachers who gently led the casualties away.

'Come here,' said Madame to the child with the fawn hair, and she came, biting her lip and holding back her tears, for this summons could only mean that she had failed.

'Dancers don't grimace,' said Madame Delsarte. She led her to the window embrasure and stabbed her cane at the pianist who broke into a march.

She was alone now with the child. Outside, snow had begun to fall. She could have been back in Russia, at the school in Theatre Street . . .

'What is your name?'

'Alexandra, Madame,'

'And who taught you to dance, Alexandra?'

'My mother.'

The voice was low, sweet, but absolutely English. Why then, this absurd sense of familiarity?

'Mothers are usually a disaster. Is yours a dancer?'

'Yes, Madame. At least she was.'

The pride in the child's voice was unmistakable.

'What is her name?'

The little girl was silent. Silky lashes curtained the downcast eyes. 'I must not say. She told me not to tell.'

'Nevertheless you *will* tell!' The old woman's face was hooded as an eagle's; she tapped with her dreaded cane on the floor.

The child stood trapped. 'Do exactly what they tell you, sweetheart,' her mother had said. 'Just do what they ask.'

She raised her eyes.

'Starislova,' she said. 'Giovanna Starislova. That was her name.'

A long pause. It was impossible that this fierce and terrifying old lady could be crying, yet something glittered in the coal-black eyes.

'Is she here?'

'She is downstairs, Madame. In the hall. She wouldn't come upstairs with the other—'

But Madame, flinging an imperious '*Continuez!*' at her

underlings, was already at the door.

It had begun many years earlier, in a now vanished world. On the fifteenth of April 1912, to be exact, with the visit of a young English officer, Captain Alex Hamilton, to the Imperial Ballet School in St Petersburg.

In Russia as *aide de camp* to his Brigadier who was heading a military delegation sent to discuss the establishment of a joint garrison in Badakhshan, that notorious trouble spot north of the Hindu Kush, he had already experienced Russian hospitality at its most lavish: at a banquet at Prince Yussoupov's palace from which guests were still being carried two days later; at a dinner in the mess of the Chevalier Guards which had ended in a dawn visit to the gypsies on the Islands; and – more decorously – at a luncheon at Tsarskoe Selo with the Tsar, his wife and four pretty daughters.

Now, politely concealing his boredom, he entered with the Brigadier, a fellow officer seconded from the Indian Army, and Count Zinov, his Russian host, the portals of the Tsar's own ballet school in Theatre Street. He was aware that an honour was being conferred on him. In Vienna, he would have been shown the Spanish Riding School with its 'white pearls', the horses of Lippiza; the Italians would have taken him to the Opera. The Russians showed him the cradle of the art they had brought to a perfection unequalled anywhere in the world: the ballet.

Not every visitor was taken to Theatre Street, Rossi's lovely silent row of ochre-coloured and garlanded buildings, whose high, bare rooms – half palace, half convent – housed the school. At ten years old they came here, small girls with anxious eyes clutching their shoe-bags, to be paraded, measured, prodded and examined and – if admitted – put through eight years of the hardest training in the world. Small vestal virgins, these girls, in their blue wool dresses, their white aprons, their relentlessly braided and pulled-back hair. They slept in dormitories, all fifty of them, moved everywhere under the gaze of a posse of governesses, were forbidden even to speak to the boys on the floor above with whom they practised their polkas and mazurkas.

Then, at eighteen, they joined the Maryinsky Ballet, to become for the twenty or so years of their working life, snowflakes, or swans or sugar-plum-fairies . . . or once, every so often, that other thing. From the door Alex was now entering had emerged Pavlova, anguished about her thinness and frailty . . . Karsavina, destined to be Diaghilev's darling . . . and that eighth wonder of the world, Nijinsky.

These hallowed ghosts were entirely invisible to Alex Hamilton as he crossed the hallway to be greeted by the formidable Principal, Varvara Ivanova. He was in every way a product of his class, trained to conceal anything which might single him out for attention. If nothing could be done about his good looks, his wide grey eyes, it was at least possible to barber and brush his hair so as to minimise its russet glint, its spring. His high intelligence he dealt with by speaking as seldom as possible. His knowledge of foreign languages – so deeply un-British – could be glossed over in a man who had, after all, won the Sword of Honour in his last year at Sandhurst. At twenty-six, it was inevitable that he should have known and pleased women, but the only emotion he had hitherto found uncontrollable was the homesickness which had attacked him when he woke, at the age of seven, in the barred dormitory of his prep school, and realised that as a result of some crime he was not aware of having committed, he was banished – perhaps for ever – from the adored gardens and streams and sunlit water meadows of his Wiltshire home.

It is perhaps worth adding that he was not musical. An unfortunate experience at *Tosca* when the heroine, after leaping off the battlements, had apparently bounced and reappeared, had left him with a distaste for opera. The only ballet he had ever seen – a *divertissement* from *Coppelia* inserted into a review at the Alhambra – had bored him stiff.

But the Principal was welcoming them in French, and the Brigadier's bulbous nose twitched at Alex, instructing him to take over the conversation. Following her through the archway, they encountered a crocodile of tiny girls in fur-trimmed pelisses – each with a neatly-rolled towel under her arm, bound for the weekly ritual of the steam bath in a distant courtyard – passed through a vestibule where a huddle of infant Ice Maidens, pursued by maids with hair-brushes, waited to be conveyed to a matinée at the Maryinsky – and were led upstairs.

Explaining the routine of the school as she went, Varvara Ivanova took them through a dining room with oil-cloth covered tables, threw open the door of a classroom to reveal a pigtailed row of girls having a lesson in notation, another in which the pinafored pupils were dutifully drawing a vase decorated with acanthus leaves . . . And down a long corridor hung with portraits: of Taglioni, the first sylphide of them all whose ballet shoes, when she retired, had been cooked and eaten by her besotted admirers . . . of Legnani, whose thirty-two *fouettés* when she first came to Russia had had every child in Theatre Street pirouetting and turning in an agony of emulation.

They had come to the heart of the building and everywhere, escaping even the heavy double doors with their crests of Romanov eagles, came snatches of music. Fragments of Brahms waltzes, of *études* by Chopin or by some unknown hack, repeated again and again, relentlessly rhythmical, their only function however exalted their source, to serve the *battements* and *glissées* and *arabesques* that were these children's alphabet.

'You will wish to see our advanced class, I imagine,' said the Principal, 'The girls who next year will leave us to join the *corps de ballet*. Some of them are already very talented.' She consulted the watch pinned to her belt. 'They will be in Room Five.'

Alex translated, the Brigadier nodded and Count Zinov pulled his moustache happily at the thought of the seventeen-year-olds. Suppressing a sigh, for he had hoped to visit a Cossack officer who had promised to show him his horses, Alex stood aside for his superiors as Varvara Ivanova opened yet another door.

The room they entered now was high and bare with three long windows, a *barre* running round the walls and everywhere mirrors. There was a white and golden stove, a portrait of the Tsar . . . a wooden floor raked like the stage of the Maryinsky. In the corner, beside them as they entered, was a middle-aged woman, ugly as a toad, coaxing with stumpy, mottled fingers a soaring phrase from a Schubert Impromptu out of the upright piano.

And all round the walls, girls in white practice dresses, one hand on the *barre* . . .

'*Continuez, s'il vous plait,*' ordered the Principal. 'These gentlemen wish to see the class at work.'

The pianist resumed her phrase and the girls, who had paused with demure and downcast eyes, lifted their heads.

'Let me have your *pliés* again,' ordered the *maîtresse de ballet*.

'One, two . . . good . . . up . . . *demi plié* in fourth . . . close. . .'

Alex looked on idly. Five girls on the far wall beneath the portrait of the Tsar; six on the wall next to the corridor . . . another six along the window. It was this row he watched absently. Two very dark girls . . . a fair one . . . one with red hair . . .

And then a voice inside his head pronouncing with ice-cold clarity the words: '*This is the one*'.

He did not at first understand what had happened, it was so patently impossible and absurd. Indeed he shook his head, as at some trifling accident, and let his eye travel again to the beginning of the row. The first girl, dark with a narrow Byzantine head; the second, dark also though a little taller; the third with that grey-eyed, blonde beauty that Pushkin gave to all his heroines; then the red-head . . . And now as he reached the girl who was fifth in line he ducked mentally, leaving a space, and came to the last one, another dark-eyed Circassian beauty.

Then, carefully, painstakingly, he let his eyes travel back to the girl who was fifth in line – and again, clear as a bell, the voice in his head said: '*Yes*'.

The fragment of Schubert gave way to an extended phrase from Bellini and the girls went into their *battements*. His face taut, Alex studied her.

She had a neat and elegant head, but so did all the other girls. Her arms were delicate and perfectly proportioned, her neck high and almost unnaturally slender – but so it was with all of them: how could it be otherwise, hand-picked and measured as they were? She moved with flawless grace and musicality, – and if she had not done would long ago have been sent away, so what was noteworthy in that? Her brown hair was scraped back off a high forehead; just one curl, escaping its bondage, cupped her small ear. Her eyes, too, were brown, but only brown – not liquid with oriental promise as with the girl who stood beside her.

Why then – for God's sake, *why*?

The music had stopped. The girls stood quietly, their feet in the fifth position, their eyes cast down.

Except for this one girl; a good girl, hitherto known for her modesty and quietness, who now lifted her head, looked directly and with an expression of the most extraordinary happiness at the handsome English officer – and smiled.

Her name was Vanni. Giovanna, really, for the route that classical ballet had taken – Milan to Paris, Paris to St Petersburg – was reflected in her ancestry. Both her parents had been dancers and came to settle at the Maryinsky. At nine, dressed in white muslin, Vanni had carried her shoe-bag through the portals of the Ballet School for her audition as inevitably as Alex, dressed in grey shorts and a blazer with towers on the pocket, had climbed into his prep-school train.

She was an excellent pupil, industrious, obedient. Her teachers liked her; she got on well with the other girls.

Then, at a quarter-past three on the fifteenth of April, 1912, a week after her seventeenth birthday, in the middle of a *cou de pied en devant*, she felt . . . something.

When the music stopped, she turned and saw in a group of people standing by the piano only one man. A man who, in the now silent room, calmly and deliberately crossed the expanse of empty floor and came to stand, as she had known he would, in front of her.

It was a piece of extraordinary effrontery. The Principal hissed; the Brigadier stared, unable to believe his eyes; the other girls giggled nervously. The Tsar himself would have hesitated thus to single out one girl.

'What is your name?' said Alex. He spoke in French, the language of the dance, and urgently for it could only be minutes before they were separated.

'Vanni. Giovanna Starislova. My school number is 157. I shall be here until May 1913, then at the Maryinsky.'

She had understood at once; given him what he needed.

'I'm Alex Hamilton of the 14th Fusiliers. My home is Winterbourne Hall in Wiltshire.'

She nodded, a frown mark between her eyes as she memorised these English names. Quickly he took possession of his territory. A small bridge of freckles over the nose, gold glints in the brown eyes, lashes which shone like sunflower seeds . . . There was a tiny mole on her left cheek; a fleeting scent of camomile came from her hair. 'She is *good*,' he thought blissfully. 'A good girl'. It was a bonus, unexpected.

'I will come back,' he said. His voice was very low, but each word as distinct as when he briefed his soldiers. 'I don't know when, but I shall return.'

She had folded her slender hands as women do in prayer. Now she tilted them towards him so that her fingertips rested for a brief moment on his tunic.

'I will wait,' she said.

Alex returned to England. Vanni was sent for by the Principal and questioned.

The questions yielded nothing. No, said Vanni, standing with downcast eyes in her blue serge dress, she had never seen the Englishman before and he had written no notes to her, made no assignations.

Then why had she smiled in that brazen manner, asked Varvara Ivanova, who could still recall the unmistakable radiance, the *intention* behind that smile.

Vanni shook her head. She did not know. But though usually so well-behaved and obedient, she did not apologise and the Principal decided not to prolong the interview for even at the mention of the Englishman, the girl became illumined, as if she had swallowed a small and private sun.

So Vanni was punished – refused permission to visit her parents for three successive Sundays – and watched. But there were no further misdemeanours. When a boy on the floor above sent her a red tissue rose from his Easter cake, she returned it. No letters came from England and at rehearsals, when the older pupils went to augment the Cupids and nymphs of the *corps de ballet* she was conspicuous for *not* making sheep's eyes at the handsome *premier danseur*, Vassilov.

If she was still watched when she returned for her last year at the school, it was for a different reason.

'There is something a little interesting, now, in her work,' said Cecchetti, the most famous dancing master in the world, to Sonia Delsarte who taught the senior class. 'And she seems stronger.'

But what he meant was 'happier'.

In May 1913, a year after Alex's visit, she left the school in Theatre Street and became a member of the *corps de ballet* at the Maryinsky Theatre. Her salary was six hundred roubles a month, her future assured. For her parents – for Vanni herself as they believed – it was the fulfilment of a dream.

Back with his regiment on Salisbury Plain, Alex threw himself into his work. In the summer he took his battalion to Scotland for manoeuvres. Getting his men fit, turning them into first-class soldiers, occupied him physically. At night in his tent he read the technical manuals which poured from the world's presses now that his profession was growing ever more complex and scientific. And when his army duties permitted he went down to Winterbourne, the estate which, since the death of his father two years earlier, had been wholly his.

It was a place of unsurpassed and Arcadian loveliness. A Queen Anne house of rosy brick faced south across sloping lawns which merged with water meadows fragrant, in summer, with yellow iris and cuckoo pint and clover. Sheltered by verdant hills, Alex's farmlands were rich and lush; the cows that grazed in the fields were the fattest, the most reposeful cows in the southern counties; his sheep moved in dreamy clusters as if waiting to be addressed by the Good Shepherd Himself. With Alex's position at Winterbourne went the position of Master of Fox Hounds, a seat on the Bench, an elaborate system of duties to tenants and fellow landowners alike.

It could not be – surely to God it could not be – that to share these duties he proposed to install a dancing girl, probably of low birth, whom he had glimpsed for five minutes in a strange barbaric land.

For as the months passed, the memory of that extraordinary encounter became more and more blurred and dreamlike. He could remember Vanni's posture at the *barre* but her face increasingly eluded him. So when his stately widowed mother told him that the Stanton-Darcys were coming for the weekend and bringing Diana, Alex was pleased. He had attended Diana's coming-out ball, sat next to her at Hunt dinners. She was twenty-one, sweet, with curls as yellow as butter, large blue eyes and a soft voice.

Diana came. The weekend was a great success. She went with Alex round the farms, the tenants took to her, his factor presented her with an adorable bulldog puppy. She was already a little in love with him – being in love with the handsome foxy-haired Captain Hamilton had been the fashion among the debutantes of her year. Yet somehow it happened that three months later she became engaged to the Earl of Farlington's youngest son, for girls with blonde curls and big blue eyes do not lie about unclaimed for long.

Alex's mother swallowed her disappointment and tried

again. Selena Fordington was an heiress – unnecessary in view of Alex's considerable wealth – but agreeable none the less: a quiet, intelligent girl whose plainness vanished as soon as she became animated. Alex liked her enormously, took her to Ascot and Henley – and introduced her to his best friend who promptly married her.

A year had passed since his visit to Russia and his longing to be ordinary, not to be singled out in this bizarre way, grew steadily. Yet the following winter he stood aside and let Pippa Latham go. Pippa, his childhood love, a tomboy with the lightest hands in the hunting field and a wild sense of humour, who returned from India a raven-haired beauty with a figure to send men mad . . .

It was time to return to Russia and lay his ghosts. His and hers, for Vanni, if she remembered him at all, was probably living under the protection of a wealthy balletomane or even married to a dancer with hamstrings like hawsers and long hair. He would take her out for a meal, buy her a keepsake . . . They would laugh together about what had seemed to happen in that high bare room in Theatre Street, wish each other luck . . . And he would return to his country a free and normal man.

Thus at the end of May 1914, having arranged to take the long leave owing to him, Alex set off again for Russia.

His host, the hospitable Count Zinov, was overjoyed to see him, but apologetic.

'It is the last night of the Maryinsky season – a gala performance of *Swan Lake*. It would be hard for my wife and me to miss it, but if you did not feel like joining us we could arrange for you to dine with friends. I know you do not care for ballet.'

Alex bowed. 'I would be honoured to accompany you,' he said.

The Maryinsky is a blue and golden theatre, sumptuous beyond belief. The chandeliers, all fire and dew, drew sparks from the tiaras of the women, the medals of the men. The Tsar was in his box with his wife and two eldest daughters. The Grand Duchess Olga had put up her hair.

In the Zinovs' *loge*, Alex joined in the applause for the conductor. Tchaikovsky's luscious soaring music began . . . The curtain rose.

Act One: A courtyard in Prince Siegfried's Palace . . . The courtiers parade in cloth of gold. The peasantry arrive with gifts for the Prince. They dance. They dance, it seems to Alex, for a remarkably long time. The King and Queen approach their son. It is his birthday, they inform him in elaborate mime; it is time to choose a bride.

But the Prince – the great Vassilov in suitably straining tights – does not wish to marry. He grows pensive . . .

The music changes, becomes dark and tragic. Swans, seemingly, are flying overhead. The Prince is excited. He will go and hunt them. His courtiers follow.

The curtain falls.

An interval . . . champagne . . . a French Countess in the next box flirting outrageously with Alex.

And now, Act Two. This of course is the act that *is* the ballet. A moonlit glade . . . a lake . . . a romantic ruin, some equally romantic trees. To the world's best loved ballet music, the doomed Swan Queen enters on her pointes. She is in a white tutu with a tiny crown on her lovely head, and on the night in question is greeted by sighs of adoration for she is danced by the fabled Kschessinskaya, once mistress of the Tsar.

The crown on her head is useful, for were she to be danced by anyone less exquisite it might not be easy at once to distinguish her from her encircling and protective swans.

Just how many swans there are in *Swan Lake* depends of course on the finances and traditions of the company, but there are a remarkable number and the discipline and precision with which they conduct themselves can make or mar this master-piece. Perfect unity, the ability to act as one is what the Russians demand and get from their *corps.* Identical in calf-length tutus, their hair hidden by circlets of feathers, their arms and faces blanched by powder, these relentlessly drilled girls would have made peas in a pod look idiosyncratic.

So now, despairing at her fate (for she is, of course, an enchanted princess) Odette glides forward. A row of fifteen swans *jeté* from stage left towards her, so far away on the vast stage that their faces are nothing but a blur. Fifteen more come from stage right. Ten swans enter diagonally from both the upstage corners. And from the centre, as if from the lake itself, the last row of girls, their fluttering arms crossed at the wrists, doing their *battements* . . .

The first swan, the second, the third . . .

At which point, the voice in Alex' head which had been silent for two years said, '*That one*'.

Two hours later he waited at the stage door among a crowd of students and admirers. The orchestra came out first: tired men in shabby overcoats carrying their instruments. Then the first group of girls, chattering like starlings, excited at the long summer break ahead . . . and another . . .

And now three girls: a curly red-head, a dark Circassian beauty and in the middle . . .

'Come on, Vannoushka,' begged the curly-haired Olga.

'No . . . you go on.' Vanni had stopped, hesitant and bewildered, like a fawn at the edge of an unfamiliar clearing. 'I feel . . . so strange.'

Alex had been hidden at the back of the crowd. Now he came forward, walked up to her, bared his head.

'We met two years ago, in Theatre Street. I said I would return. Do you remember?'

And she said, 'Yes.'

They went to Paris, the Mecca of all Russians. When they arrived, he booked two rooms at the luxurious Hotel Achilles in the Rue St Honore. They dined in its magnificent restaurant, strolled in the Tuileries Gardens. Then he took her upstairs, let her into her room and went on into his own room next door.

An hour later, leaning out of the window, he heard one of the most heart-rending sounds in the world: that of someone trying not to cry.

'What is it, Vanni?' he said, throwing open her door. 'For God's sake, my darling, what's the matter?'

She was sitting in her white nightdress on the edge of a four-poster bed. Her long brown hair was loose about her shoulders and the tears were rolling silently, steadily down her face.

'Why did you bring me, then?' she managed to say. 'If . . . I do not please you. You knew I was not pretty . . . You knew. . .'

Appalled, he began to babble . . . about marriage . . . about respect . . . he was going to the Embassy tomorrow to arrange . . .

'But it is not tomorrow,' she said, bewildered. 'It is now. It is today.'

The years of his idiotic upbringing, the taboos and conventions he had drunk in with his mother's milk dropped from him. He took her in his arms. And from that moment, all that night and the next night and the next, always and always, it was today.

They moved to a little hotel in a narrow street on the Left Bank. Their room was on the top floor, under the steep grey roof. If she leant out of their attic window – but he had to hold on to her – she could just see the silver ribbon of the Seine. It was hot as summer advanced, the pigeons made an appalling din under the eaves and they spoke of moving on . . . to the Dordogne with its golden castles and wild delphiniums and walnut trees . . . or to Tuscany with its blue-hazed hills.

But they didn't move. They stayed in Paris, dazed by their happiness, watching the city empty for summer.

It is, of course, religion that is meant to do it: meant to make people take true delight in momentariness, meant to make them aspire to goodness, to let go of the clamorous self. Alas, it is so very much more often a complete, requited and all-too-human love.

A dancer's body is a kind of miracle. She seemed to talk with her feet, the back of her neck, her small, soft ears. As she moved about their little room, learning it by heart, touching with questing fingertips the brass knobs of the bed, the chest of drawers, the buttons on his jacket as it lay across a chair, he could not take his eyes from her fluent grace. Yet she had the gift of all true dancers: she could be absolutely, heart-stoppingly still.

They lived like children. He had had servants or batmen all his life; she had been brought up in an institution. To go to the baker, buy a long *baguette,* sit on a park bench crumbling it for each other, and the birds, was an enchantment. They fed each other grapes in the Bois, spent dreamy afternoons gliding down the river in a *bateau mouche.* In the sun she grew golden; the brown hair lightened; hair, skin, eyes merged in a honey-coloured glow.

Alex disapproved. 'When we came you had eight freckles across the bridge of your nose,' he said, pulling her towards him in the Luxembourg Gardens and getting a Gallic nod of approval from the park-keeper. 'Now you've got twelve. I don't remember giving you permission to change.'

'It's happiness,' she said. 'Happiness gives you freckles, everyone knows that.'

'Rubbish! I shall buy you a parasol.'

So he bought her a most expensive sky-blue parasol, much fringed and embroidered with forget-me-nots – and the same afternoon threw it off the Pont Neuf because it prevented him from kissing her.

A wealthy and a generous man, it had been his intention to buy her beautiful clothes, present her with jewels, but here his luck was out. To the information – conveyed by Alex as they breakfasted off hot chocolate and croissants on the pavement of their personal café – that they were bound for the *couture* houses of the Rue de la Paix, she reacted with wide-eyed despair. 'Ah, no, Alex! They will take me from you and put me in booths and there will be ladies with pins!' Nor could he lure her into Cartiers, with its magnificent display of rings and brooches.

Then on Sunday at the *marché aux puces*, as they wandered between the barrows she suddenly picked up a small gold heart on a chain. On one side was engraved the word: *Mizpah*. She turned it over. 'Look, Alex; the words are in English. Read them.'

'*The Lord watch between thee and me when we are absent one from another,*' he read. He looked at her face. She was learning English quickly; she had understood. 'You want it?'

'Please!'

'It's only a trumpery thing,' he complained – but he paid, without bargaining, the absurd price the stallholder asked, and as he bent to fasten it round her neck he kissed her suddenly, unashamed, on the throat and said huskily: 'He *will* watch, my beloved. He will watch between us.'

Alex continued to besiege the Embassy, the immigration office, more determined than ever to take her back to England and arrange their marriage, but they were beset by delays. She had not brought the right papers from Russia; until her parents sent them, they were helpless.

'Incompetent, bureaucratic idiots,' raged Alex when the official he was dealing with dared to go on holiday.

But there was one absolute solution; one unfailing panacea nowadays for anything which vexed Alex. On the first night, in their room under the eaves, Vanni had begun herself to unpin her hair and he had forced down her hand and said, 'No, that's my job. That is for me to do.' Now always he would say, 'Come here,' standing with his back to the window, and she would come to him and bend her head and then carefully, methodically, he would remove one by one the hairpins with which she secured her heavy, high-piled tresses. 'Things must be done properly,' he would say, laying the pins neatly in a row on the sill. 'No cheating.' And it was only when he had laid the last pin beside the others that he allowed himself to pick her up, the cool silk of her loosened tresses running down his arms, and carry her to bed.

'Yes, but what about my soul?' she protested. 'I am after all, mostly Russian. Souls are important to us.'

'I'm mad about your soul, *je t'assure*,' he murmured. 'I see it quite clearly – a sort of soft, blue-grey colour. The colour of peace. Afterwards I will tell you. . .'

And afterwards he did tell her. He spoke to her indeed as he had not believed it was possible to speak to another human being.

'It must be reincarnation,' she said. 'That's the only way one can explain the way we knew each other, just like that.'

'Nonsense,' he murmured. 'You may have been one of Tutankhamen's temple dancers, but I'm damned certain I wasn't his High Priest.'

'No, you were certainly not a High Priest,' she said demurely, 'but perhaps you were a great Crusader on a horse . . . and you saw me in the slave market at Antioch. There were hundreds of slaves, all very beautiful, tied up in chains, but you saw me and said—'

'*This is the one*,' quoted Alex.

'Yes.' She looked at him sideways. 'You're sure it was me you wanted, not Olga? She has such marvellous red hair. Or Lydia . . . ? Someone has written an ode to Lydia's kneecaps, did you know? Are you *sure* it was me?'

'Well, I think it was you,' said Alex, lazily teasing. 'But I'm not absolutely certain. Perhaps if you would just come a little closer.'

'But I'm already very close,' she protested, not unreasonably, for her head lay against his chest.

'Not close enough.' His voice suddenly was rough, anguished, as he was gripped by one of those damnable intimations of mortality that are the concomitant of passion.

But it was not of mortality that they thought during that sweet and carefree summer of 1914. It was rather of the future that Alex spoke, lying in the dark after love – and of his home. And she would listen as to a marvellous fairy tale, learning her way in imagination out of the French windows of the drawing room, down the smooth lawns to the lake with its tangled yellow water-lilies and the stream over which the kingfisher skimmed. She learnt the names of his farms: Midstead . . . South Mill . . . and of his fields: Ellesmere . . . High Pasture . . . Paradise . . .

'Paradise!' she exclaimed. 'You have a field called Paradise?'

She heard about his dogs: the gentle huge wolfhound, Flynn, and the bull-terrier bitch, Mangle; and about the Winter-bourne oak, as old and venerable as the house itself . . .

'And there you will live, my darling, and be my wife and my love,' Alex would finish.

'Ah, yes,' she would agree, rubbing her cheek against his face. 'I shall be a great lady and pour milk into my tea and eat ham and eggs and ride on big horses in the fog,' said Vanni, whose image of England had been implanted at a very early age.

They were strolling hand in hand along the quai de Flores when a newsboy came by, calling his 'Extra!'

'What is it,' asked Vanni as Alex bought a paper.

'Just some Austrian Archduke been assassinated,' he said lightly.

'Oh,' she said, relieved. Russia had an unending supply of Archdukes who were constantly being blown up by devout revolutionaries. It was sad, of course; especially when they had been patrons of the ballet.

Alex, in the days that followed, was gayer and more light-hearted than ever, but he redoubled his onslaught on the Embassy – and at night he had to steel himself not to hurry over her hairpins, not to tumble them on the floor in his desperate need to be beside her.

They had most of July, still, to hope as the world hoped. Then Germany declared general mobilisation. France followed. And a telegram came recalling Alex.

For the rest of her life, Vanni needed no map of Hades. Not Dante's limbo with its damned and swirling souls, not the black river Styx. Just Platform One of the Gare du Nord on a bright day in high summer. A well-kept station, geraniums in hanging baskets, sunlight glancing through the glass. All around them, women sobbing and men hugging their girls . . . And Alex, in uniform again, standing quite still beside the train that was to take her back to Russia, folding and unfolding her small hands like a fan.

'It'll be over by Christmas,' they heard a young soldier say – and Alex turned his head, a look of naked envy on his face as he glanced at someone so foolish and so young.

Then the doors began to slam and as she turned to climb into the carriage he said, 'Wait!', and lifted her hat a little – a brave hat trimmed with marguerites – and pulled one silver hairpin from her hair. And then he stood back and let her go.

Vanni had three weeks before the opening of the new season during which to get her body back into shape. It was not enough, but she did it. Her parents had gone to live in the country; she moved into an apartment on the Fontaka with Olga and Lydia and she danced.

In October they gave her one of the slave dances in *Prince Igor* and the *pas de trois* in *La Bayadère*. She was made a *coryphée* . . .

Her modest success passed in a haze. She lived for letters from the front.

'There's a letter from France,' Grisha, the old doorman, would say as she came in for her morning class, his eyes shining with happiness on her behalf.

'There's a letter, Vannoushka,' Olga would whisper, hurrying into the *foyer de danse* for a rehearsal. 'Hurry, you just have time.'

Even Vassilov, the Apollo of the Maryinsky, stopped her once on the way to his dressing room to tell her that the post had come.

Alex wrote little of the danger, the horrors he saw daily. It was only indirectly that she gathered he had been promoted, had won the M.C. after only four months of fighting. It was the future – always and only the future that Alex wrote about: their marriage and their life at Winterbourne.

In the spring his letter came from England. He had been hit in the shoulder; he was in hospital; it was nothing.

Vanni rejoiced. He was in hospital; he was safe! Her exultation showed in her work and they gave her the Columbine in *Harlequinade* . . .

She had rejoiced too soon. The wound healed well, Alex refused convalescence and insisted on returning to his men. In July he was back on the Somme.

Then, on a bright October morning, Vanni came into the theatre and found Grisha slumped over his table. It was ten o'clock in the morning, but he was already drunk.

'It may not be. . .' he murmured, and picked up a black-rimmed envelope from Britain.

But it was.

His mother, swallowing her disapproval of the foreign girl who had ensnared her son, had kept her promise to him. She wrote of his incredible bravery, the devotion of his men, the last confused and horrific battle in which, until the shell that destroyed his dug-out, he had conducted himself with a heroism that was already becoming a legend. He had been awarded the D.S.O. . . .

'Oh, God, why doesn't she cry!' raged Olga in the days that followed. 'I cannot bear it!'

But Vanni could manage nothing: not to eat, or talk – or cry . . . only to dance.

One afternoon Sergueeff, the celebrated *régisseur*, found her on the deserted stage after a matinée.

'So,' he said, tapping her with his stick. 'Why are you still here, may one ask?'

She curtseyed. 'I'm sorry, Maestro.'

He examined her. What had happened to her was betrayed in a strange darkening of her hair, her eyes. 'It does not occur to you, perhaps, that you are fortunate?' he enquired.

Somehow she managed to smile. 'No,' she murmured. 'It does not . . . occur to me.'

He sat down on a stage rock and motioned her to do likewise.

'Grief,' he said. 'Sorrow . . . Everyone experiences them. Each day now, there are women who get letters like yours. Sons, husbands, lovers are killed. Their world ends. And what can they do with this grief? Nothing. It is locked inside them; useless. But you. . .'

She was looking at him, trying very hard, as she did these days, to turn the sounds that came from people's mouths into recognisable words.

'You are an artist. For you, sorrow is a force that can be harnessed. It has a use.'

Vanni shook her head. 'I'm not like that,' she said. 'I'm not a great dancer.'

'No. Not yet.' He paused. 'Vassilov wants you,' said the old man. 'That's why I came. We're giving you *La Fille Mal Gardée*.'

'Vassilov! She jumped up, incredulous. 'Vassilov wants to dance with *me*?'

So began one of the most illustrious partnerships in the history of ballet. Anton Vassilov, at the time they began to dance together, was at the height of his fame: a tall, marvellously built dancer of the old school. Vanni brought him her youth, the hunger for work caused by her all-consuming grief. He brought her authority, prestige, the glamour of his name.

The war was going badly for the Russians. Food was scarce, fuel had to be begged for. They danced now for men, many of them wounded, whose eyes had seen what no man should see and live. Yet these were marvellous nights at the Maryinsky – these last nights of the Romanov Empire when Vassilov and the little Starislova gave new meaning to the great *ballets blancs* of the classical repertoire. Men died, that awful year of 1917, with a piece of ribbon from Vanni's ballet shoes in the pocket of their tunics. She was carried shoulder-high through the streets after her first *Giselle*.

The revolution did not greatly affect the company and the new régime treated them well. No one could have been less politically minded than Vanni and her good-natured easygoing partner. Yet in the spring of 1918 they found themselves fleeing the country with forged passports, their dancers' bodies swathed in old coats, walking as if bent and stiff. On the way to a rehearsal they had rescued a little countess, who was trying to make her way into a food queue, from the sport and jeering of the crowd. Someone had denounced them as 'enemies of the people'. An anonymous phone call at three in the morning warned them that they were to be taken for questioning and urged them to leave at once.

At the Finnish border, they were stopped by the ragged peasant soldiers who guarded the new republic. One of them, searching their meagre possessions, saw the glint of the golden heart Vanni wore round her throat. (*'The Lord watch between me and thee. . .'*)

'Give it to me,' he said in his thick dialect.

She stepped back. 'If you want it, you must kill me first,' she said quietly.

He cursed, scowled – and let her go.

Then they were in Finland and free. Free to walk through two hundred miles of forest to the coast . . . and to arrive at last, on a day as foggy as any Vanni had imagined, in a grimy northern English port.

Their fame had long since spread to Europe. De Witte, that gifted impresario, built his London season around them. They had never danced better; there was a new *rapprochement* between them born of the hardships they had shared, and it showed in their work. If her Odette and Giselle now reached a new perfection, it was partly because of Vassilov's unselfish partnering. For he now loved Vanni and wanted them to marry.

'Why not?' he demanded. 'Yes, I know all about the Englishman, but it is *three years!*'

She did not know why not. He was a good man and had shown unexpected courage on their nightmare journey; he could make her laugh.

It was to please Vanni that Vassilov gave up his precious free time to go on the dismal, inconvenient tours of hospitals and army camps on which she insisted, travelling with only an accompanist, and a reduced group of girls, to perform on rickety stages to puzzled soldiers who would greatly have preferred the chorus from *Chu Chin Chow*.

But the day before she was due to dance at an army camp near Devizes she travelled alone, for Vassilov had a sore throat. She booked in at the Red Lion and the next morning took the bus to Winterbourne.

The gate stood open. The elms lining the avenue were just touched with the first gold of autumn.

She knew it all. The lake on her left with the tangled water-lilies . . . the stream . . . and yes, there – a skimming streak of blue – was the kingfisher.

The house, now. Serene, lovely – but shuttered . . . dead . . .

No, not quite. An old man, a caretaker presumably, came out of a side door towards her.

'Can I help you, miss?'

'I am wondering. . .' Her English was still uncertain and fragmented. 'Is the lady . . . Mrs Hamilton . . . The mother of. . .' But it seemed she still couldn't say Alex's name.

The old man stared at her. 'Mrs Hamilton died more than two years ago. In the winter of 1916. Had a stroke and was gone in a couple of hours.'

'I see . . . There is no one here, then?'

'No one, miss.'

Slowly she walked back across the grass, wanting now only to be gone. And then she saw his tree: the great oak he had loved so much. ('It was a whole world to me, Vanni, that tree. There were squirrels in it and little mice and hollows filled with water when it rained. I used to spend hours in that tree.')

She walked up to it and rested her back against the trunk.

And felt suddenly an incredible sense of release. It was as if the grief and anguish that had weighed her down were physically lifted from her. She felt a lightness and something else she could not at first believe.

'I'm happy,' thought Vanni wonderingly. 'Happy!'

The debt of sorrow she had owed her love was paid, then. She was free. And in that instant she saw as clearly as if she really stood before her, the image of a child: her child, a girl, fair-haired and lightly made, waiting to be born – and to dance.

So precise was the moment of her rebirth that Vanni looked at her watch. A quarter-past twelve. Then she walked lightly to the gate.

Back at the hotel, she wondered whether to ring Vassilov and tell him that she was ready now to marry him. But there was time. Everything would unfold in its own way.

Three hours later at the army camp, she danced a *pas seul* from *La Fille Mal Gardée* and a Tommy called Ron Smith, who could barely spell his own name, became a lifelong balleto-mane. Then, as she always did, she accompanied the camp commandant and the doctor on a tour of the hospital.

It was in a magnificent Palladian mansion, a little way from the camp. Long windows, high bare rooms in which men sat playing cards or writing letters, their crutches against their beds . . .

A very silent room, now, with the really sick: the shell-shock cases, those with head wounds. The room had been the private gymnasium of the nobleman who had given his house. There were wooden bars round the walls, a bare parquet floor. And rows of beds . . . eight down one side of the wall by the windows, eight by the left-hand wall, another eight facing her. Identical white beds with grey blankets, many of them screened by identical screens.

Vanni stopped. Her thoughts came to her in Russian, sometimes in Italian or French. But it was in English now that the voice in her head stated matter-of-factly: '*That one*'.

What happened next should have been easy enough to ascertain, yet to the last there were different versions. On one thing, however, everyone was agreed. The famous ballerina moved up to the third bed from the left and said in a voice from which the charming foreign hesitance was entirely absent, 'Take away the screen.'

This done, there were revealed – to the extreme annoyance of the Matron – two of the prettiest nurses (who should have been elsewhere) leaning in concern over patient Number 59613. Really, was there no limit to the fuss that had to be made over this admittedly heroic major with his medals and his amnesia? After all, other men had been decorated three times for bravery, had been grievously wounded and left for dead. Yet even in his present state, the man seemed to possess an unquenchable glamour.

But the girls were ready with their defence.

'We heard him speak, Matron. A name, it sounded like. We thought he might be coming round.'

'At a quarter-past twelve, it was,' said the second nurse, pleased to show her efficiency.

'Rubbish!' said the Matron. 'The patient's been in a deep coma ever since he was repatriated.'

To this interchange the visiting ballerina paid no attention. Instead she removed, for some reason, her small, pillbox hat and handed it to the commandant to hold as if he was a footman. Then she moved over to the bed and knelt down.

She knelt and she waited. Then, after a while, quietly and without emotion, she pronounced the patient's Christian name.

And now there was some disagreement over what happened next. That the man stirred on the pillow and turned his head was indisputable. Indisputable, too, that he smiled: a slow, incredibly peaceful smile quite without awe or incredulity.

At this point, on account of the smile, the nurses were already crying, so that their testimony is not really worth much. The ballerina, on the other hand, did not cry. Rather, as the man's emaciated but still shapely hand lifted itself from the counterpane, she bent her head so that he found, first, her high-piled shining hair.

'He was just stroking her hair,' said the first nurse afterwards; a nice girl, decently brought-up, who hunted with the Quorn.

'Oh, yeah?' said the second, who was deplorably Cockney and working-class.

And it had to be admitted that the Major's long chiselled fingers seemed to move through the brown tresses with a sense of undoubted purpose – to come to rest with what was surely a kind of familiarity on the first hairpin . . . the second and the third. It was probably just an accident – for he was still pitifully weak – that the pins should fall one by one on to the blankets so that presently the dancer's quiet, transfigured face was entirely framed in her loosened hair . . .

But if a certain disquiet nevertheless remained, if the action did not seem to be *quite* that of an English officer and gentleman, the first word with which the gallant major signalled his return to health and sanity was as reassuring and high-minded as anyone could wish.

'Sanctuary,' said Alex Hamilton, and smiled once more, and slept.

'Vanni! *Doushenka! Milenkaya!*'

For all her seventy years, Madame Delsarte ran down the last flight of stairs, and the elegant woman standing in the hall turned and absurdly, in her Chanel coat and sable muff, she curtseyed. To be pulled to her feet, embraced and addressed in a spate of Russian.

'Oh you bad, bad girl!' scolded Madame. 'To give it all up just like that! After such a *Giselle!*' She shook her head. 'How you must have suffered! What a struggle!'

Vanni smiled. 'No. There was no struggle. I never had to think, not for a moment. As soon as I found him again, all I wanted was to be with him.'

'Yes, I can see it in your face, your happiness. He must be a good man, I think, not only a brave soldier. So you have no regrets?'

'None.' But Vanni's eyes rested now, with an infinity of love, on the child who had followed Madame and stood quietly waiting on the upstairs landing.

'Is she—' she began, but found she could not trust her voice.

'She is accepted, of course,' said Madame Delsarte. She paused. Then throwing common-sense, caution, even wisdom to the winds, she put an arm round Vanni and answered the question in her former pupil's gentle eyes. 'Do not fear, *doushenka,*' she said, too softly for the child to hear. 'She is one of us. She will dance.'

THE MAGI OF MARKHAM STREET

IT WAS about the second week in December that I became really desperate about the baby Jesus.

The trouble was, I could see their point very well. Jimmy MacAlpine's point and Russell Taylor's point – and Maggie Burtt's point too, before the school doctor excluded her because of the nits in her hair. We had had real frogs from real frogspawn, real hyacinths thrusting from real black, crumbly soil, a real goldfish with – alas – real fungus on its fins. My class had a thing about real-ness – and it was I who had put it there.

So naturally for the Nativity Play, they wanted a real baby Jesus.

'A proper 'un. Alive,' said Jimmy MacAlpine, standing threateningly in front of me and sending laser beams of will-power at me from out of his violet eyes. Jimmy's mother was dead, his father in prison; so that to cast him as the Angel Gabriel and allow him to annunciate from a step-ladder wreathed in cloud-grey tissue paper had seemed the least I could do. Also, I most terribly loved him.

It was rather a place for love, Markham Street Primary School. Perhaps it was the ugliness outside – the belching chimneys of the Butterworth Chemical Works dwarfing the town; the black, greasy streets; the dank, discouraged river. You had to light it up somehow, so you did it from inside.

But that was only an excuse of course. Mr Hunter, for example, I would have loved even in a green and grassy school, a school with plate-glass windows and an abstract sculpture in the hall. I would have loved him in the King's Road, Chelsea, in a café in Greenwich Village or on the Boulevard St Michel. It didn't need adversity to make me love Mr Hunter.

He was the headmaster – superb in horn-rims, with three

unbelievably beautiful and entirely parallel lines across his forehead and the eyes of a bloodhound which has reached Enlightenment.

It was to Mr Hunter, naturally, that I took the problem of the baby Jesus.

I sought him out at break, in the beastly office which the Education Committee deemed good enough for him: processed-pea walls, a homicidal gas-fire, acres of asphalt framed in the window . . .

'Mr Hunter,' I said quickly, anxious not to waste his time. 'Do you know how I could get hold of a baby?'

Mr. Hunter blinked behind his horn-rims and came back from a long, long way away. His face was unbearably sad and because I loved him I knew that he had been thinking about his sorrow, which is the same sorrow as besets so many head teachers in the poorer English primary schools, namely the lavatories which were too few, too far away, too old . . .

'A baby, Miss Bennet?'

'For the Nativity Play.'

'Ah.'

Mr Hunter had been angelic about my Nativity Play – the more so because recently he had been away on a Drama Course. This course said that old-fashioned, rehearsed plays were right out for young children. Drama, said this course, had to 'Come Spontaneously From Within'. Whereas my play was the old-fashioned kind with the Angel Gabriel in golden wings and Shepherds with tea-towels on their heads and the Virgin Mary (if only they cured her nits in time) singing 'Little Jesus Sweetly Sleep'. And since I and my class had eaten, slept and dreamed the Nativity Play for the past fortnight and were covered in sticking plaster from fixing crowns and stars and golden trumpets, and had to wade knee-deep through bundles of straw every time we wanted to get to a cupboard, I doubted very much whether it could be classed even remotely as 'Spontaneous Drama Coming From Within'.

'There would be certain hazards with a real baby, don't you think?' suggested Mr Hunter now.

'I know, but I don't think it matters. I mean Jesus was real, wasn't he, on earth – he *did* cry, he must have done. I don't want it all prettied up. I want them to feel—'

But here I broke off because what I wanted my thirty-five awful children to feel about the birth of Christ was something I couldn't put into words. So I looked at my reflection in Mr Hunter's horn-rims and wondered whether if I hadn't been wearing a badge which said 'I am Superman's friend' and a chain of glass beads which Jimmy MacAlpine had almost certainly shop-lifted for me from Woolworths, not to mention a decayed chrysanthemum from Russell Taylor's Dad's allotment, I might have found favour in his eyes.

'What about Mrs Burtt?' asked Mr Hunter, rubbing his nose, a gesture he performed with unbelievable grace.

It was a good question. Mrs Burtt could generally be relied upon to do a baby every year – but of course this year some interfering person from the Family Planning had been at her.

'Or Mrs Taylor?'

But as I explained to him, Mrs Taylor too had chosen this year of all years for her sabbatical.

In the end I had to tear myself away from Mr Hunter, the issue unresolved, and go to the staff-room where Miss Crisp, who taught the top class, was busy crunching up a custard cream between her even white teeth and despising me.

In the matter of the all-pervading love at Markham Street, Miss Crisp was quite definitely the exception that proves the rule. She was related to the Butterworths who owned the vast Chemical Works and therefore virtually the town – so that she 'obliged' rather than taught. She was neat and composed and never wore badges proclaiming that she was Superman's Friend or belonged to the Lollipop League. Her class always seemed to be sitting in orderly rows looking at the blackboard and hamsters never got loose in her Wendy House because she didn't keep any. What is more, on Friday *her* Register added up neatly in all directions and when Mr Hunter came to check it she would lean over him complacently, revealing acres of calm and creamy bust.

We worked hard on the Nativity Play all the next week. Lacking the real thing, we had cast the best doll we could find for the baby Jesus, but really it was no good pretending it was a success. There was a static, glassy quality about its pinkly shining face which was the absolute antithesis of the warm radiance the part required. And when Maggie Burtt, still sticky around the head but mercifully restored to me, leant over the manger and said 'Shut yer bloomin' mouth,' instead of 'Hush, my baby' I found it hard to chide her as I should.

In the afternoon, walking home to my digs on the other side of the town, quietly saving Mr Hunter from fire or pestilence or flood, I would succumb to sudden and terrible lusts . . . These lusts were not what you think they were, though I had those too. They were lusts for Jonathan Tobias Butterworth.

Jonathan Butterworth was possibly the most beautiful thing in the whole town – always excepting the three marvellous parallel lines which swept across Mr Hunter's forehead – and really he had reason to be. His father, after all, owned the Butterworth Works and was worth millions, and his mother – acquired by Mr Butterworth during a business trip to the States – had been a famous model.

He was a gorgeous baby, the kind you find on Renaissance ceilings: silky, dandelion-coloured curls; dimples; a sudden stomach-turning smile . . . A natural for a Nativity Play. Almost, one might say, heaven-sent.

The Butterworths, when not living it up in Menton or Acapulco, inhabited a great grey turreted and crenellated mansion separated from the busy road by a high beech hedge. I passed this house on the way to and from school and again at weekends when I went to visit Jimmy MacAlpine who was in a children's home nearby. Now, with the beech leaves curled and withered, I caught agonising glimpses of this clean and reverent-looking baby lying in his high black pram. There were days when he was so close to the road that I could have put out a hand and grabbed him – and Tantalus had nothing on me then.

Once I suggested to Miss Crisp that in view of her relationship with the Butterworths she might like to borrow him for me. It was a joke, but not apparently a good one.

'What, expose him to all the dirt and germs down here! You must be out of your mind!' she said – and grabbed as usual the last of the custard creams.

By the end of the last full week of term I knew that the play was going to be a complete and utter flop. They just couldn't seem to feel the awe, the reverence . . .

'Fear not,' Jimmy MacAlpine would yell lustily from his

step-ladder at a Maggie Burtt about as fearful as a haggis.

''Ere, 'ave some gold,' mumbled the Magi, thumping their offerings like sacks of coal across the baby's chipped and china feet.

I must say Mr Hunter, whose cool, austere and Christian name was Charles, was marvellous. Never once did he say that he had told me so. Never once did he even *hint* that 'Drama Should Come Spontaneously From Within'. And as he picked his way across my classroom that last Friday, dodging collapsible stable doors and avoiding deformed angelic harps, and took with gentle hands the maimed and bleeding thing that was my register, I thought that two hundred rose-pink, low-level toilets with onyx cisterns would not have been too good for him.

By the morning of the performance I had reached that bottomless pit of gloom and apprehension which is reserved for people who get mixed up in producing plays.

And then, just as I was tottering towards the staff-room for morning break, a small boy panted up to me and handed me a note. And when I had read it, hope – no longer a stranger – uncurled inside my sleeping breast. Not only hope, actually, but an idea – rather a *good* idea – though it involved certain risks. So busy was I working it out that I didn't even hear the usually deafening sound of Miss Crisp crunching with white and even teeth, her custard cream.

Mr Hunter was letting us use the hall, at the end of which was a raised platform which made (though it was curtainless) a splendid stage.

By two-thirty the mothers were in their place, the other classes with their teachers had filed in behind them. I pinned on Maggie's mantle for the third time, muttered final instructions to Jimmy MacAlpine and went to the piano out in front. Mr Hunter nodded. I broke into 'A Virgin Most Pure'.

And the play began . . .

I shall never forget it, never! I couldn't see a lot from where I sat at the piano but I could hear and, by heaven, I could *feel*! And even before Jimmy, pale with excitement, had finished annunciating from his ladder, I knew it was going to be all right. Better than all right. A triumph!

All the awe, the wonder I had tried to get across and failed,

were there right now. Joseph leading Mary into the stable with
a sudden, startled look – a look of conspiracy – as though this
birth was a marvellous secret they both shared. Maggie Burtt
herself, crooning over the crib, half-dotty with tenderness. The
shepherds pushing, jostling for a view of the manger . . . Long,
long before the Magi rode in and laid their gifts with fearful
tenderness beside the crib, there wasn't a dry-eyed mother in
the hall.

As a matter of fact, I was a trifle misted-up myself. Which is
why, thumping out, 'Oh Come Let Us Adore Him' for the final
tableau, I did not at once take in the fact that two enormous
blue policemen had entered the hall and were walking, grimly
purposeful, to Mr Hunter's side.

Almost immediately I began to feel sick. So it seems did
Jimmy MacAlpine, for he broke from the tableau on the stage
and dived for my skirt, wriggling off his wings as he came. His
flight was the signal for the other children to jump off the
platform too and seek the shelter of their Mums. One didn't
trifle with policemen at Markham Street.

From the empty stage, the forgotten manger, came a single
sound: 'Gaa!' And then again, imperatively: '*Gaa!*'

I lifted my head. Something was wrong. Very wrong.

Mr Hunter leapt on to the platform and the two policemen
followed. There was a moment's frozen silence. then: 'Will you
come here, please, Miss Bennett?' called Mr Hunter, and there
was something in his voice that I had never heard before.

I dislodged Jimmy and climbed up. Then I stood looking
down at the manger.

Something was wrong all right . . .

There he lay on a snow-white lace-edged cushion, his silky,
dandelion curls adorably tumbled; his dark, measureless lashes
framing the night-blue eyes . . . Lay there, smiling his celestial
gummy smile, flexing his shell-pink toes and crowing in
uncontainable ecstasy. No wonder the play had been a
triumph!

'It's the Butterworth baby all right,' said one of the
policemen.

'Did you know that this baby was stolen from its pram earlier
today, Miss Bennett?' said Mr Hunter, his voice as grey and
relentless as winter rain.

'Of course she knew it! She stole it herself! She as good as told
me she was going to!' Miss Crisp had broken from the audience

and was pointing at me with a shaking finger.

'I saw her myself,' she continued to shriek. 'I saw her at dinner-time sneaking in something wrapped in a shawl.'

The second policeman turned half apologetically to me. 'Seems as someone did see you, Miss, coming down the hill. . .'

I looked over to where Jimmy MacAlpine, pale and shaking, was crouching by the piano. I didn't understand anything, not anything at all.

No, that wasn't altogether true. One thing I understood all right. The cold, hostile, accusing look on Mr Hunter's half averted face.

'Yes, that's right,' I said. 'I did it. I stole the baby from his pram.'

Later they made me go to the police station and asked me a lot of questions. Mr Butterworth was there, blue-jowled and ferocious and though no harm had befallen his baby, there was talk of prosecutions and summonses and a lot of other things I scarcely heard and didn't try to understand.

I was frantic by the time I got back to school, but it was all right. Though the children had all gone, 'Our Les' was exactly where I had left him, tucked into his cardboard box in the corner of the Wendy House.

I pulled it out and looked at him.

All right, so he was no beauty. Was in fact the ugliest baby I had ever seen . . . He had scurf; he had spots and in the stumpy blob which passed for his nose, the mucus bubbled like soup.

Still, he was a baby, a *real* baby and when Mrs Burtt's cousin's sister-in-law had sent a message that morning to say I could have him for the play I'd been overjoyed. So had Jimmy, when I swore him to secrecy and showed him how to put the baby in the manger just before the play began. Jimmy adored secrets – he'd been enchanted at the idea of surprising the others, and where anything living was concerned I knew him to be one hundred per cent gentle and one hundred per cent safe. In the Children's Home, it was Jimmy they put in charge of the younger ones.

So why, why? Why had he left 'Our Les' to snore in the Wendy House and gone to such crazy and dangerous lengths to secure a substitute?

I fetched the thermos and the bottle 'Our Les's' mother had

given me and gave him a feed. Then I went for his clean nappy.

It wasn't on the shelf where I had left it. Instead, a crumpled and soiled object lay rolled-up on the floor near by. Jimmy had changed him, then? Better make sure . . .

I undid the pins. And then, because I knew Jimmy like I knew Mr Hunter (and for the same reason) I understood everything. It was my fault, of course. Everything was my fault. I simply hadn't checked the facts. I had made an assumption about 'Our Les' and the assumption had been crashingly unjustified. And in stressing as I had done throughout the year the strength and vigour, above all the *masculinity* of Our Lord's life on earth I had made sure of one thing. Never in a hundred years would Jimmy MacAlpine allow the part to be taken by a *girl*!

It was almost dark by the time I had taken the baby home and returned to school. Only in Mr Hunter's office a light still burned.

It didn't take me long to scribble my resignation and take it across to him.

'This is what you've been waiting for, isn't it?' I said, slamming the paper down on his desk.

Mr Hunter gazed at it through the horn-rims I would never see again.

'I had hoped you would resign, certainly,' he said. 'The truth is—'

He was interrupted by the shrill, insistent ringing of the telephone. 'Wait!' he commanded and picked up the receiver. I watched his eyebrows shoot up as he listened, doing shatteringly beautiful things to the lines across his forehead which I had always loved so much.

'Miss Bennett is with me now,' he said presently. 'Perhaps you would like to speak to her yourself?' He put his hand over the mouthpiece and turned to me. 'It's Mr Butterworth. As far as I can gather, he wants to give you vast sums of money. Apparently when they got back with the baby they found there'd been an accident on the road outside their house. A lorry skidded on a patch of ice and slewed into their garden. If the baby had been in the pram, he would probably have been killed.'

Dazedly I took the receiver. Miracles make me nervous and this one was too close to the bone in every way. 'Mr Butterworth? Miss Bennett speaking. Listen, Mr Butterworth,

I don't want anything for myself. No, really . . . But there is something that's needed for the school. Badly needed.'

And very carefully, giving precise instructions – for I too had read the catalogues – I told him.

Then I put down the receiver.

'Good-bye, Mr Hunter' I said, stretching out my shaking hand. Mr Hunter ignored it; evidently my incredible nobility had completely stunned him and no wonder. How many men, after all, receive two dozen, low-level pedal-flush toilets at the hands of a girl they have wronged, humiliated and dismissed?

'I was wondering,' said Mr Hunter, still ignoring my outstretched hand, 'how Jimmy MacAlpine got the baby into school?'

'Russel Taylor's brother's box-cart,' I said absently. I had found it abandoned in a corner of the yard. Then I stared at Mr Hunter.

'You mean, you *knew*?' I shrieked. 'You knew all the time and yet you just stood there and let me *resign*?'

'Caroline,' said Mr Hunter – and my hitherto detested Christian name rang in my ears like a celestial glockenspiel. 'You have no idea what a strain it has been having you on my staff.' He rose and took down his coat. 'I'll clear up the business, of course. I just didn't want Jimmy to get pounced on before I'd had a word with the child care people.'

'There were extenuating circumstances,' I said – and explained about 'Our Les'.

Mr Hunter smiled, then he put on his coat and steered me gently out of the door. Glorifying the huddled town, the shadowy chimneys, the Evening Star rose trembling in the Christmas sky.

'I was wondering,' said Mr Hunter, whose marvellous cool, austere and Christian name was Charles, 'whether one might ultimately interest you in a more . . . orthodox way of getting hold of babies?'

I turned and looked at him. 'I am only interested,' I said primly, 'in one particular kind of baby. The kind with horn-rims and parallel lines across its forehead.'

Mr Hunter took my arm and drew it tenderly through his. 'Curiously enough,' he said, 'that's precisely the kind I had in mind.'

It was just eleven months later, at the beginning of November, that Alexander Dominic was born. Though lacking at birth the spectacles I'd craved, he came, otherwise, up to my wildest dreams. But when I offered him, beaming with pride, to the girl who had taken over my class, she turned him down flat. She wasn't doing a Nativity Play, she said. She had been on this course. 'Drama', she said, 'Should Come Spontaneously From Within. . .'

THE LITTLE COUNTESS

IN THE early years of this century my grandmother (whose name was Laura Petch) became engaged to a Mr Alfred Fairburn. A month later she set off for Russia to be a governess.

'Oh,' I said, anguished, when first I heard the story, 'wasn't it awful for you both, being separated so soon afterwards?'

My grandmother, who was very old by then, gave me a look. 'In those days, my dear,' she said, 'people knew how to *wait*.' What with her brave sister Gwendolyn more or less permanently chained to the railings in Hyde Park because of women's rights and her father a doctor in the London slums, my grandmother felt she wanted to *achieve* something before she settled down – and achieve something, in a sense, she did.

So, aged twenty-two, she travelled alone to Moscow and on still further in a slow and stuffy train through endless birch forests and shimmering plains, and even then her journey was not finished, for she took an old wooden boat down the Volga ('Yes, my dear, the *Volga*,' said my grandmother as I sighed) and at last reached the little village of Yaslova on the estate of her employers the Count and Countess Sartov.

And there, on the landing stage, was the whole family to meet her.

The Count, ruddy-faced and smiling, standing beside his Countess, a pale, plump woman who peered anxiously across the sun-dappled water. Their three little boys, Vashka, Mishka and Andrusha, wearing identical sailor-suits and far more interested in the arrival of the boat than of the governess. Petya, the eldest son, all but grown-up, standing aloof; self-absorbed and dreaming.

But it was at the figure of the only girl that my grandmother looked hardest, as she walked down the gangway beneath her parasol. At the Countess Tatiana, aged sixteen, in her white dress and pink sash, for the little Countess was to be her special care.

Grey, gentle eyes; long, dark gold hair; a wide mouth. Typically Russian features, and as she stepped forward to shake hands and greet her governess in the perfect French the family all spoke among themselves, she could have been any well-brought-up Russian girl.

'I'm Tatiana,' said the little Countess, 'but everyone calls me Tata,' and she smiled. At which my grandmother stepped back a pace instinctively. For it occurred to her that it might be difficult not to love the Countess Tata, and to love anyone in this wild, vast country was not what she had intended.

Though she missed her parents, her brave sister Gwendolyn and of course kind and patient Mr Fairburn, my grandmother settled in quite easily to life at Yaslova. In the morning she taught Tata English and supervised her other lessons. In the afternoons she took her for walks, or they went rowing on the lake, or they played croquet. Often they were joined by Petya, the literary and dreamy eldest son, or by Vashka, Mishka and Andrusha whose tutor – an aged and decrepit scholar – usually fell asleep over a volume of Pushkin after lunch.

It was only in the evenings that my grandmother began to feel the strain. For just when she began to think of a light supper and an early night after the day's work, everyone at Yaslova woke up. The Count came in from the stables. The Countess, a devout and dedicated hypochondriac, left her bed. Petya abandoned his books, neighbours arrived by *troika* or on horseback and the samovar was carried out on to the veranda which ran the length of the house.

And there, drinking interminable glasses of tea with raspberry jam and being bitten by mosquitos, everybody, said my grandmother sadly, just sat and sat and sat. Sometimes they talked of the hopelessness of Russia's destiny; sometimes they discussed the total uselessness of their beloved 'Little Father', the Tsar. Occasionally the old tutor would read aloud from Pushkin and everybody would explain to my grandmother (in the French they all spoke, even to say their prayers) how much more beautiful, inflected and sensitive the Russian language was than any other language in the world. And no one, said my grandmother, sighing, *ever* went to bed.

Because she had been careful to read the works of Chekhov, Dostoyevsky and the rest before she came, my grandmother was not really surprised to find that beneath the pleasant routine of a country summer everyone at Yaslova boiled darkly and deeply with hopelessness, yearning and despair.

Darkly and deeply they might boil, but not in secret – and this was because of the diaries. Except for Vashka, Mishka and Andrusha who were mercifully too young, everyone at Yaslova kept a diary. Count Sartov kept a diary. His Countess kept a diary. Petya, their literary and dreamy eldest son, kept a diary. As for the little Countess Tata's diary, it was currently running at volume twelve. And in spite of the beauty, inflectedness etc. of the Russian language, all their diaries were in French.

Though very young, my grandmother – then as now – was a model of rectitude and although everyone left their diaries lying about, she would have died rather than read a single word. After a few weeks, however, she found that this was giving the most bewildered offence.

'But did you not read in my diary my views on Lermontov's poetry?' enquired Petya during an evening session on the veranda.

'Surely I mentioned my symptoms in my diary?' said the Countess, surprised, when my grandmother enquired about the progress of an ailment.

'But, Miss Petch, I wrote it in my *diary*,' wailed Tata when set a composition on the countryside. 'Such a beautiful description of the Zarestry woods!'

The discovery that she was supposed to read all their diaries in addition to her other work depressed my grandmother, but she stuck to her task assiduously. And it soon became clear to her that the Sartov family were in a fairly bad way.

'I live only for poetry! I long only to dedicate my whole being to expressing the truth in words. And yet I am doomed to kill and to teach others to kill,' wrote Petya.

'Why are you doomed to kill?' enquired my grandmother, who had dutifully read this passage on her way to bed.

'Petya is to go into the army next year,' explained Tata. 'He will join the Cadet Corps and be a dashing soldier.'

'It was my grandfather's dying wish,' said Petya and his eyes grew dark.

The Countess Sartov's diary expressed a more physiological

turbulence. 'My head ached all day. A throbbing seemed to go through from my temples to my ear-lobes and it was as though a leaden weight pressed on my stomach', would be a typical entry in the diary of Tata's mother.

The Count's diary my grandmother was always inclined to skip a little. Not that the Count, too, didn't have his troubles.

'For the fifth day we brought Old Bull out to the cow, and again – nothing! Oh, the cursed inaction of all male animals!' was the kind of thing my grandmother had to contend with from the Count.

But of course it was Tata's diary which distressed my grandmother most. For she had been right about Tata; it *was* impossible not to love her. Generous and passionate, open and selfless, Tata in her diary burnt the pages with intimations of a great and dedicated love.

'Oh, to find someone to whom I could belong totally, someone in whose depths I could lose myself!' wrote the little Countess.

And my grandmother would shake her head and sigh, for Tata, it seemed, was destined to be the wife of Prince Kublinsky. And in Prince Kublinsky it would have been hard to discern depths enough to float a tea-leaf.

He was a plump, lardy young man with enough physical signs of dissolute living greatly to disturb my grandmother, who was a doctor's daughter. But his family was old and immensely aristocratic; his father had owned the souls of three thousand serfs and his attentions to Tata, now that he had decided it was time to carry on his line, were considered by all the Sartovs to be a great honour.

And this was the state of things when, about six weeks after my grandmother's arrival at Yaslova, the old scholar who was tutor to Vashka, Mishka and Andrusha quite suddenly died.

He died, it was generally agreed, an enviable and truly Russian death, falling asleep on the stove they lit for him even in summer and failing to wake. But admirable though it was, his death created problems, not the least of which were Vashka, Mishka and Andrusha running wild and driving everybody mad.

So a new tutor was engaged from Moscow. And on a hot grey day in early July, my grandmother went with the rest of the family to the landing stage to meet him.

The boat landed. Nikolai Alexandrovitch leapt lightly on to

the wooden jetty and my grandmother's heart plummeted right down to her neat kid boots and stayed there.

The new tutor was young. He was tall and lightly built and slender. He had large, dark, unutterably expressive eyes, a passionate mouth and leaf-brown hair with copper glints in it.

'Oh dear,' thought my grandmother, watching him bend gracefully over Tata's outstretched hand. 'Oh dear, oh *dear!*'

And as was so often the case with my formidable grandmother, she was perfectly right.

Any lingering hopes she might have had about the new tutor were shattered on the first night when he came and joined them on the veranda. Nikolai was polite but not servile, shy but not tongue-tied and when requested to read aloud from Pushkin did so in a voice of such beauty and depth that even my grandmother (who still understood very little Russian and was getting a bit of a thing about Pushkin) found herself carried away by the sheer beauty of the sound.

Very soon, all her worst fears were realised. Not that Tata's family, deep in its own despairs, seemed to notice anything. The Countess Sartov's diary continued to reflect the state of her liver; Petya mourned yet again his coming incarceration in the army; the Count remained obsessed by the inadequacies of Old Bull. It was thus left to my grandmother to note that Tata was quietly, deeply and heartbreakingly falling into the shattering glory of first love.

'Today I spoke with Nikolai Alexandrovitch about Pushkin. We think so much alike, it is amazing!' wrote Tata. Or: 'Is it not extraordinary? Nikolai Alexandrovitch, too, likes nothing better than to walk in the rain!'

Like the most formidable duenna in fiction, my grandmother watched the young tutor for signs of licence or disrespect. There were none. Nikolai behaved perfectly. Only his pallor, a barely perceptible change in his voice when he spoke to Tata betrayed him. Soon it became impossible for him to remain on the veranda when Prince Kublinsky called and ran his slug hands absent-mindedly up and down Tata's arm. Even so Tata's innocence, Nikolai's integrity might still have saved them had it not been for the picnic in the Zarestry woods.

To my grandmother, accustomed to striding briskly over the Downs with a cheese sandwich in her pocket, the Sartov picnics were a nightmare. There never seemed to be less than three *troikas* and two neighbouring families with whom no one, by the end of the day, was on speaking terms.

And there was the picnic samovar. Even fifty years later, when she described it to me, my grandmother's voice trembled with hatred for the picnic samovar: a huge brass, convoluted beast which lived in a special shed, took hours to light and then sent terrifying sparks over the tinder-dry forest.

It was because of her struggles with this fiend that my grandmother was careless enough to allow Tata to stroll off alone. An hour later, when everyone assembled in the clearing, there was no sign of her.

The forests of Central Russia are not Hyde Park. The Count roared, the Countess blanched; search parties were assembled. And my grandmother, half-demented with guilt, found herself struggling through the undergrowth with Nikolai Alexandrovitch.

Try as she would, she could not in her long skirts keep up with him. So that it was Nikolai, striding between slanting rays of sunlight towards her, that Tata – lost and lonely and bewildered, with wild cornflowers in her hair – saw first, and she ran forward and threw herself into his arms.

It was impossible, my grandmother said, to blame Nikolai in any way. He didn't even *kiss* the girl, just put his arm round her to steady her and murmured something, not in his polite and easy French but in low and throbbing Russian. Even so, as my grandmother came up to them and saw the expression on both their faces, she realised that all was now well and truly lost.

Though she knew she was failing in her duty, my grandmother didn't read Tata's diary the day after the picnic. It was all she could do to bear the pain in Tata's eyes, while the young tutor's cheekbones looked as though they would tear through his face and Vashka, Mishka and Andrusha had to be carried to bed each night, so violent were the games he played with them.

For time was running out and Prince Kublinsky was growing impatient. He detested the country and was anxious, as the summer drew towards its close, to get his affairs settled and return to Moscow. His visits became more frequent, his moist hands moved ever further up Tata's trembling arm. And at the party given to mark Tata's name day, he asked formally for the Countess Tatiana's hand in marriage and was granted it. After which happy event, the Sartov family plunged into total and utter gloom.

'I cannot like Kublinsky,' wrote Petya, 'but what does it matter? We are all victims, all born to sacrifice. . .'

And: 'Give me strength to endure it,' wrote Tata, smudging the page with her tears. 'God give me strength.'

It was August now and the days were shortening. While still weighed down by their own particular sorrows, the Sartovs began to share in a new and general despair.

'Soon now we must return to Moscow,' sighed the Countess.

'We are always so sad when we leave the country,' mourned Tata.

'Only here is there air to breathe,' agreed the Count.

They began to pay long sad farewell visits to their favourite haunts.

'This is the last time we shall ride along this lane,' Petya would sigh, or, 'Let us pick our last blackberries,' the Countess would suggest mournfully. Even Vashka, Mishka and Andrusha were liable to burst into howls of despair as they punted 'for the last time' across the lake or picked a final crop of mushrooms. And wherever they went, through birch woods, along the banks of the river, Tata and Nikolai walked as far apart from each other as they could and, if they were forced by the narrowness of the path into proximity, they flinched as if someone had struck them.

Even so, said my grandmother, she would have behaved beautifully right to the end if she had only ever been able to get any *sleep*. But even when at last she was allowed to go to bed (and the idea always caused deep distress) she still couldn't sleep because her room was above the veranda and it was often three or four in the morning before the last of the visitors dispersed.

On the night she finally broke, she had just dozed off when she was woken by a scene of passionate farewell between a neighbouring landowner and the Count.

'Good night, my little pigeon,' said the landowner moistly. 'We meet too rarely, Vassily Vassilovitch,' replied the Count. After which, overcome by vodka and emotion, they began to sing sad songs taught to them by their wet-nurses from Nizhny Novgorod.

It was during the refrain of one of these, which went '*I love your dreary, vast expanses, Oh, Holy Russia Mother Dear*,' that something in my grandmother quite simply snapped.

She became suddenly and violently homesick. She also became extremely cross. The homesickness took the form of a craving for scrambled eggs, a longing for her quiet, icon-less bedroom on Richmond Hill and a desire to look again on Mr Fairburn's calm and well-remembered moustache.

The crossness took a different form. My grandmother rose and from her bureau drawer she took out the large black fountain pen which had been a farewell present from Mr Fairburn. Then she put on her dressing-gown and crept downstairs.

The Countess Sartov's diary was the one she came across first.

'What a sad day!' the Countess's latest entry read. 'I had a pain in my chest and worried about Tata who looks so pale. Even so, all would be endurable if we could remain here in the peace of the countryside. But soon, now – Ah, God, how soon – we must return to Moscow!'

My grandmother unscrewed her fountain pen. For a moment she hesitated. Then, after the Countess's last entry, she wrote in large, clear letters and in English a single word. After which she moved on into the library.

Petya's diary was among a jumble of books on the birchwood table: 'The leaves have begun to fall from the lime tree along the drive. Each day brings my doom closer. But what help is there? All must be as it must be. I must become a soldier.'

Once again my grandmother unscrewed her fountain pen and once again she wrote the same single word against Petya's last entry. Then she went out on to the veranda.

Tata's diary was under a cushion on her favourite wicker chair.

'How shall I bear it?' poor Tata had written. 'How shall I bear the endless, empty years without Nikolai? Yet there can be no hope for me. I *must* marry the Prince.'

And once more my grandmother wrote the same single word against Tata's last entry and closed the book.

She was on the way upstairs when an unfamiliar notebook caught her eye. Opening it she saw with a sinking heart that it was the diary of Nikolai Alexandrovitch. Staunch Slavophil that he was, the young tutor had written his diary in Russian which she could not read. Still, from the wildness of the scrawl and the frequent repetition of the Countess Tata's Christian name, she felt perfectly justified in adding the same, single word to the end of his diary also.

After which she went upstairs, packed her portmanteau, laid out her travelling clothes and got into bed.

Petya was the first to burst into her room at dawn. 'You have written in my diary!' he announced, wild-eyed.

'Yes,' said my grandmother, sitting up in bed.

'Where I have said I must be a soldier you have written "WHY?".'

'Yes,' agreed my grandmother.

'Why have you written "WHY"?' stormed Petya. 'You know it was the dying wish of my grandfather that I become a soldier.'

My grandmother settled herself against the pillows. 'Was he a good man, your grandfather? A man to respect and—'

'You have written in my diary!' declared a shrill and agitated voice as the Countess Sartov, grey plaits flying, entered the room. 'Here, where I have written that we must return to Moscow, you have written "WHY?".'

'Yes,' said my grandmother.

'Why?' shrieked the Countess. 'Why have you written "WHY"?'

'Well,' said my grandmother, 'I wondered why you must return to Moscow when you all like it so much better here.'

The Countess stopped pacing. 'But we always return to Moscow, isn't it so, Petya?' She ran back into the corridor. 'Sergei,' she yelled to her husband, 'come and explain to Miss Petch why we must return to Moscow.'

'We always return to Moscow,' said the Count, entering with a heavy tread. (Old Bull had still not done his stuff.)

'Father, was my grandfather a good man?' interrupted Petya.

'A good man? Your grandfather!' yelled the Count. 'He was a louse. A swine! When I was six he locked me in a cupboard for two days. Once he killed a serf with his bare—'

'Then I can see no reason why you need be bound by your promise to him,' said my grandmother briskly. 'As for returning to Moscow, I suppose that's because the house is not habitable in winter?'

'Not habitable in winter?' roared the Count, turning to his wife. 'Did you hear that, Annushka? Why, the stoves in this house would heat the Kremlin. They would heat the Kremlin without the slightest—'

'You have written in my diary!' came a deep and passionate voice from the doorway. 'Here, where I have written I may never hold the Countess Tata in my arms, you have written "WHY?".'

'That's right,' agreed my grandmother patiently.

'Why have you written "WHY"?' demanded the young tutor,' when you know that it can never be?'

'I suppose your father was an illiterate serf and so on?' enquired my grandmother.

Nikolai looked surprised and said no, his father had been – and actually still was – headmaster of a Boys' Academy in Minsk.

'Well then, I take it that you are penniless and futureless?' prompted my grandmother.

Nikolai turned his marvellous eyes on her and said that as it happened he had been left a little money by an aunt and was going in the autumn to take up a lectureship in Russian language at the University of Basle, in Switzerland. He had, he said, hopes of a Professorship fairly soon.

'Well then,' said my grandmother.

The Countess, who had been in feverish conversation with her husband, now turned round sharply. 'What are you saying, Miss Petch? Tata is engaged to Prince Kublinsky.'

'Madame, you must forgive me for speaking plainly but I am a doctor's daughter,' said my grandmother. 'And in my opinion,' she went on steadily, 'you would be advised to look . . . very carefully . . . into Prince Kublinsky's health.'

The Countess blanched. 'No! Oh, my God, it is not possible. Yet I have heard rumours . . . His early dissipations . . . Oh, my poor Tata!' She paused, then rallied. 'Even so,' she said, 'it is out of the question that Tata should marry Nikolai Alexandro—'

'You have written in my diary!' announced the Countess Tata, arriving in the doorway bare-footed, tangle-haired and devastating.

'Tata, Grandfather was a louse,' yelled Petya, 'so I need not be a soldier!'

'We're staying in the country, we're staying in the country,' sang Vashka, Mishka and Andrusha who had appeared from God-knows-where, and began turning ecstatic somersaults.

But it was at Nikolai, standing perfectly still in the centre of the room, that Tata looked.

'Come here,' said Nikolai. 'Come here, Tata.'

He didn't use her title, nor did he go to her but waited, his head up, until she came to him.

'We're going to be together, *doushenka*,' he said, taking her face between his hands. 'I promise you this. We're going to be together always.'

In spite of all entreaties, my grandmother insisted on leaving as soon as transport could be arranged. Her homesickness persisted and she felt she had done what she could.

When she reached London, Mr Fairburn was at the station to meet her.

'How kind of you, Mr Fairburn,' she said, allowing him to help her from the train.

'I wish,' said Mr Fairburn earnestly, 'that you would call me Alfred.'

My grandmother realised that this was probably the most passionate speech that she would ever hear from him.

'Weren't you disappointed?' I asked, remembering the mighty Volga, *troikas* and a little Countess hopelessly in love. 'Didn't it all seem rather tame?'

My grandmother said, no. One should know one's limitations, she said. And call him Alfred she did.

A QUESTION OF RICHES

JEREMY WAS seven when he first went to boarding school, his expensive new grey shorts enveloping his skinny knees, a roll of comics for the journey smudging in his tight-clasped, bird-boned little hand. Even Matron, jovial by profession, felt a pang as she unpacked the belongings of this patently unfledged fledgling and wondered whether another year in the nest would have done any harm.

Except that in Jeremy's case there wasn't really any nest. His father, one of the finest climbers of the decade, had died trying to help an injured companion on a distant, still unnamed Himalayan peak. Jeremy's mother, gay and accomplished, had married again within two years – this time, for solid worth and safety. Jeremy's stepfather was a mining engineer, kind, decent and magnificently unimaginative. When his firm sent him out to the Copper Belt in Central Africa, it seemed obvious to him that what Jeremy needed was to be left behind in a good English prep school.

And Jeremy's school *was* good. When he wrote his weekly letter to his mother out in Africa, his pen digging holes in the thin blue air-mail paper, it was pointed out to him that to describe one's homesickness was a bit *selfish*, didn't he think? So he wrote instead, in his huge, sloping script, of cricket matches and other suitable topics suggested on the blackboard. After a while, too, he stopped crying under his pillow at night because, as Jenkins minor said, he was simply disgracing their dorm. And gradually, as the weeks crept by, he began to forget. He 'settled'. Really he had no choice.

Fortunately there was no problem about where Jeremy should spend his holidays because he had grandmothers – a full set. There was his mother's mother, Mrs Tate-Oxenham whose husband, Jeremy's grandfather, sat on the Board of not fewer than seven major business enterprises. Mrs Tate-Oxenham lived in the centre of the most fashionable part of London in a tall house filled with valuable antiques and had a housekeeper, a chauffeur and a cook. Jeremy called her 'Grandmother' in full because abbreviations, she said, were slipshod: one was never *that* short of time.

Then there was his dead father's mother Mrs Drayton; she was a widow and managed on her pension. She lived in London too: in a single room, in a shabby peeling house on the 'wrong' side of the river. Jeremy called her 'Nana' but not when Mrs Tate-Oxenham was around because it made her frown.

It was to 'Grandmother', that Jeremy went first when his school broke up for the summer. He had never actually stayed with Mrs Tate-Oxenham before, so that at first he took the uniformed chauffeur who had been sent to meet him at the station for some kind of admiral or chief of police.

'Mind you sit still!' said this lordly being, settling Jeremy into the huge black car with its silver fittings and the rug made of a whole dead zebra lying on the seat. 'We don't want anything kicked, do we?'

Jeremy wouldn't have dreamt of kicking anything. Indeed, after a while the mere effort of sitting up straight was all that he could manage, for the great car was almost hermetically sealed against draughts and long before they drew up at the tall house in the hushed street, Jeremy was feeling agonisingly, almost uncontrollably car-sick.

Grandmother had cut short a committee meeting to greet him and was waiting in the hall, beautiful and composed with her upswept silver hair, and it was she herself who showed him round the house.

Jeremy had never seen a house quite like it. It was so quiet you couldn't hear your feet at all in the deep, deep carpets, nor any noises from the street. All the windows had two pairs of curtains – a thin white pair and a thick velvety pair tied back with cords – and even then there were shutters so that outside it could have been any kind of weather or any time of day.

And everywhere, on the mantelpieces, on the walls, in alcoves all up the stairs were museum-ish sort of things: Chinese dragons, and carved statues and dark pictures of people stuck with arrows.

Jeremy's own rooms were at the top of the house, a whole suite of them: bedroom, bathroom and sitting-room all to himself.

'No one will disturb you up here,' said Grandmother briskly.

'No one?' said Jeremy in his thread of a voice, averting his eyes from a grinning bronze head on the bookcase behind which, he was pretty certain, THINGS were already mustering for the night.

'No one,' said Grandmother – and sent for the housekeeper to help him unpack.

At his grandmother's, Jeremy had a lovely time. He knew he was having a lovely time because everyone constantly told him so.

'It isn't every boy gets a car like this to ride around in,' said Clarke, the chauffeur, who often had instructions – when Grandmother had one of her committees – to take Jeremy for a drive. Very interesting drives they were, too – or would have been: to Buckingham Palace or Hampton Court or Richmond Park, except that long before they got there, Clarke would be obliged to draw up in an empty side street and stand with his back turned while Jeremy was violently and humiliatingly sick.

'I bet there's not many little princes eat better than you do in this house,' Mrs Knapp the housekeeper would say, helping Jeremy to get ready for lunch.

And Jeremy, agreeing, sat very straight, his damask napkin sliding relentlessly across his knees, and chewed gratefully on dark slices of grouse in quivering aspic; swallowed, meticulously, his Russian caviare; didn't even splutter when what looked like a perfectly ordinary doughnut turned out to be filled with liquid fire.

In the hot, softly-lit department store where Grandmother bought him more grey suits and good white shirts and stripy ties, the assistant was almost overcome by Jeremy's good fortune, as was the waiter in the restaurant with the gold tables and potted palms where she took him when she met her friends afterwards for tea.

And Jeremy really *was* grateful, everyone agreed on that. Even Grandfather, in the few moments he spent in his own house, found nothing to complain of in the docile, quiet little boy. Except at bedtime . . .

'Getting that child upstairs to his rooms – you'd think he was going to his execution,' said Mrs Knapp. But otherwise his good manners, his evident gratitude pleased everybody. Clearly, he was a child who appreciated gracious living.

It was because of this that Grandmother, after a few weeks, felt compelled to give him a word of warning.

'We are fortunate, Jeremy, in having been able to give you a good time during your stay with us. Now, however, I'm afraid the time has come for you to move on.'

She waited for a sign of regret but Jeremy's eyes – those huge, dark, incurably underprivileged-looking eyes, remained obediently on her face.

'As you know, your mother wanted you to divide your time equally between us and your other grandmother.'

Jeremy nodded.

'I want you. . .' She broke off, unable to find suitable words. 'You will find . . . things different there. Mrs Drayton is. . .' Again, rejecting the unmentionable word 'poor', she floundered. 'You must not be spoilt or difficult to please, Jeremy. You must try to *adapt* yourself.'

And so, for the last time, Jeremy was packed into the big, closed car and Clarke drove him slowly across London to Nana's house.

Mrs Drayton, waiting at the window, saw the great car inch into the street with a stab of apprehension. It was so huge, so opulent and in the back Jeremy, poker-straight in his grey suit, looked as remote and aloof as some miniature diplomat isolated from the world. How would he get on here? Though she had managed without lunches now for over three weeks, the pile of coins she had saved towards Jeremy's entertainment seemed laughable.

But when she opened the car door she forgot her fears.

'Car-sick?' she said. 'You poor chap! Your father was just the same.'

And calmly inviting the lordly Clarke in for a cup of tea, she drew Jeremy gently into the house.

'Nice little place you've got here,' said the chauffeur, and there was no trace of condescension in his voice.

Jeremy, looking round, agreed wholeheartedly. It was just

one room and not all that big, with a single window opening out into the bustling, sunny little street, but this one room was so cunningly worked out! Red and white checked curtains slid back and behind them there was a little cooker and a sink. In one corner was a dresser with blue and white cups and a geranium; and the sofa they were sitting on turned itself most intriguingly, as Nana showed them, into her bed.

'Where will I sleep, Nana?' asked Jeremy when Clarke had gone.

Nana, who had been unpacking his case, straightened herself and looked at him anxiously. 'Well, love, I've made up a bed for you behind the screen there.'

The screen had pictures of parrots and humming-birds on it and Jeremy had already admired it. Now he peered behind and found a camp-bed, a proper khaki one like explorers had, with crisp white sheets turned back.

'You mean I'm going to sleep in the same room as you?' he said slowly. 'You're going to be in the same room as me all night?'

Nana reddened. This was worse than she had feared. 'I've only the one room, you see,' she said quietly. 'But you won't see me—' She broke off. 'Jeremy, what is it?' She pulled him towards her. 'There, don't cry, my pet. Maybe I can go and share with Mrs Post upstairs.'

Jeremy looked at her through his tears. 'Oh, gosh, Nana, you are silly!' he said. 'I want to share a room with you more than anything else in the world.'

There now began for Jeremy one of those periods which makes old gentlemen say that the sun always shone when they were young, the grass was greener and the sky a never-to-be-forgotten blue.

He and Nana lived off the land. Each day they took the cocoa tin from behind the spotted dog on the mantelpiece and counted out their spending money. Lots of money, it seemed to Jeremy: pennies, three-penny bits – far more money than he had ever seen in his other grandmother's house. Then they did something called budgeting. Jeremy liked budgeting very much because what it really meant was *deciding* things. For example, you'd decide to go to the park and feed the ducks and take a packet of sandwiches – that was clear. But a deck-chair for another ninepence each? Or sitting on the grass and having the money for an ice-cream?

That was an easy one, but others gave Jeremy many deliciously complicated moments of deep thought. A ride on the tube all the way to the Natural History Museum? Or get off two stops away and walk the rest, which meant sevenpence over, and that was a comic under his pillow at bedtime? Nana never *interfered* but sometimes when the agony of choice was almost too much she might nudge him gently towards a solution.

'I *think* there are those pavements with cracks on them on the way to the Museum,' she would say, and Jeremy would perceive immediately that this meant playing 'the first to step on a crack is a nitwit', and decide in favour of walking and a comic at bedtime.

To Jeremy it seemed as if Nana knew – and owned – the whole of London; perhaps the world. There was St James's Park where they sat for hours, laughing at the Canadian geese and the little ducklings making ripple arrows on the butter-smooth waters of the lake. Once Nana said there would be a surprise when they came round the corner – and there was a whole band of soldiers in scarlet and gold playing wonderful thumping music. A band they didn't even have to budget for, because it was free!

Then there were the pigeons in Trafalgar Square – they were free too – more pigeons than Jeremy had ever seen. If you stood still and held out the scraps that Mr Oblinsky had saved for Nana, you could *cover* yourself in pigeons. You could even have pigeons sitting on your *head*!

Sometimes they would find a bench in a nice crowded place like Leicester Square and play people-spotting, and the good thing about Nana was that she never cheated to let you win. If she saw more men with curly black beards in the set time, or more women with grey hair and poodles, well then she said so and ate the bull's-eye peppermint they kept for a prize without fuss.

And when they got back at the end of such a busy day there was still lots more to do. Jeremy would unfold the card-table, set it under the window and lay it while Nana cooked. The food at Nana's was *fantastic*! Whole plates of potato cakes or cinnamon toast or an apple peeled and quartered, with little triangular bits of cooking cheese stuck in each bit so as to make a boat with sails.

And the odd thing was that while staying at his other grandmother's *he'd* been the lucky one, here it was agreed by Mr Oblinsky, and Mrs Post who lived upstairs and by the people in the shops that it was Nana who was the lucky one. Terribly lucky, having Jeremy to stay!

Now, when Jeremy returned to school, he had three weekly letters to write. The one to his mother was shy and stilted because she had become as distant and longed-for as a mirage. The one to Grandmother, Mrs Tate-Oxenham, was the 'proper' letter, the one with the cricket match and his form position and the achievement of Rutledge minor in the 100-yards. But the weekly letter to Nana sprawled and spread and was one long question. Had she been to see the pigeons lately? Was the geranium growing? How was Mr Oblinsky's cough?

During the autumn term the school gave a long weekend off at the end of October. Once again Jeremy divided his time between his grandmothers and once again it was to 'Grand-mother', to Mrs Tate-Oxenham, that he went first.

At Grandmother's, Jeremy began being lucky straight away because she took him to something called a 'Private View', which was a lot of people standing very close together, drinking and smoking, in a room with pictures on the walls. The next day she had a bridge party and Jeremy was allowed to walk carefully about the room offering trays of canapés to the ladies as they played.

The day after that he went to Nana's.

At Nana's the folding table was set out with newspaper spread over it, and on it sat two big turnips and the kitchen knife.

'It's Hallowe'en,' explained Nana when she had hugged him. 'We're going to make the most horrible turnip lanterns in the whole street!'

And they did. They were so horrible that when they'd propped them on the window-sill with candles in them, Mr Oblinsky, returning from work, almost fainted; and all the children passing by said 'Cor!' and stopped to look.

The next day they got up very early, walked to the Common and found the last of the year's conkers buried under a pile of leaves. When he got back to school, Jeremy didn't string up the conkers to fight with but kept them in his pockets and weeks later when he took them out he didn't see them as hard and dry and shrivelled, but as shining and fresh as they had been on that October morning.

For the Christmas holidays, Jeremy was to fly out to Africa.

As the time drew near he became almost demented with excitement. Three weeks, two weeks, one week – and then he would see her. His *mother* . . .

The suitcases were packed; the grey-suited, ecstatic little boys were hurling themselves into their parents' cars – when the telegram came.

A garbled telegram but one thing was clear. There had been some political trouble in the copper mines. Rioting had broken out in the villages and Jeremy was not to go.

He sat hunched on his suitcase, his legs dangling over the bright airline labels, and listened politely while this was explained to him, and even the arrow-swift boys running through the hall to their Christmas freedom stopped when they saw his face.

'Where shall I go then?' he said at last in his mouse of a voice. 'Where shall I spend Christmas?'

Matron peered again at the telegram, which had undergone some strange sea-changes in its journey from the dry and dusty plains of Central Africa. 'Wait a minute,' she said, 'I'll go and talk to Mr Danworth.'

When she came back from the headmaster's study she was brisk and decisive. 'It's all settled, Jeremy, and there's nothing to worry about. You're to go to your grandmother's. To Mrs Tate-Oxenham's. There's lots to see in London at Christmas; she'll give you a lovely time. We've sent a telegram and Mr Danworth is sending you up in his own car with Ted to drive you,' continued Matron – and all but bundled him out, because there was something in his eyes she preferred at that festive season not to see.

The Head's car was not as bad as Grandmother's and Ted – who acted as boilerman, groundsman and general factotum at the school – was a more approachable character than Clarke. All the same, to Jeremy, sitting wraith-like and silent beside Ted, the inevitable happened soon enough.

'Please could you stop the car?' he asked.

Outside it was freezing cold with a gusty, boisterous wind straight off the snow-spattered hills. First it shook Jeremy, his teeth chattering with cold and nausea and despair. Then it blew through the car and scattered the papers on the dashboard . . .

'Darn it! I've lost the address,' said Ted when they had driven on again. 'Your grandma's address. Must have blown away when we stopped back there. You remember it?'

'I've got two grandmothers,' said Jeremy, his voice almost inaudible.

'Well, the one we're going to, silly.' Searching his mind for what he had overheard in the school office, Ted elaborated. 'The rich one. The one who's going to give you a lovely time.'

A slight tremor ran through Jeremy's skinny frame.

'The *rich* one?' he repeated wonderingly. 'Are you *sure* I'm going to the rich one?'

'Well, it stands to reason, doesn't it? You wouldn't want to bother the other one, not at Christmas time?'

Something had happened to Jeremy, something which made Ted turn his head for a second and give him a puzzled look.

'Oh, yes, I know the address of the *rich* one,' said Jeremy, his voice suddenly loud and strong. 'I know the address of *her* all right.'

And so it was that Nana, sitting quietly by the window and foolishly imagining, as people will at Christmas time, that the person they love best will somehow defy space and time and come to them – looked up, and gasped and saw that it had happened. That Jeremy was running towards her into the house . . .